THE REUNION

Recent Titles by Claire Lorrimer from Severn House

CONNIE'S DAUGHTER
THE RELENTLESS STORM
SECRET OF QUARRY HOUSE
THE SHADOW FALLS
A VOICE IN THE DARK
BENEATH THE SUN

Non-fiction

HOUSE OF TOMORROW

WEST GRID STAMP

NN		RR		WW	
NT		RT		WO	✓
NC		RC		WL	
NH		RB		WM	
NL		RF		WT	
NV		RS		WA	
NM		RW		WR	
NB		RV		WS	
NE					
NP					

THE REUNION

Claire Lorrimer

This first world edition published in Great Britain 1997 by
SEVERN HOUSE PUBLISHERS LTD of
9–15 High Street, Sutton, Surrey SM1 1DF.
This title is a revised, reset, and entirely rewritten version
of *Three Loves* first published under the name of
Patricia Robins in 1948.
First published in the USA 1997 by
SEVERN HOUSE PUBLISHERS INC. of
595 Madison Avenue, New York, NY 10022.

British Library Cataloguing in Publication Data

Lorrimer, Claire, 1921–
    The reunion
    1. English fiction – 20th century
    I. Title
    823.9'14 [F]

    ISBN 0-7278-5168-3

Typeset by Palimpsest Book Production Limited,
Polmont, Stirlingshire, Scotland.
Printed and bound in Great Britain by
Creative Print and Design Ltd., Ebbw Vale, Wales.

2 0 MAY 1997

Chapter One

1948

Lee stepped off the bus and started threading her way through the crowded streets of the little market town towards Harrington's tea-shop, a faintly amused smile tilting the corners of her beautifully curved lips. When Lee smiled it changed the whole character of her face. In repose, she could not be called beautiful, or pretty, although the intensity of her normal expression would always be arresting and therefore attractive. Brown-eyed, brown-haired, she would have been quite ordinary save for that expression and the extreme pallor of her face. Only when she smiled was she beautiful and one noticed nothing but that rich, generous expressive curving of her mouth.

Lee's amusement was at her own expense. It seemed fantastic that at twenty-five, she should have remembered and kept a childish promise made at fifteen, coming thirty miles from London to do so at extreme inconvenience to herself. Just beginning to make a name for herself in the artistic world, Lee had more work waiting to be done than even a six-day week and late hours could absorb. It seemed that this post-war world had need of commercial artists and she, in turn, had need of the work. Entirely self-supporting since the death of her parents a few years previously, Lee had thrown herself heart and soul into her work, and now, at last, results were forthcoming. But to spend the best part of a precious day trailing down from

1

London to Harrington Heath to keep a promise made ten years ago was surely a fantastic waste of time!

Nevertheless, she had come, not knowing whether the others would keep the appointment, but just in case they, too, had remembered and given up valuable time to see her.

Strange, she mused, how this little town brought back so vividly memories of ten years ago. In her mind's eye, she saw three schoolgirls in tunics and regulation coats and hats, striding down this same street, arm in arm, confident of the future, of themselves, worried about nothing but the cost of the huge tea they were to eat at Harrington's tea-shop, and later, swearing undying friendship throughout the years to come.

Sally, Clare, Lee, inseparable companions through their school-days, joyously flouting the saying that 'two's company, three's none!' Writing chain letters when they had left school to go to their different homes, Sally to the country, Clare back to Scotland, Lee to London; losing touch when the war had broken out and finally, for the last six years, no word, no sign, no news.

Lee recalled Sally's impulsive voice, heedless of the other people seated at tables around them, saying,

"Whatever happens, let's meet again, here, ten years from now. Of course, we'll probably see heaps and heaps of each other after we've left school, but all the same, in case we don't . . . what about it, Lee? Clare?"

And they had promised. She, Lee, had remembered. As she pushed open the door of the tea-shop, Lee could not help wondering anew if the others had remembered, too.

Clare sat down at one of the empty tables, casting a quick look at her watch. She was early, but it didn't really matter. She would rather enjoy watching the door, trying to recognise among the faces of the newcomers, those girlish faces of her school companions. Of course, they would be changed, she told herself. She herself had

2

changed. At school she had been tall, lanky, a head and shoulders above the other girls in her own age group. Her dark hair hung in straight, lanky strands and the clear blue eyes stared around her always with a hesitant, self-conscious and uncertain gaze.

Clare smiled. Really, her face had not changed so much, but the dark hair now hung in a loose page-boy round her shoulders, undoubtedly more flattering than those black rats-tails. At sixteen she had ceased growing and had filled out a good bit so that her five-foot-ten no longer seemed too tall. She knew she had a good figure and good taste in clothes – that she was according to modern standards, reasonably well-dressed, good-looking, attractive. This knowledge had helped to banish the inferiority complex of school-days and now, although still shy with strangers, she was by nature calm, placid, outwardly cool and inwardly calm. It took a good deal to shake her poise, but somewhere deep within her, Clare felt the warning note telling her that when one day she fell in love, everything would be different. She was not quite certain how she knew this, but in any case, it did not worry her. Up until now, she had never fallen in love. She had a large number of friends of both sexes, but they were nothing more than friends, and the few young men who had asked her out had never been very certain of themselves and had almost welcomed her refusals to repeat the occasions.

"I suppose I frighten them, or something," Clare had once said vaguely to a girl friend. And did not doubt that the answer had been near the mark:

"You're so calm, so unruffled, Clare. You make one feel – I don't know – a little as if life doesn't really touch you. That's enough to chill any man's ardour!"

Perhaps life hadn't really touched her deeply yet. But one day it would. It was that very certainty which gave Clare her calm, her poise, her placid outlook. Now, she gazed around her unworried over the possibility that the other two might not turn up. If they did, then she would be wonderfully pleased to see them. If they didn't – well, it was pleasant to see the little town again and to revive school memories.

She wondered what Lee was like now. She had been such an odd little girl – always scribbling – drawing things. Hopeless at mundane subjects such as arithmetic and Latin, she had shone brilliantly in anything artistic – music, painting, dramatics. What would Lee have made of the last ten years? Had she fallen in love? Was she married? Somehow Clare did not think so. Lee was not the 'settling' sort. Nor, for that matter was Sally – funny, vivacious, impulsive, podgy little Sally.

Clare smiled. Just the thought of Sally was enough to bring laughter to anyone's face. Sally inspired happiness, cheerfulness, goodwill. Of course, she had always been in hot water at school. Whenever there was mischief done, Sally would be behind it! But it was so easy to forgive her. Blonde, blue-eyed, rosy-cheeked, she was a lovable child, a little too plump to be called pretty, but cuddlesome fitted her perfectly. Imaginative, quick-witted, Sally was one of the most popular girls in the school. She would always be popular, Clare thought. But with her quick-silver nature, never happy to stay doing one thing for long, it was unlikely that Sally had settled down to a hum-drum married life. It was far more possible that she had a multitude of admirers and laughingly danced her way among them, favouring first one then another – unless some film-star hero had carried her off to a romantic paradise in Tahiti!

Clare's musing came to an abrupt halt as the door pushed open and Lee's unmistakable figure came into view.

"Jumping jehosaphelt, I'm late!" Sally cried, fidgeting in her seat next to the driver. "Mark, dear, do step on it! Never mind the speed limit . . . oh, dear, we should have started sooner!"

4

The tall, dark-haired young man at her side gave her a quick smile.

"Darling, I hate to say it, but who wasn't ready when I called for you?"

Sally's young, happy laugh rang out.

"I know, Mark. But do hurry, there's a poppet."

She searched frantically in her handbag and pulled out a powder compact and dabbed her pert, tip-tilted nose, smoothed the curly fair hair away from her forehead, and finally lit a cigarette, momentarily relaxing against the leather seat.

"Of course, I'm quite round the bend to be worrying like this," she said more to herself than to the young man seated beside her who was her fiancé. "The other two probably won't be there. Still, I hope they are. I'd like to see them both again. I want to ask them to our engagement party, Mark. Darling, what shall I wear?" And without waiting for his answer, she went on, "I think I'll blue my coupons and get something absolutely brand new. After all, it is an occasion. Mark, do you think we shall be happy? I think we will. I'm nearly always happy. I wonder if the other two are happy. You'll like them. Lee is very unusual – at least she was as a child. I expect she's even more so now. Different from the others. Still, Clare's probably more your type. She's rather placid and easy-going – a safe sort of person. She's got an inferiority complex like yours, too. At least, she had . . . she's not very pretty but there's lots beneath the surface once you get to know her . . . Mark, what are you thinking?"

She studied the firm, tanned face of the man beside her with half-exasperated curiosity. One never did know what Mark thought, and he was nearly always deep in contemplation. In fact, she often forgot he was there. Still, even though it took him time to express his thoughts in words, they were usually worth hearing. Mark was very, very much in love with her and so he always said wonderful things. It was such fun being in love, and being engaged. Shane would have to get engaged, too. Shane was her twin brother. Everyone said they were as alike as two peas in a pod, and they were, really, except that Shane was well over six foot and she, Sally, only five five! And Shane always smoothed his hair down so that you couldn't see the curls. He was an attractive person. All her girl friends fell for him. He got along very well with Mark, too, though of course, they were very different. Shane was like herself. Mark was quiet and thoughtful and reliable. He made her feel safe and secure, and his intensity was nice, too. Or perhaps that was the wrong word – it was exciting. Rather like playing with fire, except of course, she wasn't playing. Mark had been in love with her ever since he was a little boy in the next door garden and everyone had expected them to fall in love and get married. After a year away from home in one of the women's services, Sally had returned and things had blossomed into a more romantic vein and now, happily, they were engaged, unofficially until next week, when it would be announced at the party.

"Mark, what *are* you thinking?" Sally asked again, remembering that she had, as yet, had no answer to her previous question.

Mark grinned down at her.

"I was thinking, Sally, that even if these two school friends of yours were the most beautiful creatures in the world, they still would not be as pretty or nice or attractive as you!"

Sally laughed happily, and snuggled closer to him, her mood now sentimental and purring, like a contented kitten.

"You are nice, too, Mark!" she said softly. Then jerked upright and clutched Mark's arm. "We're there, Mark. There's the tea-shop. Pull up that side. Oh, I do wonder if Clare and Lee are there. I'm dreadfully late – nearly half an hour. Perhaps they've gone . . ."

"Calm down, Sally," Mark said slowly, as he pulled

the car in to the side and parked it behind a large Ford. "They'll be there."

But Sally was already across the street and half-way through the door. With an affectionate grin, Mark locked up the car and went slowly after her.

Clare and Lee had finished their tea and were smoking as they discussed old times together. After the momentary strangeness, they had found one another much as they had expected and had already decided to follow up their reunion with further meetings.

Sally they had long since given up, but Lee, who had been constantly looking around her, recognised her other school friend as she burst breathlessly into the tea-room.

"Lee!" called Sally, unaware and uncaring of the curious glances from the people at neighbouring tables. "I *am* glad to see you. And Clare!"

She hurried over to them and sat down at the table, laughing excitedly in between sentences.

"I thought you'd both have gone if you'd ever come!" she told them. "Lee, you haven't changed a scrap! Or Clare. Yes, you have. You're both grown up and terribly chic. Are you married?"

"Calm down, Sally, old thing!" Clare said with her quiet smile. "We'll order some tea for you and then you can tell us about yourself."

"Oh, goodness, there's Mark!" Sally exclaimed. "Still, he'll be quiet and let us chatter."

Lee and Clare exchanged amused glances and turned towards the doorway where Mark stood, looking rather anxiously around for Sally.

Lee's first impression of Mark was complimentary. Sally could certainly pick the good-looking ones, she thought. Clare, in a sudden rush of shyness, formed no first impression of Sally's young man. Hazily, she heard Sally making the necessary introductions. The next moment, Sally had squeezed him in between them on the

7

sofa seat and Clare could only see his profile, turned away from her towards Sally.

The remainder of the tea-party became a confused riot of voices, laughter, reminiscences, with Sally and Lee doing most of the talking. Mark, Clare noticed, was doing all the listening. His eyes seldom left Sally's sparkling, vivacious little face; he had ears only for what she had to say. Once or twice when Lee spoke of Sally at school, he turned to listen to her. Only once did he address Clare, and then to say, "It must have been fun for you being at school with Sally. I'll bet she led you into all sorts of mischief!"

She answered him. She must have done. But she could not remember what she said. One thing and one thing only was she aware of and that so acutely that it blinded her to every other happening and being in the room – the man beside her. For the first time in her life, she felt her whole body tingling with a curious nervous reaction – to his voice, his eyes, the touch of his hand as he took his teacup from her.

What in heaven's name is wrong with me? she asked herself angrily. He's attractive, of course, but that's no reason to fidget becuse he's sitting so close to me. He's Sally's friend. And obviously deeply in love with her. Why should I be feeling like this?

But the questions, the introspection were all dream-like and cloudy. Only the heavy thudding of her heart was real – the odd tingling in her nerves and the desire to get away, away from everyone – the crowded tea-shop which suddenly seemed too small to hold everyone – from Sally's voice, and Lee's – from the man sitting beside her so near that it was only by an effort on her part that their elbows did not touch.

"Clare, you're lost in a day-dream!" she heard Sally's voice. "You're just the same as ever. I want to hear all about you. What you're doing – and everything."

"I'm not doing anything exciting, Sally," she answered

with an effort. "I'm still in Scotland, helping Mother run the house and look after my sister's three babes. They're quite a handful and of course we haven't any help. I do a bit of secretarial work for Father, too. In fact, I really ought not to have come away but I – well, we made the pact and I just didn't want to break it."

"I'm glad you didn't, Clare," Sally cried, leaning across Mark to place her hand on Clare's arm to give it a friendly squeeze. "What's more, you're not going back yet, either. Is she, Mark?"

Mark nodded his head.

"You've got to come to our party next week, Clare," Sally went on. "And you, too, Lee. You must both be there or it just won't be a proper party at all. Now you will come, both of you, won't you?" she pleaded.

Lee laughed.

"Sally, my dear old thing," she said. "I'm a busy businesswoman these days. I haven't time for parties, much as the idea appeals."

"But it's more than that," Sally burst out. "It's my engagement party."

"Engagement!" Lee echoed. "Why, Sally, congratulations. I never guessed. You're not wearing a ring."

"Oh, it's not official yet," Sally laughed. "We're announcing it at the party, aren't we, Mark?"

"That's right, darling," he said. "But I must say it won't come as much of a surprise. In fact I don't know anyone you haven't told the 'secret' to."

Sally and Lee laughed.

"Oh, well, darling, I can't help telling people things when I'm happy!" Sally said. "Clare, what on earth are you looking so stunned about? Don't you think I'm old enough to get engaged or something?"

Lee spared Clare an answer as she said, "You're not a day older than when we last saw you, Sally. Is she, Clare? If Mark's a sensible man, he'll wait a long while before he marries such an impulsive, frivolous-minded little girl."

Sally laughed, knowing Lee was teasing her. Clare, looking at Mark, noticed a slight frown crease his forehead, but it passed almost immediately and when he spoke, he was smiling again.

"Oh, she'll grow up quickly enough once she's married!" he said. "Being a housewife these days adds years to a woman, I'm told – especially since she's marrying a poor man."

"Now Mark, don't be silly," Sally reproached him. "You know very well I'm the daughter of a *very* wealthy father. We've had this all out before. As I don't like housework, I shall pay for a maid. Now that's fair, isn't it, girls?"

Mark did not look too comfortable having the financial side of his marriage discussed so openly and Lee changed the subject with her usual tact.

"Well, since it's your engagement party, Sally, of course I'll come, even if I lose three new commissions to do so."

"And you, too, Clare?"

"Well, I don't see how I can," Clare said quietly. "You see, it means staying in London till next week and—"

"You'll come and stay with me, Clare!" Sally said, remembering that Clare's parents had never been very well off and that it might be difficult for Clare to afford a London hotel for a week. But Clare shook her head.

"No, Sally, dear, I really don't think I ought to. Mother expects me back. Besides, you'll be busy getting ready for the party and—"

"Why not come and stay with me, Clare?" Lee suggested. "I've got a tiny flat in the Chelseaest part of Chelsea, but there's plenty of room if you don't mind sleeping amongst the easels."

Clare looked from Lee's face to Sally's and felt trapped. She didn't want to go to the party. It seemed crazy not to want to, when she led such a quiet life in Scotland and it would be fun to wear evening dress again. But it went deeper than that. Something inside her was warning her not to go – some sixth sense, if there really were such a thing. Her grandmother, who came from the Highlands, was supposed to have had something of the sort, and very occasionally, she, Clare, *had* had premonitions. Once it had come to her when she had been shopping in a town. She had felt that one of the children was in danger. First she had ignored it, but the feeling had become so strong that she had taken a taxi home, to find the eldest child had fallen out of the nursery window and was suspended by her clothes on the spike of the balcony one floor below.

Her mother had been in the garden with the other children and the child's cries might never have been heard in time but for her return. She had never mentioned the reason for it to anyone, but it remained very vividly in her mind. Now the same odd, strong feeling was with her, warning her that unhappiness lay in wait for her at Sally's home.

"Really, Sally, I think—" she began, when Mark's voice broke in as he said, "Do come, Clare. Sally won't be really happy unless all her friends are there. She has spoken about you so often and – well, do come, please."

Clare looked up and her blue eyes stared for one instant into Mark's brown ones. At that moment, something happened to her that caused all the blood to rush to her face and recede again, leaving her weak and helpless beneath his gaze. Her will was no longer her own. Her very soul no longer was hers. For some strange, unaccountable reason, this friend of Sally's, Sally's fiancé, held her powerless to do with her as he would. She was his, utterly, completely, and his wish was her law.

"All right, Sally," she said breathlessly. "I'll come, but I think it would be better if I stayed with Lee. Then we'll travel down together on the night of the party. I'll

11

telephone Mother tonight and I expect she'll get someone in from the village to help with the children."

She did not hear Sally's or Lee's happy replies. She only heard Mark's voice, saying, "I'm so glad, Clare. Sally's going to be pretty busy playing hostess and I shall need some company. Sally's girl friends frighten me to death and I shall be counting on you and Lee."

"Better not do that, Mark!" Lee said, laughing. "I'm hopeless at a party. I always get the urge to go and draw someone or something. Besides, I can't dance."

"Then can I count on you, Clare?" Mark asked with pretended anxiety.

"Yes!" said Clare. "You can count on me."

Long afterwards, when Sally and Mark had driven away and she and Lee were drinking a last cup of tea before bed, Lee turned to Clare and put a hand on her arm.

"You know, Clare, you don't have to go to the party." she said without explanation.

Clare looked up, the blood rushing into her face again. "What do you mean, Lee?" she asked quietly.

Lee lit a cigarette and walked across to the huge studio window, staring out across the rooftops at the twinkling lights of London.

"Because, my dear old thing," she said affectionately, "you may not know it yet, but it's perfectly clear to me, and probably to anyone except Sally and Mark, that you've fallen for the guy. No, don't talk about it. I'm no fool, and nor are you, Clare. Sally's going to marry him and he's desperately in love with her. It won't break her heart if you don't go. It might break it if you did."

"Lee, I still don't altogether understand!" Clare murmured, knowing that Lee was probably right – that she had thought of nothing else but Mark, Mark, Mark ever since he had disappeared from her sight six hours ago; that already she was counting the hours until she could see him again.

"I mean this, Clare," Lee went on. "In my view, Sally and Mark aren't really a pair. He's too quiet, too steady-going for her. She's too impulsive, too headstrong, too inconsistent for him. But that doesn't matter so much. They think they are in love and that does matter. It might stand a chance – unless Sally met 'the person' – the one big love that comes into everybody's life once and once only. The trouble is, my dear, that Mark is 'the person' for you, but Sally isn't 'the person' for Mark. If I'm right so far, then you're in for untold unhappiness if you go on seeing him. I wouldn't want to see you hurt – unnecessarily."

"But Lee," Clare cried passionately. "How can anyone fall in love – all in a few minutes like that? It's absurd. You don't meet a strange man in a tea-shop one minute and know he's 'the person' as you call it the next. It can't be love. It's just physical attraction, biological reactions, or whatever scientists call it."

Lee turned round and faced Clare with a strangely pitying look in her eyes.

"You aren't the type, Clare, to be swayed by physical things. If I asked you, could you tell me how tall he was, the colour of his eyes, the shape of his face? No, it's his voice, the way he looks, the expression in his eyes – himself. Isn't it, Clare?"

"Yes!" Clare whispered. "Lee, have you been in love, this way?"

"Yes. He was killed in the war," Lee told her. "That's how I know. I felt it just as you felt, Clare. What I'm so afraid of is that, being a woman, you, too, will take a chance. You see, the man I loved was married. We met too late. The war gave us a few brief months and then it took him from me. I would have lost him anyway, but – I thought it worth it."

"Was he in love with you?" Clare asked.

Lee shook her head.

"No, he loved his wife. I was just a friend. So you see,

Clare, you've got to decide, too. Do you want Mark, just as a friend? Or will you cancel the party?"

Clare was silent for a moment, but she knew her mind had been made up long ago, years, centuries ago. Lee was right. She loved Mark. Because it could never happen again, she had to see him – just once more. Only once.

"I'll go, Lee," she said, knowing that for all her premonitions – for all Lee's warning – she had no choice.

Chapter Two

Lee and Clare and Sally were getting themselves ready for the party in Sally's luxurious bedroom. Clare, used to her own rather spartan, austere furnishings, had been amazed to see the quilted satin bedspread, the silk brocade curtains and fine Irish linen sheets, silver-backed hairbrushes and all the expensive perfumes and make-up of pre-war days.

"It's practically all from America!" Sally explained. "You know Daddy is working with one of the big USA film companies now. Of course, in a way, all this luxury is a necessity. The Americans expect this sort of thing and Daddy says we've got to keep up appearances for the sake of the business – not that we can't afford it. He's making packets!"

"How about income tax and super tax?" Lee queried.

"Heavens knows!" Sally said vaguely. "Anyway, it means dollars for the country so I suppose it's in the national interest. Pop is terrifically patriotic so I don't think he'd live like this if it weren't for the good of the country."

Lee, dressed and ready to go downstairs, sat in an armchair, smoking from a long jade cigarette holder. She looked very beautiful, very sophisticated, in a long, figure-fitting green lamé dress, gathered at the hips in the fashionable line.

"You're like a *Vogue* cover, Lee!" Sally cried in admiration.

"It's very exotic," was Clare's comment. "Only *you*

15

could get away with a dress like that, Lee. I certainly couldn't."

She, herself, wore a simple pale blue brocade dress, cut low at the neck to reveal her white throat and shoulders. She, too, looked lovely but her beauty was more simple, less studied than Lee's. It suggested something deeper than surface charm and was, in its way, typical of Clare, herself.

Sally struggled into her white muslin dress with its flounced dancing skirt and tiny pink bows dotted round the Victorian neckline. She smoothed the yards of material into soft lines and surveyed herself in the mirror.

"I think this dress makes me look too young!" she remarked with a tiny frown. "I think I'd rather have your dress, Lee."

Lee laughed.

"It wouldn't suit you, Sally. Besides, your dress looks quite lovely – sweet seventeen, fresh, innocent, youthful – all the right things for an engagement party. It's almost bridal. Mark will love it."

"Perhaps you're right," Sally said. "As a matter of fact it was a bridal gown, used in one of the films Daddy directed and sent over from America. I did think of keeping it for my wedding but I couldn't wait to wear it. Besides, we mightn't get married for ages and ages. Mark says he's not earning enough to afford to marry me yet. Isn't it silly, when I have so much money of my own?"

Clare, unwilling to enter this discussion, turned to the long mirror and recurled her hair into its long page-boy smoothness. Acutely conscious of every word that passed between her two friends, she heard Lee saying, "Mark must be allowed to have his pride, Sally, and even if the idea of a man supporting a wife is a little old-fashioned nowadays, I still think it's an admirable outlook. Whoever holds the purse strings invariably wears the pants, and that, after all, is a man's privilege."

Sally brushed her fair curly hair vigorously.

16

"I suppose you're right, Lee. Still, I don't want to wait till I'm an old maid before I start living my life. I want to experience everything while I'm still young enough to enjoy it. I want to have a husband and keep house and travel and possibly have children, too. There are hundreds of things I want to do and life's so short."

"Nonsense, Sally. You're young, and so is Mark. There'll be heaps of time for all that later. You're so impatient, child! Isn't it enough to be in love, happily in love? Isn't just having Mark enough for you?"

Sally's reply was cut short by a knock at the door. She jumped up, the seriousness gone from her blue eyes as they flashed an expectant smile.

"That's Shane!" she cried. "He has a special knock. Can he come in, girls, or aren't we ready?"

Lee and Clare nodded their heads and Sally opened the door to admit her twin brother. There was, indeed, the most extraordinary likeness between him and Sally, in spite of the tremendous disparity of their sizes. Shane's large, powerful figure seemed to fill the room, dwarfing even Clare's height. Beside him, with his arm around her waist, little Sally looked even more a child.

"Hullo, girls!" he greeted them. "You must be Lee and Clare. Sally's talked about you such a lot I'll bet I can guess which is which." He turned to Lee, looking at her from laughing blue eyes that were exactly like Sally's. "You're Lee, the artist. I'm genuinely interested in painting, although you mightn't think it. In fact, I even dabble a bit in oils."

Lee looked at him with interest, thinking:

He's like a young Apollo with that fair curly hair, those huge shoulders and perfect physique. I'd like to draw him. I wonder if he really is interested in art?

"Yes, I'm Lee," she said. "I'd love to see your paintings. Most of mine are water colours. I'm a commercial artist, you see, and I do mostly book-jackets and illustrations for children's books and that sort of thing. But my heart is in oils and I only do the other stuff because it's a financial necessity."

"Let's get together and have a chat about it," Shane said easily. "Once the party is under way, I'll seek you out and we'll retire to my studio for a chin-wag. Now, you're Clare!"

He moved over towards her and held out his hand.

"You're every bit as attractive as Sally said you were!" he remarked unexpectedly.

Clare flushed and withdrew her hand nervously.

"Thank you! I – I'm very pleased to meet you," she replied formally.

Without taking his eyes from her, Shane said, "May I have the first dance, please? Sally says dancing is my only accomplishment. If I don't tread on your toes too heavily, I'll have the supper dance, too, if you can spare it, and all the rhumbas!"

Clare, unused in her Scottish home to such open flattery was uncertain which way to take Shane's remarks. Was he teasing her?

"I'm afraid I can't rhumba," she said quietly. "But I'll try the others."

"Fine!" said Shane. "I'd better be getting along now. Pop wants me to see the champagne is properly iced. He doesn't trust the hired butlers! I must say, I wish old Rory would send us a dozen cases of fizz every day!"

And with a laugh which was a complete male replica of Sally's he turned and left the girls alone again.

"Rory's the American film director!" Sally explained. "I say, Clare, you have made a hit with Shane. It must be your aloofness or something. He's terribly spoiled and a bit conceited and no wonder, really. All the girls fall for him. I expect you will too. Don't you think he's attractive? It would be fun if you and Shane got together. I do so want him to get married, too. We've always done things together and I'd really hate to get married before he did!"

Lee, seeing Clare's flushed face, said quickly,

"Honestly, Sally, you treat love as if it could be turned on and off like a tap! I wouldn't have said Shane was a bit Clare's type."

"Why ever not?" Sally asked. "I've never met a girl who didn't find him attractive."

"Nobody's arguing that point!" Lee assented. "But there's a big difference between attraction and love. Clare would never—"

"Do I have to be discussed like this?"

Clare's voice rang out with unusual sharpness and conscious of her taut nerves, she hastened to force a laugh.

"Anybody would think you were trying to marry me off," she said lightly. "I don't want to get married – not for ages, anyway. Still, I think your twin is awfully nice, Sally, Don't you, Lee?"

"He quite knocked me sideways!" was Lee's abrupt comment.

The other two girls stared at her, but seeing their glances, she smiled.

"His attraction is purely from an artistic point of view," she told them. "I'd give my eyes to be able to paint him. I'd like to do him as a young modern Apollo, standing with his head against the skyline—"

"Now, Lee," Sally interrupted, with her eyes sparkling, "my brother wouldn't be a bit happy to think your only interest in him was as a model for a painting. Anyway, this isn't the time to go artistic on us. It's a party – my engagement party and you're to be as lighthearted and happy tonight as I am."

Lee stood up and put her arm round the younger girl's shoulders.

"Of course, Sally dear!" she said. "Tonight I shall be frivolous and with your permission and to please you, I shall flirt outrageously with your Shane, unless, of course, he is too tied up with Clare."

Sally and Clare laughed and the three girls left the room arm in arm and went slowly down the wide, beautifully carpeted staircase together.

A man broke away from the group in the hall below and came forward to meet them. With her heart leaping in sudden quick jerks, Clare recognised Mark. He was looking at Sally and the expression of his eyes spoke more quickly than his voice.

"You look beautiful!" he said slowly, and then, turning to the other girls, he smiled and said, "I'm so glad you could come. I hope you've enjoyed your week in London, Clare."

She managed to make some reply, her eyes meeting his only for a brief second. But he turned from her almost immediately and spoke to Sally again.

"I'm glad you wore white," he said. "I brought you these to wear in your hair."

"Ooh, how scrumptious," said Sally, tearing the tissue paper from the double spray of white roses which she hastened to fasten in her hair. She stood on tip-toe and kissed Mark on the cheek.

"Now, now, you two!" called Shane as he walked across the room towards them. "The night is yet much too young to start that sort of thing. Come along and have a drink."

He linked arms with Clare and Lee, and followed by Mark and Sally, they went towards the improvised bar to sample the iced champagne, as Shane suggested.

The large hall filled gradually with guests. Clare and Lee were introduced to Sally's mother and father whom they had met once before at parents' day when they were still at school. They were charming people, and neither Clare nor Lee could find anything to dislike about them. Rich as they undoubtedly were in these post-war times when so many people were struggling for bare existence, they were nevertheless simple, charming people, and, as Mark told them aside, the most generous couple he had known.

"Sir Dennis personally supervises the estate and gives all his employees huge bonuses," he told them. "And although he's such a busy man and such a great man in the film business, he always has time for the so-called nonentities. Of course, he spoils Sally and Shane, but who wouldn't! He's a man the country could be proud of, although there are plenty of people who say unkind things about him – those who see him living in the lap of luxury and don't know the ins and outs. Actually, he pays colossal sums of money to the government in super tax as well as providing them with dollars, and if with all that, he can still maintain this sort of a house and accompanying luxuries, then all I can say is good luck to him. He works for it."

"I see you like your future father-in-law," Lee said with a smile.

"I certainly do," Mark agreed. "All the same, I do wish, selfishly, of course, that there wasn't quite so much money in the family. It makes me feel I have no right to ask Sally to live in comparative poverty with me."

"Nonsense, Mark," Lee reproached him. "What she loses financially, she'll gain by having a husband like you. She'll be rich in love and happiness and that's all that really matters."

"I wonder if it *is* all that matters to Sally," Mark said rather quietly, more to himself than to the two girls. "I don't know, but . . . well, she's alway been used to so much. It's not as if she has ever had to do without anything she wanted in life before. I hate to think that I can't give her even half as much as she has been used to having."

Clare listened in silence, remembering Lee's words to her that night in the studio the day she had first met Mark.

'You'll only cause yourself unnecessary pain, Clare.'

Yes, it was a very bitter sweetness, listening to Mark as he talked of the girl he loved. Bitter because she was

21

not that girl; sweet because she knew now, even more clearly than she had known it the other day, that she loved him; that every word he spoke only proved him the more worthy of love and respect.

"Hey! You're looking much too thoughtful, young lady!"

She looked up and met Shane's twinkling blue eyes.

"I'm sorry," she said. "I was in a day-dream, I'm afraid."

"Then wake up, my beautiful maiden, and make good your promise of yore!" said Shane. "You promised me the first dance, remember?"

Clare had to admit that Shane was a wonderful dancer. It was a strange experience to feel herself held close in a man's arms, his face touching her hair every now and again, their bodies matching perfectly in rhythmical movement of the dance, her head against his shoulder. Social life had been non-existent of late.

How wonderful if this were Mark! she found herself thinking, and checked the thought instantly.

As the tune changed to a slow, sentimental waltz, Shane's arm tightened a little around her waist, but Clare remained stiff in the circle of his arm, and he loosened his grip immediately as if aware of her inward withdrawal. He looked down at her with an odd expression in his eyes.

"You're a funny girl, Clare!" he said abruptly. "Not like Sally's other friends. Most of them expect a man to flirt with them. You're different. I'm glad. One gets so fed up with easy conquests."

Clare was surprised at his frankness, but she liked him for it. She said, "I'm always accused of being stand-offish and straight-laced . . . but somehow I just can't flirt – even if I try. Perhaps it's my Scottish upbringing, or maybe I'm a prig!"

"That's absurd," Shane retorted. "Why shouldn't you be choosy?"

22

"It isn't that. It's just that . . . I always wanted to keep those feelings for someone I really loved . . ." she broke off, biting her lip as Mark's face clouded her imagination.

"What a lucky man he'll be!" Shane remarked. And then, with an unmistakable touch of Sally's impulsiveness, he added, "Clare, you're the first girl I've met who has admitted to feeling this way. You're different. I knew it as soon as I saw you. Now don't look so surprised—" he said with a smile as he saw the expression on her face "I'm not suggesting I can suss out your secret thoughts. I've hardly spoken more than two words to you and only seen you for the first time this evening. It's just that I think you're rather a special person and I'd like it if we could get to know one another better. Could we?"

Clare could not fail to recognise the obvious sincerity in his voice, but something within her warned her that she must go carefully with Shane. Like Sally in temperament, he might well rush impulsively into some new idea, some new emotion. It might even be that with Sally becoming engaged, he felt he, too, should start to think more seriously about love. Premature though it undoubtedly was to judge his feelings towards herself, she knew that Shane found her attractive – different from his usual girlfriends. Equally, she knew that she could never fall in love with him.

"I hope we'll be good friends, Shane," she said quietly, "but I'll be going back to Scotland tomorrow. I doubt very much whether we'll have the chance to get to know one another better."

"Suppose I were to make such an opportunity?" Shane questioned pointedly. "I could always come to Scotland, you know."

"Of course I'd be pleased to see you," Clare said formally. "But it would be a long way to come and besides, you would find it very dull up there. We live very simply and there's nothing to do."

"It wouldn't be dull if I could be with you, Clare. I think you're the most intriguing person."

Clare was spared the necessity of replying to Shane's remark for the dance ended and couples were moving over towards the bar. They were joined almost immediately by Sally and a young American whom she introduced to Clare as Lyndon Rea. He was a nice-looking boy, young, but socially mature, and Sally introduced him as a film actor.

"He's been given the lead in *Follow My Leader*," she told them. "In fact, he's going to be a star pretty soon, aren't you, Lyn?"

"Sure hope so, honey!" Lyndon Rea said.

Clare noticed that Sally had a large spray of orchids pinned to her dress, and although Mark's roses were still in her hair they were dwarfed by the magnificence of the spray which, she supposed, this young film actor had given her in true American style.

I wouldn't want to wear another man's flowers, she thought. Shane, too, seemed to be thinking the same thing.

"Trying to make Mark jealous?" he teased his twin sister.

Sally looked at him in surprise.

"Of course not, stupid," she retorted. "Besides, Mark knows very well that Lyndon never comes to the house without bringing flowers. It's an American habit, isn't it, Lyndon?"

At that moment, Mark joined them. His glance went immediately to the orchids on Sally's dress and Clare was certain that a tiny frown creased his forehead. Shane and the young American went over to the bar to collect drinks and Clare, standing a little apart from Sally and Mark, could not help overhearing his voice.

"Really, Sally, I don't see that you have to wear them. I know they are beautiful, but—"

"Mark, don't be such a silly!" Sally interrupted with

24

an affectionate laugh. "If I'd thought you would mind, I'd never have put them on. Would you rather I didn't wear them?"

"Of course not, if you want to!"

"Mark, you're being difficult. Who wouldn't want to wear orchids like these? You know I never receive orchids unless Lyndon brings them. Surely you're not jealous?"

"It isn't that, Sally. It's just that you shouldn't *want* to wear them."

"Mark, you know I love you – terribly!" Sally's voice rang out. "I'd rather wear your roses than any old orchids, but Lyndon would have been dreadfully hurt if I'd chucked them away."

The sharpness left Mark's voice and his tone was almost inaudible to Clare as he said tenderly, "The flowers don't matter, Sally. All that matters is you. Come down to the summer-house for a few moments – please. I want you to myself just for a minute or two."

"Mark, I will – but not just yet. I promised the next dance to one of Father's friends. I'll come down afterwards. How's that?"

"I'll wait for you, darling," was Mark's answer.

The music started up again and Sally moved away to find her partner. Mark took the drink Shane had brought him and disappeared through the french windows. Clare stood there with Shane, conscious of a sudden loneliness.

"Are we going to sit this one out?" he asked her, "or shall we dance again?"

Unwilling to face any more of his personal questions at that moment, Clare pleaded for a rest and, followed by Shane, went across to a secluded corner where she found Lee with another young man, who went off in search of drinks.

Shane and Clare sat down and chatted to Lee. Soon enough the subject of painting came up and Clare was left to her own reflections. Looking for Sally among the dancers as they passed, she thought of Mark, down in the summer-house, and wondered again how Sally could be so casual about the orchids. There was nothing coquettish in Sally's make-up, nothing premeditated. Clare was sure that Sally had not wilfully made Mark jealous. It was just thoughtlessness.

I'm siding with Mark! she told herself. And really it has nothing to do with me at all. I ought not to have overhead that conversation. Could she have avoided it? she wondered. Or had she purposefully listened, trying to find the possibility of a rift between the two?

She tried to quieten the voice of her conscience. It's not like me to spy and scheme. I won't do it. All the same, if Sally and Mark were to . . .

She caught herself up quickly, and tried to concentrate on Lee's remarks, Shane's replies, but her thoughts wandered again. Mark really did love Sally, there was absolutely no doubt about that fact. And Sally loved Mark. She had said so, and if Sally's way of loving was not Clare's way, it was nevertheless real to Sally – and to Mark. . . .

Sally broke in on her reflections as she hurried up to her.

"Look, Clare, I've got to go and see if the supper table is all right. Mother insists I check over details with her. I promised Mark I'd meet him in the summer-house, but there just isn't time. Could you be a darling and pop down and explain? I know he'll understand. When Mother wants something it's now or never!"

And she hurried away before Clare could make an excuse.

I can't go down there – in the dark – alone with him, she thought wildly. Lee can go. I won't. I just won't!

And then the absurdity of her fear struck her.

I've got nothing to be afraid of! she told herself. Only my own feelings, and the sooner I face up to them, the better. The sooner I put Mark out of my mind and my heart the better, too, and I won't do that by avoiding him.

Sound common sense was uppermost as Clare went through the french windows and stepped out into the garden. There was no moon and the stars gave barely enough light for her to see the faint outline of the summer-house at the far side of the lawn.

The grass was wet under her light dancing slippers and the night air was cool against her flushed cheeks. Somewhere down beyond the lawn, a night owl gave out its eerie screech and a shiver went down her spine. Something within her made her want to race back to the light and the noise and the people, and yet something else made her go forward.

Outside the summer-house, she paused, and then with a sudden squaring of her shoulders, she stepped into the dark interior. At that moment, before she could speak his name, Mark's arms were round her, and his lips were on her mouth in a long, searing kiss.

For a moment or two, she struggled against him, knowing in an instant that he had thought her to be Sally, but in this embrace, with his mouth burning against her own, her whole heart went out to meet his, and before she could realise her disloyalty, her wrongdoing, her arms went instinctively round his neck and with all the pent-up emotion within her, she gave back kiss for kiss, to the man she loved.

Chapter Three

Clare was the first to regain her senses. Against the confused riot of emotions that assailed her, realisation of her own actions was uppermost. She pushed away from Mark and cried breathlessly, "Please, don't. It's not Sally. It's Clare. She sent me down to tell you she couldn't come. I'm so sorry . . ." She turned from him and ran back towards the house.

Mark stood like a statue, unable to speak or move. That long, incredibly passionate kiss had disturbed him deeply, and the fact that it was Clare, not Sally, whom he had held in his embrace was even more disturbing.

How fantastically stupid of me! he thought wildly. I never stopped to find out if it was Sally.

The mistake had been understandable. Sally had been wearing white – Clare pale blue. In the dark, and because of his impatience to hold Sally in his arms, he had never thought to study her clothes.

Clare! What must she think of him! Embarrassment held him in grip and he sat down heavily on the wooden seat within the summer-house. With hands that were still trembling, he lit a cigarette. Of course, he might have known it wasn't Sally . . . she had never returned his kisses quite like that – never with that same ardent response. Sally always laughed, teased him a little and he had never allowed himself to reveal the extent of his feelings for her for fear of frightening her. She was somehow so young, so innocent. Just now, aware of the emotion of the girl in his arms, he had lost a little of his own self-control and so they had both been carried away – and now, to discover that it was Clare, Sally's friend . . .

He put the palm of his hand against his burning forehead and tried to think more clearly. For the first time, it struck him that Clare had not mistaken *his* identity – and yet she, too, had responded. Surely she was not the type of girl to let any man kiss her, especially her friend's fiancé? And with such depth of feeling? Clare, as he had summed her up the other day in the tea-shop, had been a quiet, thoughtful girl. There was nothing flirtatious about her. He was certain he had not been mistaken in her character. What then could explain that passionate response?

There seemed to be no answer to Mark's probings for an explanation. It never occurred to him that Clare loved him. After all, he had known her so short a while – only seen her twice in a lifetime and then he had hardly noticed her.

Filled with perplexity, he walked slowly back towards the house, uncertain of what he should say to Sally about those last ten minutes, if indeed anything should be said; what he should say to Clare when he came across her indoors. Should he apologise? Or should he make no reference to it?

Disliking scenes of any description, Mark decided that it would be best to forget the whole thing. Clare, no doubt, was just as embarrassed about it as he was. There must be some reasonable explanation and, if so, Clare could make it if she chose.

Mark could not help but wonder, as he went in through the french windows, what Sally would say were he to tell her what had transpired. She would probably treat it as a great joke. All the same, he would selfishly be pleased if, hearing the facts, she were to feel just a little jealous.

Upstairs in Sally's bedroom, Clare lay with her head buried in the pillow, the softness of the linen cool against her flushed cheeks. Lee sat in the armchair surveying her in silence. She had been standing at the french windows trying to drink in some fresh air when she had caught sight of Clare, racing across the lawn from the summer-house, and had known immediately that something had happened to upset her. With her usual tact and foresight, she had taken Clare's arm and led her upstairs, where Clare had flung herself onto the bed, waiting until such time as she felt ready to talk.

Eventually Clare lifted a tear-stained face and Lee was able to make some sense out of Clare's spasmodic sentences.

"It was dreadful of me, Lee!" Clare ended her story, her voice a litle calmer now. For the first time in her life and for the second time this evening, she had completely lost her self-control. (So this, thought Lee, is what love can do to a girl like Clare!)

"My dear, you're making a mountain out of a mole-hill!" she soothed her friend. "After all, the initial mistake was Mark's. You broke away from him, didn't you, as soon as he gave you a chance?"

"Yes . . . but, oh Lee, I kissed him back. He must have known . . . realised . . . I don't know it happened. At first I tried to struggle against him and then . . . well, I just gave in and, Lee, it was so wonderful . . . so incredible. I've never kissed any man or been kissed like that before. I love him, Lee, with every part of me. How could I help responding?"

"Of course you couldn't!" Lee replied in her calm voice. "Anyway, there's no harm done. It was just a case of mistaken identity. Mark won't think about it again and you must just try and forget it ever happened."

"Forget?" Clare cried involuntarily. "How could I forget?"

"To outward intents and purposes, you must," Lee went on. "Surely you don't want Sally or Mark or anyone else to know how you feel about him?"

"No!" Clare whispered. "That's what I'm afraid of, Lee. Mark *must have guessed.*"

"My dear old thing, why should he?" Lee asked. "It seems to me that it would be the last thing to enter Mark's mind. He's not conceited. He'd never believe he was capable of arousing such feelings in anyone, other than Sally. He probably thought you were looking for somebody else – a secret nocturnal tryst or something!"

But Clare could draw no comfort from Lee's flippancy. "He knew I was looking for him. I told him Sally had sent me down to say she couldn't come."

Lee shook her head. Clare certainly had made a mess of this party, she thought. Mark had no reason to suppose that Clare was in love with him. If he thought about it at all, he would assume she had had a bit too much to drink, although Clare hardly gave that impression to people, even to those who did not know her well. She was too quiet, too reserved. Either way Mark must be made to think that, or he might really begin to wonder how Clare felt.

"Clare, you'll be going home soon," she said. "You may never see Mark again. This isn't such a tragedy, after all. You mustn't take it so seriously. Let Mark think you're the sort of girl who might get carried away by the party spirit, or something of that sort. You must joke about it. Tell Sally before he can; let him see that it meant nothing to you so that he'll think he was mistaken about your reactions. Knowing Mark even as slightly as I do, I'll lay you a wager he is only feeling thoroughly embarrassed at the moment and wondering how to face you after making such a fool of himself."

"I couldn't talk about it – pretend it meant nothing, Lee," Clare cried desperately. "How could I when it was the most wonderful moment of my whole life – wonderful for that brief second when I could imagine Mark loved me, too – horrible when I remember that he loves Sally. Oh, Lee, I'm trying to think of Sally, too. Suppose she doesn't take it so lightly when she finds out?"

Lee stood up and went to Clare, sitting down on the bed beside her.

31

"You know Sally as well as I do," she said. "You *know* she'll treat it all as a big joke. In fact if you weren't in love with Mark, it might even *be* amusing. At any rate, you've just got to pretend it was nothing to you – nothing at all, do you understand, Clare? Either that or you'll have them guessing your real feelings. Now make up your face and come downstairs with me. We'll tell Shane first and then Sally when Mark is with her. Shane will probably tell her for us . . . you've just got to put a good face on it, Clare, and act the part. Come to think of it, it wouldn't be a bad idea to flirt a little bit with Shane. He seems attracted to you and he'd enjoy a little attention. Have the next two or three dances with him and let Sally and Mark see you both. Dance cheek to cheek with him if he wants it. Shane won't mind, and to tell you the truth I rather envy you. Underneath that frivolous exterior, he's a deep-thinking person, sincere and nice. I like him. And he really is interested in art. You know, I asked him to come up to town next Wednesday and see some of my work. He's promised to sit for me, too."

Clare, forgetting her own misfortunes, was struck by the tone of Lee's voice. Usually inclined to be flippant, there was a new note of softness in it and she could not help asking if Lee was, after all, a little more attracted to Shane than she had first admitted.

"Perhaps I am!" Lee said with a half smile. "I think he's very charming and I'd like to see more of him but don't" she added seeing the expression that crossed Clare's face, "get any match-making ideas about us. You're almost as bad as Sally! Besides, even if I did go crazy enough to allow myself to fall in love again, it wouldn't be with someone who has designs elsewhere."

"What on earth do you mean, Lee?" Clare asked.

"My dear, he never stopped talking about you the whole time he was with me, except when we discussed art. Wanted to know where you lived, how old you were, everything I knew about you. Sally was right when she said you'd made a hit. You know, Clare, Shane would make a good husband. He's spoilt of course, and a little conceited. But underneath it, he's good. How typical of life that you should meet him too late. Now with your heart filled to the brim with Mark, you'll never be able to think about Shane as a possible husband."

"No!" Clare agreed, almost inaudibly. "I couldn't fall in love with anyone else. I'll never marry anyone else, Lee. I always knew it would happen this way and nothing could have changed it after those first few minutes of knowing him. What happened tonight hasn't made things any worse than they were from the start."

Only that Clare would find it harder than ever to forget him, Lee thought. "We must go down before we are missed, and find Shane," she said.

It was a very nervous Clare who followed Lee downstairs; a very silent one when Shane joined them.

"I've been looking for you both," he said. "Where have you been?"

"Gossiping!" Lee returned brightly. "Girlish gossip in Sally's bedroom."

"Is it repeatable?" Shane asked, his blue eyes twinkling. "By the sound of your voice, I gather it was quite funny."

"It was rather, wasn't it, Clare?" Lee prompted.

Clare forced a smile to her lips and nodded her head.

"As a matter of fact, Sally sent Clare down to the summer-house to give Mark a message and the ardent Mark mistook Clare for Sally and kissed her soundly. Nearly frightened the life out of Clare until she discovered who had attacked her."

"I thought you were looking a bit pale, Clare," Shane said. "I do think it's rather funny, though. I must tell old Sal. Tease her a bit to see if she gets jealous."

"You know very well she has no need to be jealous of Mark!" Lee replied laughing.

"Well, I'll tease old Mark, then," said the irrepressible

33

Shane. "Have him over the coals for being unfaithful to my twin sister. Not that I blame him, though."

Clare, feeling his glance on her, kept her eyes from his face. Then, remembering Lee's advise, she looked up and met Shane's gaze. There was no mistaking the admiration in his eyes. Lee was right, then. Shane did find her attractive! How complicated everything was. As if it were not enough to cope with the repression of her own feelings, it looked as if she might well have Shane on her hands, too.

Shane, however, refused to remain silent or serious for very long. He linked arms with the girls and marched them into the dining-hall where the other guests were already enjoying a buffet supper. Shane, catching sight of Sally and Mark, took the two girls over to them, and waggled a long brown finger impishly at Mark.

"You Big Bad Wolf!" he teased. "Do you know what he's been up to, Sal? Kissed our Clare in the summer-house just now. Thought it was you, Clare said, but I don't believe her for one minute. What are you going to do about it, Sal? And what have you got to say for yourself, Mark? You frightened Clare out of her wits and I won't stand for it!"

Mark looked from Sally to Clare, a little anxiously but with a growing ease from his embarrassment. He had not broached the event to Sally as yet and had been worrying a little. According to Shane, however, it was to be the joke of the evening, and would be, too, if he knew his future brother-in-law. Well, that would clear the air. Poor Clare looked a little embarrassed too.

"I'm really sorry, Clare, Sally!" he said in his slow, quiet voice. "It was dreadfully stupid of me. Both of you being in light coloured dresses and it being so dark . . ."

"I'm not at all sure I should announce our engagement, Mark," Sally treased with mock severity. "In fact in grandmother's day, that kiss you gave Clare would have obliged you to marry her or else ruin her reputation. Maybe you two should get engaged instead."

34

"Sally, please!" Clare begged. "It was so stupid. Do let's forget all about it. Poor Mark wasn't to blame so do stop teasing him."

Sally laughed and linked her arm with Mark's, giving it a little squeeze.

"All right. I'll forgive you this time, darling," she said affectionately. "But only because Clare has asked me to. You must say thank you to her like a good boy."

Mark and Clare smiled at one another, both a little shyly, but the tension was gone.

Shane said, "You may forgive him, Sal, but I don't. I won't have men kissing Clare in summer-houses. Have you for a duel, Sir!"

And he struck a fencing pose at which they all laughed.

"Really, Shane, I don't see where you come into it," Sally told her twin. "Clare isn't your property."

"Then by the right of chivalry!" Shane retorted. "Clare, will you have me as your knight protector?" And he held out his arm to her with mock gallantry. Clare, playing the part Lee had set her, put her hand on Shane's arm, and forced a flippant reply, and then, to her great relief, they turned of mutual accord to the supper table.

Supper over, dancing was resumed, and Clare allowed Shane to take her back to the ballroom to teach her the rhumba. The next dance was a waltz but before Shane could lead her away, Mark cut in, asking Clare for the pleasure.

"With your permission, of course!" he said to Shane with a laugh.

Shane moved off having gained a promise from Clare that she would reserve the next dance for him, and then Clare found herself in Mark's arms again, drifting round the room to the sentimental strains of 'The Anniversary Waltz'.

"Sally's dancing with that American chap," Mark said after a moment or two, "so I thought I'd take this

35

opportunity of making my apologies to you. I *am* most dreadfully sorry, Clare."

"Please don't think of it again," Clare said quickly. "It doesn't matter in the least. I was a bit surprised, naturally, but I realised it was a mistake . . . honestly, I'd rather forget the whole thing."

"Yes, so would I!" Mark agreed, looking down at her with a smile. "You know, Clare, I think we two are the only ones to have been upset by it. Sally and Shane seem to think it was a big joke."

"Well, it was, really, wasn't it?" Clare managed to force from her lips.

Mark was silent for a moment.

"Yes, I suppose it was!" he said rather doubtfully. "All the same, the whole thing puzzles me rather. I mean it's strange how the darkness can cloud outlines! One would think an inner self would have warned me you weren't Sal. I suppose I never stopped to think."

Clare thought it time to change the conversation which seemed to be getting too personal for her to stand with her nerves as taut as violin strings. She said, "Do you believe in telepathy, between people who love one another, Mark?"

He thought for a moment, and then said, "Yes, if they are really united in heart, mind and soul. But that must be a difficult accomplishment. It doesn't exist yet between Sally and myself. Temperamentally we are very different. Sally skims over the surface and I probe too deeply. I wonder if we will ever find the happy medium so that we can be perfectly united on common ground. Don't think I am reproaching Sally," he hastened to add. "As you know, I absolutely adore her. It's just that I'd like her to take life a little more seriously, and I must learn not to take it quite so much so."

"Can people change their inner selves?" Clare asked. "Can one ever alter one's innermost feelings?"

Something in her tone surprised Mark. Clare was

36

certainly not an ordinary girl. She was intelligent and thoughtful and in some ways, her mind seemed to run along the same lines as his own. He was glad she was Sally's friend. In spite of the awkwardness of that meeting in the summer-house, he felt that they might yet become good friends.

Before he could answer her question, the dance ended and Shane was beside them in a moment.

"Enough, my good fellow!" he told Mark. "I am now claiming my promised dance."

Mark laughed and went off to find Sally, and Clare, listening only half-consciously to Shane's light-hearted chatter, followed Mark in her thoughts, fighting against the bitter feelings of jealousy that assailed her just to think of him holding Sally in his arms, his face against her hair; Sally who belonged to him. . . .

The dance was interrupted suddenly by Sally's father making a formal announcement of his daughter's engagement.

"I don't think it's much of a secret if I know my Sal," he said, an arm round Sally's shoulder as she stood between him and Mark on the platform by the small band that had been playing dance music all evening. "Anyway, for those of you who don't know, I have great pleasure in announcing my daughter's engagement to young Mark, here. Let's wish them both jolly good luck."

The guests surged forward towards the platform, reaching for Sally's and Mark's hands, offering their congratulations. Clare stood alone, watching them, watching Mark, seeing with a deadly pain in her heart, the glow of happiness and pride on his lean, brown face. Tears forced their way into her eyes and she bit her lip, fighting against them.

I must go and congratulate them, too, she thought, and then she felt Shane at her elbow, saying gently, "Why so sad, Clare? It's not good thinking of what might have been!"

37

She looked up at him in sudden fear. Had Shane guessed after all how she felt about Mark? But he dispelled her fear with his next remark.

"It's never any use raking up old loves," he said. "Forget about the fellow, Clare, whoever he was. He couldn't have been worthy of your love. Turn your mind to the future, to a new love. One must live in the present, not the past."

Strange words from Shane, and how poignant, even although he had mistaken the reason for those tell-tale tears. He had imagined she was recalling some unhappy love affair. He did not know how true were those words of his, 'One *must* live in the present'. This was the present, this moment of jealousy and pain and anguish. Neither the past nor the future could alter it. Tomorrow she would be on her way to Scotland and these brief meetings with Mark, his kiss, his words to her, their dance together, would all be imprinted on her memory to be lived and relived.

"Forget him, Clare," came Shane's voice.

"I can't!" Clare whispered, unable to prevent the words from escaping her lips.

"You can and you will!" Shane replied, his grip on her arm tightening. "I'm going to help you, Clare. Listen to me. You'll probably think I'm quite mad. Most of the family are. It's probably the Irish in us! But I'm sane enough now. I know I only met you tonight, but when I saw you first of all in Sally's room, something inside me turned over and over and a vague idea formed at the back of my mind. That was four hours ago. Ever since then, the idea has been growing and forming itself and now I'm quite sure, crazy as it may seem to you . . . Clare, I want you to be my wife. Will you marry me?"

Clare turned, and stared at him aghast.

Chapter Four

"Oh no, Shane, no! I couldn't!" Clare cried involuntarily, drawing away from him.

"Because of the other fellow?" Shane asked quietly.

Clare nodded her head, tears blinding her eyes with a sudden, burning swiftness.

"Look, we can't talk here, amongst this crowd," Shane said. "Come up to my studio, Clare . . ." and as she seemed to be hesitating, he added with his quick smile, "I shan't try to make love to you. I'm not quite such a fool."

He smiled at her again, and reassured by his obvious friendliness, Clare allowed him to lead her out of the dance room, away from Mark and Sally and the happy, congratulatory crowds.

Shane's studio was beautiful. Originally the attic of the house running along the length of the roof, one sloping wall had been taken down entirely and replaced with a huge unbroken pane of glass. It was uncurtained and from the doorway in which she stood entranced, Clare could see nothing but milliards of twinkling stars and the faint orange crescent of the moon against the velvety black sky.

"It's beautiful, Shane!" she whispered.

Shane closed the door behind them and switched on one of the standard lamps. The room itself sprang into a soft light and Clare stared round her in amazement. There were easels, canvasses, paintings everywhere, all colourful and living. There could be no doubt about the fact that Shane had talent. Lee would be fascinated. Her own little Chelsea studio, where her work only added to the confused jumble, was dwarfed by the magnificence of this one and Shane's was spaced out so that one could fully appreciate the colour, line, and detail of every painting.

"It's quite a little home up here!" Shane told her, moving over to a corner of the room where there were two comfortable armchairs each side of the fireplace. Behind a screen, painted by Shane himself, there was a small electric cooker and a cupboard with china, plates and some tinned food.

"This is my own private domain!" Shane said, showing Clare to one of the chairs and disappearing behind the screen to put the kettle on for a cup of coffee. "Nobody is allowed in here except Sally who occasionally whisks round with a duster. You know, Clare, since I had the attic converted five years ago, only Sally, yourself and Lee have been inside this room. Even Mother and Father are excluded, except of course when they first saw it. So you can consider yourself, and Lee, too, highly honoured."

"I do!" Clare told him with a smile. "What fun it must be, Shane, to have a place like this – all of one's own. At home, in Scotland, I have my own room, bedsitting-room really, but everyone comes in and out of it as they please. You see, it's rather a small house and my mother and father and my brother, Douglas, and my sister and her husband and their three babes all live there, too."

"Quite a clan existence," Shane remarked, bringing out a tray with a coffee pot and two cups and saucers. "It must be fun."

"It is, in a way," Clare agreed. "But it's hard work, too. You see, we lost all our money in the war. Father had a business mostly tied up in Norway, and of course the Germans just took it over. Before they left, they burned everything, the factories, stocks, everything connected with it and Father's income was so depleted that he has only been able to build it up again by very slow degrees.

So he and my brother and brother-in-law and my elder
sister who was a fully qualified shorthand-typist, are all
working together; and Mother and I look after the house
and children. We can't afford any help and as Mother is
getting old now, there's always so much to be done."

Shane poured out the coffee, listening in silence. Ever
since his school days, he had lived in comparative luxury,
and had never in his life wanted for anything. This studio
itself had cost nearly a thousand pounds to build and
furnish and his father had written out a cheque probably
with more ease than Clare's father would have handed
out sixpence pocket-money to one of the children.

It seemed so wrong, when one looked at it in that light.
He, Shane, had never done so before – just taken everything
for granted and been grateful to his father in a nondescript
way. This party that had been thrown to celebrate Sal's
engagement and the money spent tonight on champagne,
hired butlers, lobsters, the band, decorations with gladioli
everywhere at ten shillings a dozen! – would no doubt keep
Clare's family on their feet for a year.

"How old is your brother, Clare?" he asked suddenly.

"Twenty-three!" Clare told him. "Father meant to put
him through university but we just couldn't afford it
when the war was over. So Doug has been in business
since then."

"I've never had to earn a penny in the whole of my
twenty-five years!" was Shane's comment.

Clare looked up at the note of self-deprecation in
his voice.

"But you work, Shane. Just look round this room."

"Work I enjoy doing, not work I have to do," Shane
argued. "It makes me feel rather ashamed of myself."

Clare took the cup of coffee he handed to her and
forgetful of her own thoughts and worries, she was
thinking now only of the expression on Shane's face.

"That's stupid, Shane," she told him quietly. "It's no
blame to yourself that your father is doing so well out

of the film business. It's certainly no shame on your father. Mark said he was doing more to put this country back on its feet than most of the other well-to-do people put together. Besides, I think every artist who is really talented should have the opportunity to work unharrassed by financial troubles."

Shane ignored her last remark and said thoughtfully, "You know, I like Mark, Clare. He's a thoroughly good type in every sense of the word. Sometimes I think he's too good for our Sal – not that I'm belittling Sally," he hastened to add. "It's just that – well, she's as spoilt as I am and Mark's much too good for her. He'll just go on spoiling her. I sometimes wonder if she wouldn't be better off with some man who kicked her around a bit!"

Clare remained silent. The sound of Mark's name was enough to start her heart beating again in those quick uneasy jerks. She clenched her hands at her side, hoping that Shane would not observe any change in her face as he talked. Little did Shane realise what his words meant to her . . . and she couldn't tell him; couldn't beg him not to go on because she loved Mark, because she hoped deep down inside herself that he was right; that Sally would be better off with somebody else.

How mean and despicable she was becoming! she told herself angrily. Why should she consider herself more worthy of Mark than Sally – gay, vivacious, adorable little Sally, who had never and would never harm a hair of anyone's head, unless it were by unintentional thoughtlessness.

"Do *you* like Mark, Clare?" Shane asked suddenly.

Clare kept her eyes on her coffee cup.

"I haven't known him very long," she prevaricated, "I think he seems very charming."

"He's a damn sight more than that," Shane said quickly. "I've never liked another chap as much as I do old Mark. The trouble is, he's so confoundedly fond of Sal. He's not the type to fall in love lightly."

42

"Why should that be a trouble?" Clare questioned, her calm voice belying her inward feelings.

"Oh, I don't know," Shane replied after a moment's consideration. "Sal's in love with him, too. But they are so different, don't you agree with me, Clare? I mean, they must love in such different ways."

"Opposites are supposed to attract," Clare said. "I think they probably do very often, and I don't see why, as long as their interests are the same, they should not complement one another. Mark will steady Sally's impulsiveness, and she will laugh him out of his serious moods."

"Perhaps you're right," Shane agreed. "It's certainly true that opposites attract. I always imagined at the back of my mind, falling for a girl like Sally. And yet—" he looked up at her with a strangely shy smile, "I seem to have fallen for you with a big enough bump, Clare, and we couldn't be more opposite, could we?"

"No!" said Clare quietly. "But our interests aren't the same, either, Shane. You build your life round your art and I haven't a streak of artistry in me. I'm just born to be a plain housewife. Domesticity comes easily to me and I enjoy that sort of thing."

"What *do* you want out of life, Clare?" Shane asked abruptly.

"I wanted a home, a husband, children – that's all!" Clare told him, her voice nearly inaudible.

"Wanted? Don't you still want those things?"

"No, not now," Clare replied with difficulty.

"Because you can't have them with the man you are still in love with?" Shane surmised.

Clare nodded her head.

"Then it wasn't as far back in the past as I had thought," Shane said, more to himself than to her. "Clare, I haven't any right to ask questions and I'm not going to. It's obvious that you do love this man and that either he doesn't return your love which I can hardly credit, or else he is already tied elsewhere. In either case, surely

43

you realise that you can't spend the rest of your life thinking about him – wanting him?"

"I don't see any alternative, Shane," Clare cried, all the pain and wonder of her feelings for Mark re-awakened by Shane's remarks.

"But of course there is, Clare," Shane retorted, leaning forward in his chair to look at her with flashing blue eyes. "You yourself say you were born to be a mother, have a home and a husband to look after. You cannot deny yourself those things for ever just because of this man. It isn't fair to yourself, or to him, making him responsible for such dreadful waste."

"But I could never love anyone else!" Clare cried. "I always knew that when I fell in love it would be for always. There couldn't be anyone else in the world I should feel that way about – there never was until I met him."

The desperately unhappy cry, wrung deep from within her, struck Shane with an unexpected rush of pity. He was no longer thinking selfishly now of his own feelings. He wanted more than anything in the world to take Clare in his arms and comfort her and in some way relieve her suffering. Sensitive as he was beneath that gay, light-hearted exterior, he could not bear to see any human being so wretched, so unhappy.

Swept away by his own impulsiveness, he stood up and pulled Clare to her feet, folding her in his arms before she knew his intention. But there was no passion in his embrace, only a deep tenderness, so that Clare, at first intending to break from him angrily reminding him of his promise not to make love to her, found herself suddenly clinging to him, the tears flowing down her cheeks, her slim body racked with sobs that she could not account for. Perhaps it was just the nervous strain of the whole evening, or tiredness, or both. She did not try to find reasons, but allowed herself to give way for those brief minutes, drawing comfort from Shane's arms, his strength, his kindliness.

Presently, he released her, and drawing a handkerchief from his pocket, handed it to her with a smile. Clare sat down in the armchair again, ashamed now of her outburst, her lack of self-control. Her whole behaviour this evening was so foreign to her that she could not really believe it was she doing and saying these things.

"I'm sorry, Shane," she whispered, her voice husky from the tears. "I've been behaving like an hysterical schoolgirl. I'll pull myself together."

"You don't have to apologise to me, Clare," Shane told her gently. "Besides, I expect you're tired. It's well known that human resistance is at its lowest ebb about this time of the morning. It's nearly one o'clock, you know."

Time! Clare thought. How fantastic and unreal it was. So much could happen in so little time; so much had happened that it seemed an eternity since yesterday. Seven days ago she had been in Scotland, happy, contented in a placid, easy sort of way and the days had drifted by, seemingly only a few minutes passing. Then she had met Mark and every moment of every day since then, she had lived each second so acutely and with such awareness of her living them, that they had turned themselves into hours, days, years. There was no accounting for the passing of time. People always said that it was the great healer. Would she, many years hence, look back on these minutes and remember them without pain, without emotion, with only the barest interest? It did not seem possible, and nor did the prospect comfort her. A future which held no Mark, no love, was not one she could look on with happy expectation.

"How expressive your face is, Clare!" Shane broke into her thoughts. "One can almost read your mind. I would like to paint you as you were just then . . . and yet I think I couldn't do it. I could only paint you with a smile on your lips – a Gioconda smile. Will you sit for me one day, Clare, one day when you can smile again? I should

45

like to do you against your native background – in a plaid skirt perhaps, with a shawl over your shoulders, a bunch of heather in your hair and colour in your cheeks, and an aurora of the hills and the wind and the scent of heather about you."

Clare looked at Shane in surprise. How right Lee had been in her quick summing up of him. There were depths to his character which one would never believe of him, meeting him socially. Strange that he could live in a world of hothouse comfort and luxury and yet deep within him, hold so much poetry and love of nature and the real things of life.

"You're thinking me a fool!" Shane said with a self-conscious laugh. "I apologise."

"No, Shane, I wasn't!" Clare cried quickly. "I was thinking – how nice you are!" she added simply and with a shy smile.

Shane jumped up from his chair and sat down on the rug in front of the fire at her feet.

"You know, Clare, I wasn't so crazy when I asked you to marry me downstairs just now," he said softly. "I know now that you couldn't love me – I wouldn't expect it anyway – you're far too special to fall for a chap like myself . . . no, don't interrupt me! But I might be able to help you to forget him – to find happiness again; a different sort of happiness, perhaps, but at least you wouldn't be lonely. And I should make no demands on you – just that you talk to me and sit with me like this in the evening; and admire my paintings sometimes!" he added with a smile. "In return I would love you with all my heart and you should have everything you wanted of life to replace the one thing you most want. If you liked, we could travel, go to Spain, Italy, America, or we'll bury ourselves in the Highlands and I'll paint the hills and lochs until there isn't one I haven't done . . . Clare, we could be happy together. I'm sure of it. Won't you give it a trial?"

For a brief moment, Clare allowed herself to be swayed by his ardent voice, by the faint hope that perhaps Shane was right – that his would be the best way to forget Mark. Married to Shane she wouldn't have time to think; no long days walking alone on the hills at home thinking, remembering. No horrible moments of jealousy seeing her sister and brother-in-law laughing happily together, in love, loving their children; no moments of fear that she was getting old and life was passing her by.

And then she thought of Shane and his feelings and without hesitation she said gently, "Marriage has got to be a two-sided affair, Shane. I know you could give me a great deal but that isn't enough. I would have to feel I was giving you something, too, and I couldn't! What could I give that would make you happy? I would only make you unhappy because you would know that I was wanting to be with someone else."

"I'd take a chance on that last remark!" Shane cried quickly. "You wouldn't want a ghost for ever. And Clare, you underestimate yourself. You could give me so much. Already you have inspired me to get down to some serious work in real earnest. My mind is bursting with new ideas, new paintings, paintings of you in all your moods. And you're different, in every way. I've never met a girl like you before. I've never felt this way about any girl before."

"Shane, don't you think perhaps that is the reason you think you care for me?" Clare asked steadily. "You're confusing this – this inspiration as you call it, with love . . ."

"Don't you think then, that one can fall in love at first sight?" Shane asked, little aware of the effect of his words on Clare.

I fell in love with Mark at first sight! she was thinking. How can I answer Shane's question when I have done the same thing. My love for Mark is real. Is there any reason why Shane's love for me should not be real, too?

She passed her hand wearily across her hot, tired eyes, unable to find words. Shane, seeing her hesitation, pressed his point.

"It *is* possible, Clare!" he cried. "And you know it."

"Even if it is so, it doesn't alter anything," Clare replied. "You know I'm in love with someone else, Shane. Running away won't cure that. I must fight it out alone. If I succeed, perhaps things could be different. I don't know."

Shane was silent for a moment or two. Then he spoke again.

"I think you're right, Clare, about facing up to things," he said slowly. "Running away never helped anyone. But – forgive me for probing again – this affair of yours you have admitted to me is a hopeless one. Are you then facing up to it in your own mind, or are you running away from life so that you can bury yourself in memories?"

Clare flushed, knowing that once again, Shane was near the truth. Was she after all, not planning an escape back to Scotland where she could re-live, in an orgy of self-pity, the wonder and pain and every moment of these few brief days of knowing Mark? Was that facing up to things? Supposing she were to agree to become engaged to Shane? He would want her to stay on here, in the house where Mark was nearly always around, in his company, seeing him, hearing him, fighting with herself to subdue her feelings. She might even find in time that Mark was not so perfect after all. When all was said and done, she knew incredibly little about him. Actually speaking, she knew Shane the better of the two. Supposing Lee had been right when she said last week up in her flat that it was difficult to distinguish between attraction and love, and that it was possible her feelings were not so deep-rooted as she had imagined? Then she would be free of Mark. She could go back to being herself and be happy and peaceful and perhaps, too, she might discover eventually that she loved Shane. He was, without doubt, the most charming person. One could not help but like him . . .

That, Clare told herself, was one alternative to 'running away' as Shane put it, and therein lay the possibility of peace of mind and happiness again. And the other possibility . . . ?

Clare faced the truth and knew that deep within her had existed the hope that eventually Sally and Mark might decide there was too much incompatibility for them to go through with their marriage. Horrid as it was, she had to admit that it was the truth. And if she were to continue being honest with herself, she would have to admit, too, that such a possibility existed only in her own mind, put there by wishful thinking. She had assimilated those few words of Mark's when he said he and Sally had not yet got to know one another well enough to meet in perfect understanding; Shane's words just now, 'Sally's in love with him, too, but they're different;' that and her own selfish desires.

Hating herself more in this moment of self-revelation than she had ever had cause to do in her life before, Clare thrust all such hopes from her as if they were hot coals burning her finger-tips. With sudden resolution, she said, "Shane, there is something I must tell you. I never meant to tell anyone, except Lee, who guessed. But you must know the truth. You'll probably hate me, or else you will think me crazy. But I think you ought to know – I'm in love with Sally's fiancé – with Mark."

She closed her eyes, unwilling to see the expression that she was sure would cross Shane's face. He was Sally's twin; Mark's friend. What must he be thinking of her?

She waited for him to speak. After a moment, he said, "That makes sense now, Clare. What an utterly hopeless and ghastly thing to have happened. Poor Clare! I'm most dreadfully sorry." He paused for a moment, lost in thought, then went on, "I don't see why it makes so much difference, Clare. You couldn't help falling in love with

him. There's no blame attached to you for that. When . . .
Was it tonight, when he kissed you?"

"No!" Clare whispered. "It happened the other day, last
week, in the tea-shop. I knew from the first moment."

Silence fell again and then Shane said, "Are you sure,
Clare? I mean, you've only seen him twice, haven't
you?"

"Don't *you* believe in love at first sight?" Clare countered. "I'm as sure I love Mark as you are certain that you
love me – more sure, I think, because I've been fighting
against it, knowing it to be hopeless."

Shane reached over and took her hand from where it
lay on the arm of the chair, and gently he uncurled the
clenched fingers.

"Then, surely you see, Clare, that I am right? Don't
run away back to Scotland. Stay here a little while.
Face him! Study him. Try and find things you don't
like about him. Force yourself to see him with Sally
and to see how happy they both are so that you know
quite certainly and irrevocably that Mark isn't for you.
If you go away you'll only magnify the whole thing to
such an extent that even if it had all been imagination,
you would never let yourself believe it. Give yourself a
chance to get over it. Give me the same chance, Clare," he
added with a smile. "We're both in the same boat, really,
aren't we, except that you are not quite so far beyond my
reach as Mark is beyond yours. Perhaps Fate meant it to
happen this way and we shall end up happily together.
At the worst, we can still only find ourselves in the same
position."

There was a great deal of common sense in Shane's
suggestions, Clare told herself. Perhaps he *was* right.
With Shane's help, she might learn to feel indifferently
about Mark; and if Shane's interest in her was simply
because she was different from his usual girlfriends, then
that novelty would wear off, too, and they would both be
fancy free again.

"An engagement won't hurt anybody, Clare – a long engagement between us. If it's a dismal failure, nobody will be surprised if we break it off. After all, they will probably expect it, seeing how quickly we will have become engaged. Clare, give it a trial. We've nothing to lose, and so much to gain. Will you?"

Chapter Five

"All right, Shane. But not tonight. I couldn't face all those people. Leave it until tomorrow."

"You won't think better of it in the cold, grey light of dawn?" Shane asked anxiously.

"Even if I do, I'll stick by my word," Clare promised.

"I'm going to make some more coffee!" Shane said suddenly, jumping to his feet. "I think we need it."

Clare was immensely grateful to Shane that he had not, from some inner tact, tried to kiss her. She could not have stood being kissed again that night – not after the summer-house and Mark. Shane went up in her estimation and Clare did not feel so crazy making such a decision as she had expected she would. Shane was a dear – and he seemed to understand so well; with his help, perhaps everything would turn out right after all.

There was a sudden knock on the door, and Shane said in surprise, "Who on earth could that be? Nobody ever comes up here, unless it's Sal."

Clare was relieved when Shane opened the door to reveal Lee.

"Sally sent me in search of you," she said. "She thought you might be up here. The party's nearly over, you know."

"Come in, Lee," Shane said. "We're making coffee. Would you like some?"

"More than anything in the world," Lee replied with her odd little smile. She went over and sat down beside Clare.

"Well, old thing, how have you enjoyed yourself?" she asked, pulling out her long jade holder and lighting a cigarette.

Clare met Lee's enquiring gaze with some uncertainty. "It's been a lovely party!" she answered formally.

Shane poured out the fresh coffee and said, "Clare, let's tell Lee what we have been discussing. I think she'd understand – and approve."

Lee raised an eyebrow and Clare met Shane's gaze which seemed to her to be saying, You've got to face them all tomorrow, Clare. Why not try out your self-control on Lee? I'll help you.

She nodded to him, and Shane told Lee exactly what the position was about himself, Mark and Clare.

"So we're getting engaged tomorrow," he ended. "We shan't ask anybody else what they think of the idea, but I think both Clare and I could do with a straightforward comment, Lee. If I'm not mistaken, we'll get honesty from you."

Clare, watching Lee's face, was uncertain whether she had seen any trace of surprise, disapproval, dismay there. Lee was so self-confident and controlled. Until she spoke, it was impossible to know *how* she felt. She seldom let her expression give her away.

"My poppets, I think it's a wonderful plan," she said at last. "As you say, an engagement can always be broken. In fact, the original intention of an engagement as I see it, was that it should be a period of trial, of getting to know one another better. You and Shane can do that and if at the same time it cures Clare of Mark, then so much the better. As a matter of fact, I came to tell you that Sally was insisting we stayed the weekend. She seems to think it stupid to go back to town on a Sunday, and I must admit, I don't think I should get much work done tomorrow, or rather today, by the time I got home. I'm quite ready to stay but I wasn't sure whether you would be, Clare. Now it seems the best thing for us all. I must go back on Monday, but I expect your mother would understand if you prolonged your holiday, Clare. You haven't had one this year and you need it."

"Mother did say she was managing all right with the girl from the village," Clare said thoughtfully. "The trouble is the girl is so unreliable. She's quite liable to say she's tired of work for the moment and rush off home without warning."

"Then you could always take the night train home," Shane said. "Or come to that, Father would charter a private plane for you in an emergency."

"You see, Clare?" Lee said with a laugh. "This is fairyland. You clap your hands and like Aladdin, you find anything you want to hand."

Clare smiled and Shane jumped to his feet.

"I think we'd better go downstairs again," he suggested. "It is Sal's party and she'll be furious with me for appropriating the two prettiest girls at the dance for so long."

But when they did go down, most of the guests had gone and Clare, her eyes searching involuntarily for Sally and Mark, noticed that they had disappeared, too.

"The two love-birds are saying good-night!" Sally's mother said. "I think I shall go to bed, now. I'm very tired."

She kissed Shane and nodded to the two girls.

"Sally tells me you're going to stay on tomorrow," she said with her charming smile. "I shall be most pleased if you will."

"Thank you!" Clare and Lee said together. "Good-night."

"Good-night!" she said, and went up the broad staircase to bed.

Shane said suddenly, "Are you too tired, Father, or could I borrow a few moments of your time before you go to bed?"

54

"Of course, my boy, of course," said his father. "We'll have a nightcap. What about the girls?"

"I'm for bed!" Lee said. "Thank you very much for a wonderful party."

"It's been marvellous," Clare said, realising that to all intents and purposes, she was speaking to her future father-in-law. It did not seem possible and together with her intense tiredness, everything seemed to have taken on a dream-like quality.

Lee and Clare went up to their room together. Within a few minutes, they were undressed and in bed, and not long afterwards, Clare could hear Lee's steady breathing and knew that she was already asleep.

In spite of her tiredness, or perhaps because of its intensity, she, herself, could not sleep. Try as she might, she could not still her imagination, and although she struggled against it, her mind saw all too clearly Sally's white-clad figure standing somewhere in the moonlight, held in Mark's arms; saw him kissing her with all the longing and passion with which he had kissed her, Clare, in the summer-house.

At last, mercifully, she heard Sally's light step on the stair; heard her own door open softly and Sally's voice whispering, "Are you both asleep?"

And then, receiving no answer, she closed the door behind her and went into her own room.

Then, finally, Clare was able to turn over and fall instantly into a deep sleep.

In her own room, Sally flung her clothes onto a chair, and jumped into bed, snuggling down among the cool sheets, stretching her hot little toes which ached from so much dancing, as far down, where it was really cold, as she could reach them.

What a party it had been! she thought. Now she was really and truly engaged to Mark. Dear Mark! It was such fun being in love with him – and that last embrace just now in the moonlight – it had been a little frightening in a way, but thrilling, too. Mark certainly loved her very deeply. Much more than Lyndon. Of course, Lyndon was in love with her as well, and made no bones about it. He was fun, too, and a much better dancer than Mark. Although Mark was good at the slow things, he couldn't do all the nice rhumbary ones, or the old-fashioned waltz.

Sally stretched herself like a kitten, sleep stealing over her. Why didn't Englishmen dance cheek to cheek? she mused. It was much more – well, much more something! It did all sorts of odd things to you and it wasn't surprising she had let Lyndon kiss her. It was naughty of her really, she supposed. Still, it had been early on in the evening and she hadn't been engaged then, at least, not officially. All the same, Mark wouldn't have like it if he'd known, but after all, he'd kissed Clare so that made them all square.

She wondered suddenly whether he had enjoyed kissing Clare and was a little perturbed at the thought. Then she put it from her. She knew only too well that she had no need to be jealous of Clare. Mark loved her, Sally, as devotedly as – as a slave. Now Lyndon loved her in quite a different sort of way. Sally wasn't at all sure that it was love after all. He started by treating her as if she were a child. When she got annoyed, he just laughed at her, then kissed her. And when she broke away from him, telling him it wasn't fair to Mark and that she was in love with him, he just laughed again in that maddening way of his and said, "You'll see, honey. You're my girl. I'm quite happy to wait."

"I'm going to marry Mark – soon!" she had stormed at him angrily, hating him for his possessiveness and the maddening certainty of his voice; his self-assurance.

"Marry him, then, my beautiful!" Lyndon had said. "You'll come to me in the end."

"I won't!" Sally had cried, stamping her foot. "And I don't believe in divorce. I'll never leave Mark once I marry him."

"You will if you ever do marry him!" he said, and turned on his heel and left her.

How furious she had been with him! How she hated him at that moment. But sometimes he was different and then try as she might, she couldn't help but like him. He was really quite attractive with his auburn hair and hazel eyes, and that incredibly tall, lithe figure. His slow, southern drawl was attractive, too. Socially, he was much more fun than Mark, but when it came to deeper things, Mark won every time. Now Mark nearly always let her have her own way about things, even if he started by being stubborn. Mark had a strong streak of stubbornness in him, but Sally knew how to get round that. She only had to tease him a little, or laugh, or kiss him and then he always gave way. Mostly, of course, he wanted to do the things she liked doing so it didn't matter very often.

Come to think of it, Sally mused, I still haven't convinced Mark about the monetary side of marriage. After all, why should they both live on his meagre salary when her allowance, which Father had said he would continue, could double that amount. Then they could live very happily and travel and have a car and a nice house and a servant. It would be much more fun, not just for her, but for Mark, too. Why couldn't he see that? All Mark could see was his own side of the picture.

"I want to support my wife myself," he had said firmly. "Not share that responsibility with your father."

"It's just pride!" Sally had told him, and Mark had unexpectedly agreed with her.

"Maybe that is just what it is," he said. "I should lose my self-respect, Sally, if we did things the way you want them, and soon enough, you'd lose your respect for me, too."

"All you care about is your pride!" Sally had said almost in tears with annoyance. "You don't really care whether

I'm happy or not. If you really loved me, you'd see it my way."

Mark had taken her into his arms, then, and kissed her so hard that it had hurt.

"You know how much I love you, Sally," he had whispered fiercely. "That's the reason I'm not giving in to you this time. I know in the long run that we'll be happier; that I'm right about this."

She hadn't answered him but had stood there silent and impassive in his arms, her lips pouting, her eyes sulky. Mark had been most upset. He grew upset very easily. He'd turned her face up to his so that he could look into her eyes.

"Listen to me, Sally," he'd said. "Maybe in a way you are right, too. You've been used to so much and it wouldn't be fair to make you do without all those things – just because I wanted you to."

"Don't be sarcastic, Mark!" Sally had flared back. "I suppose you're implying that if I loved you I'd be prepared to give up everything for you."

"I didn't say that and I didn't mean to imply it," was his cool rejoinder. "But since you've brought it up, Sally, maybe it does boil down to that. We've plenty of time to change our minds. Would you rather call the whole thing off?"

The argument had gone farther than Sally had intended, and she certainly didn't want to lose Mark. With sudden misery, she had burst into tears and then Mark's arms went round her again and he was apologetic and contrite, and had said, "Sally, darling, you don't think I'm trying to back out, do you? You know I love you – just how much I love you. It would break my heart if I were to lose you. That is what makes me so selfish about you. I haven't the courage to let you go to the sort of life I know you ought to have. I want you so much for myself . . ."

He had kissed her passionately and Sally had sobbed a little just for the comfort of it because she hadn't been

58

miserable any longer; and then she had dried her eyes and kissed him on the tip of his nose and told him she loved him too. And so it had all ended up happily – except that they hadn't got much further with her own plans for their financial arrangements.

"Oh, well!" Sally thought sleepily. "There's plenty of time for that."

Mark wanted to be married in the spring, and before then she could bring him round to her way of thinking. As for Lyndon – the sooner he went back to America the better. In fact he should have gone a month ago, only he had purposefully prolonged his visit.

"I'm not going back without you, honey," he had said.

What a conceited ass the man is! Sally thought indignantly. Let him stay and find out for himself that he means nothing at all to me. In fact I shall send him an invitation to my wedding to Mark. Serve him right!

With which amusing thought, she turned over again and like a child, fell instantly asleep.

* * *

Sunday morning dawned sunny and clear. Shane was up first and breakfasted alone and then went out into the sunshine because he wanted to do some thinking. Life had suddenly become a much more serious affair than hitherto, and he was going to start this very day to view it as such, he thought as he walked past the summer-house. What a fantastic party it had been last night! Everything seemed so much more rational in the sunshine. Nothing mattered quite so terribly when the sky was azure blue and the birds were chattering away in leafy green trees. At night, emotions invariably grew magnified until they were out of all proportion before daylight came again. Perhaps that was why God had created night and day. When one really thought about it, everything to do with nature had a purpose.

A rabbit scuttled across the green close-cut lawn and Shane watched it with delight. Lucky rabbits! No emotions for them. They just ate, mated and lived happily ever after! It was curious how, sooner or later, everybody and every animal, bird, fish, insect always found themselves a mate in the end. Somehow, until last night, he'd never really thought about marriage, or only as something rather improbable tucked away in the future. He didn't consider himself the marrying sort. Somebody had once said artists shouldn't marry. But that was nonsense. Artists wanted wives just as much as anyone else.

Sally had started the ball rolling with her engagement to Mark. Then he had suddenly realised that when she was married and went off with Mark (not that she would be going far) it would be devilishly lonely around the house. Sal was great company, and always ready to come up to his studio at a moment's notice to give an opinion on his work and a little encouragement. She had sat for him a good deal, too. Then, once the idea of Clare as a prospective wife had crossed his mind, it had grown steadily throughout the evening until he had realised that this was the perfect answer. It seemed, in fact, as if Fate had everything arranged. After all, Sally might never have gone to meet her two schoolfriends in that tea-shop. In fact, she did say she hadn't time, and then at the last moment had changed her mind. And then because the engagement party coincided, Sal had asked the two girls home, otherwise he might never have met them.

Actually Shane mused, Fate might have meant him to fall in love with Lee. But it had been Clare who attracted him which was surprising really, when he stopped to consider that his mental picture of his future wife had been someone like Sal – light-hearted, amusing, carefree – all the things Clare wasn't. But there it was. No one could account for love. This morning, he decided, he would tell the rest of the family that they were to be engaged.

Shane's father had been a bit surprised at the suddenness of this decision.

"Clare seems a very nice type of girl," he said. "I've nothing against her, Shane, if you're sure. It seems so sudden, though. You've only just met the girl!"

"I know!" Shane had answered. "But I'm crazy about her, Father, and anyway, an engagement can always be broken. Neither Clare nor I wish to be married right away. We both want plenty of time to get to know one another better."

"In that case, my boy, I'll raise no objections," his father had answered. "And let's hope a broken engagement won't be necessary. I must say, it's nice that you and Sal should both find someone else at the same time. Your mother and I were afraid you might get a little lonely what with Sal being so much with Mark these days. You twins have always been such inseparable companions, haven't you?"

Relieved to find his father so acquiescent, and understanding the reasons, Shane was sure his mother would be pleased, too – and Sal. She'd been trying to find him a suitable girlfriend ever since she had met Mark. The trouble had been that he really rather disliked most of Sally's female friends. Then suddenly she had produced two very nice ones. Lee was a curious person, but charming. He felt very much at ease with her. They were both artists and understood one another.

As Shane walked back to the house, he told himself he was to be congratulated at having acquired such a good friend in Lee and such a wonderful girl as Clare at the same time.

In the dining-room, the objects of Shane's thoughts were breakfasting alone together. Clare's meal was only an apology for one. Lee, eating heartily, remarked on the fact and asked Clare if there was anything wrong.

"You're as white as a sheet, old thing," she said affectionately. "Hangover?"

"Of course not, Lee; I only had two glasses of champagne the whole of last night."

"Worrying, then?" Lee asked.

Clare nodded her head.

"Come on, out with it!" Lee said. "A trouble shared is a trouble halved, so they say."

"Lee, I can't go through with this engagement!" Clare burst out suddenly. "I can't. I don't love Shane. I can't get engaged to him. I can't!"

"Steady up, Clare," Lee said gently. "I suppose this is the result of viewing things in the cold grey light of dawn. If you really mean it, why not go and tell Shane. It hasn't been made public yet so no one but ourselves will know."

"And his father!" Clare cried. "Shane spoke to him first thing this morning. That means his mother probably knows by now, and Shane's bound to have told Sally. Besides, I promised him I wouldn't go back on my word."

Lee didn't reply for a moment. Her mind was busy with Clare's problem. The whole affair was absurd in a way. If only Clare had not been such an intense person . . . if she could only have found Mark mildly attractive and then ceased to think about him again, instead of falling straight over the precipice! Still, she, herself, was a fine one to talk. A few years ago, she had done exactly the same thing. Now she had too much self-control to allow it. That, in itself, was something to be thankful for. Just supposing she, finding Shane as attractive as she did last night, had allowed herself to think about him in a serious light. A fine shock she would have had in the early hours of the morning to find Shane and Clare getting engaged! No, no sudden emotions for Lee. Next time, if ever she allowed a next time, it would be a gradual thing, founded perhaps on friendship, ripening into love. And knowing all along that there would be no complications.

Lee gave herself a quick shake. She wasn't trying to

62

sort our her own problems now, but Clare's. Clare hadn't learned self-control – not regarding her emotions. A first love always cuts more deeply. Perhaps next time, Clare would be more cautious, too. Still, the fat was truly in the fire at this precise moment. Not only had she fallen in love quite hopelessly, but she had got herself engaged to a man she didn't love and now, presumably, knew she never could love.

"Clare, nothing you said last night, nothing Shane said, and none of the circumstances are altered. Last night you felt that Shane might help you to get over Mark. Shane was prepared to take a chance on whether or not you grew fond of him eventually. Personally, I think his hopes of a solution are the best possible ending to the whole thing. Surely you haven't started to hope all over again this morning that Mark and Sally will break their engagement?"

"No, it isn't that!" Clare answered. "It's just – well, just that it seems so crazy to tie myself up to a man I don't even know in order to extricate myself from a measure of unhappiness. Surely one shouldn't even get engaged with the idea of breaking it?"

"Of course not!" Lee agreed. "But why should it be broken? You can't say for sure that Shane isn't right, can you? Perhaps you will change your mind about Mark. Perhaps one day you'll wake up one morning and know as suddenly as you knew about Mark, that you love Shane. But I'm not going to say another word, Clare. It isn't for me to decide your life for you. I've no right to, and my advice may be totally wrong. One human being cannot determine the course of another's and be sure that it's the right path. You must make up your own mind. If you're afraid of the result of telling Shane you want to break it off, I'll tell him for you. You can take the next train home and that will be that. And if it's what you really want, deep down inside you, then go, my dear. But don't be too long deciding. Sally

63

will be down soon, and Shane, too, probably. Which is it to be?"

For a long fraught moment, Clare hesitated, then, afraid that a lack of courage was the only reason for this morning's doubts, and unwilling to admit to such a thing, she said quietly:

"I'll go through with it, Lee. I've nothing to lose."

Chapter Six

I suppose she's right, Lee told herself during the long silence that followed Clare's decision. Shane's a charming person and is obviously deeply attracted to Clare. An artist needs someone like Clare who never intrudes when she isn't wanted, and yet is around when you do want her. She knew, herself, how pleasant it had been this last week, having Clare's company in the flat. She had never really considered until then how lonely she had been, living by herself. Clare was the sort of person who would listen to a violent burst of artistic temperament and then without flaring back, go quietly off to make a cup of tea! And what was more, she did not bear one a grudge for it afterwards.

Yes, Clare was a good type of character to go with Shane's nature. She would be the background to his vivid foreground. She would look after him and give him peace and quiet and understanding. But would she give him the stimulus every artist needed? Would Shane find he must go elsewhere for his inspiration once the novelty of Clare had worn thin? More important still, would Shane make Clare happy?

Lee frowned at the uncertainty of her own thoughts. Clare, after all, asked little of life – a home, a husband, children. Shane could fulfill those needs. But could he fill that need deep down within Clare for love – a genuine lasting emotion coming from the heart and not from reason? Could Shane, in fact, replace what Clare thought Mark could bring to her life?

Why not? Lee then asked herself. After all, just what is love? Only a figment of the imagination. One considers oneself in love, and the physical senses build up the idea and then in one's own mind, it becomes a reality. I was in love, or thought I was. And yet I can be happy without him. If I'm honestly truthful about it, I really only think about him occasionally. If my love had been real, I'd not be able to feel like this. So if I can be mistaken, why not Clare? And if she can imagine herself into love with Mark, then why not out of love and into love with Shane?

She laughed suddenly aloud and Clare, unable to read her thoughts, asked her to explain the joke.

"Just life!" Lee said vaguely. "It's such an intangible thing. Once one starts looking for facts, there's nothing there at all. After all, how do we know we exist? How do we know we aren't somebody's dream?"

"Somebody's nightmare!" came Sally's voice from the doorway. "I've got a head like nobody's business. Lee, how you can discuss such subjects at breakfast, I just don't know!"

"Because, my poppet, it's not so far off lunch time," Lee replied. "Nearly eleven o'clock. And you'd better brace yourself, my child, because Clare has some startling news for you."

Sally perked up instantly. The anticlimax of the party had been the chief cause of her depression. Anything startling or exciting would soon put her back into the party spirit.

At that moment, Shane came in through the french windows and said brightly, "Hullo, Sal. Has Clare told you our news?"

Sally looked from one to the other with dancing blue eyes.

"I see she hasn't," Shane went on. "So apart from Lee and Father, Sally, I would like you to be first to know that Clare and I are unofficially engaged."

66

Sally gave a joyous little laugh and rushed round the table, first to hug Shane and then Clare.

"Oh, it's wonderful, really great!" she cried. "Lee, isn't it exciting? Shane, it's just what I *hoped* would happen. When are you going to be married? Soon? Let's have a double wedding, Clare. That would be fun!"

"Steady on, Sal!" Shane said. "Neither Clare nor I intend rushing things. You seem to forget we only met for the first time yesterday. We hardly know one another!"

He smiled at Clare in such a friendly, disarming manner, that she did not have to force the smile in return.

"And none of this spreading of the news, Sal!" Shane went on. "Enough people will think we're mad to get engaged a few hours after we met. We don't want the whole village buzzing with it, too. It's to be a secret, do you understand, Sal, a secret? I doubt if she knows what that word means," he said aside to Lee with a grin.

"Oh, no, I promise I won't tell a soul!" Sally vowed. "Not Mother or Father or even Mark."

"Mother and Father already know, and there's no reason why you shouldn't tell Mark," Shane replied rather sharply. "He's almost one of the family now, anyway."

"Then I'm going to ring him up," Sally cried, but Shane put a hand on her shoulder.

"You eat your breakfast, first!" he said. But then Sally heard Mark's voice in the hall and nothing could stop her. She flung down her napkin and rushed out of the room. A minute later, she returned, hopping up and down beside Mark, her arm through his.

"Aren't you going to congratulate them, Mark?" she cried, prodding his arm impatiently.

Mark's gaze went slowly to Clare. Try as she would, Clare could not keep her eyes on her plate, and she looked up at him, straight into his eyes. Her heart jumped violently and the colour flooded her cheeks. For one brief second, she was quite unconscious of the other people in the room. There was only herself and Mark, and the same repeated glow inside her and heady excitement because this was the man she loved. Every time she saw him again, she felt the same inward shock, the same reactions. And something in her heart gloried in it. She had found her man, her love. That it was too late didn't matter. Part of her was fulfilled just by the knowledge that love had come to her at last.

And then she became aware of the others, aware of the fact that she had been staring at Mark, heaven alone knew for how long. What must they be thinking – Lee, Shane, Sally? The colour welled into her cheeks again and she dropped her eyes in an agony of self-consciousness.

Sally gave her happy little laugh.

"Don't be so embarrased, Clare. You're blushing like you used to do at school! Mark, do hurry up and congratulate them, or Clare will think you don't approve, or something."

"What nonsense!" Mark said hastily, recovering from his surprise. "It was just the unexpectedness of your news, that's all. My heartiest congratulations to you both."

He sat down at the table, although he had already eaten, listening with only half an ear to Sally's chatter, the background of the voices. The other half of him was trying to recover from his surprise. It had almost been a shock. How wrong one could be in summing people up. He would never have credited quiet, shy, intelligent Clare with an appalling action like this. She must be mad! It was typical of Shane, of course. It was the Irish in him, and in Sally, that made them both follow their crazy impulses on the spur of the moment. But for Clare to become engaged to a man she had only known a few hours – it just didn't make sense. Or did it? Perhaps after all, it did. Supposing Clare had been going to meet Shane in the summer-house, leaving it late to deliver Sally's message and assuming he, Mark, would have gone? That might explain all sorts of things – her surprise, her reactions, her confusion afterwards. It put a different construction on the girl altogether. That kiss was certainly not the product of a light-hearted flirtation. Could it be that Clare was one of those girls who was out to marry for money? Heaven alone knew, Shane had enough of it. And being an only son, he would eventually come into a small fortune – not even a small one, come to that!

No! Mark rejected the idea with a sudden repulsion. Why should he misjudge the girl, or cast aspersions on her motives? He was marrying Sally who had just as much money as Shane. Still, Mark argued with himself, Sally knew how much he hated the idea. And anyway, it hadn't been an overnight affair like this. Perhaps Clare had fallen in love with Shane at first sight. It did happen – at any rate in books.

He looked across at Clare who was staring out of the window, and was like himself, lost in thought. Her face was pale now and there was no trace of the colour that had come so suddenly into her cheeks. Had that been the blush of a guilty conscience, or was Sally right when she had accused Clare of being shy and self-conscious – quite a different thing. Sally, surely, should know Clare better than he did, but Sally, on the other hand, was so confoundedly trusting. Shane, too. They took people on trust at sight and often realised afterwards that they were not quite so nice underneath. Look at that fellow Lyndon. Charming enough fellow to meet. Even he, Mark, had been taken in at first. But he wasn't a fool and he could see now what the American was up to. He wanted Sally and meant to get her. Darned cheek! Mark thought jealously. Sally was his girl and just because this fellow worked with her father and was a coming film star, and had already packets of money which he flashed around the place (those orchids, for instance, every time he came to the house!) – that didn't make Sally his girl. She loved him, Mark, and if Mark had anything to do with it, it was going to stay that way.

With instinctive honesty, Mark knew that he was not being entirely fair. Lyndon was not going behind his back. He was, on the contrary, flaunting his suit. Not that it made it any pleasanter for Mark, but at least the fellow wasn't underhand. Mark knew exactly where he stood and knew what he was fighting against. That made it, in a sense, an equal fight. All's fair in love and war, so people said, and presumably Lyndon had as much right to fight for Sally as he had. An engagement wasn't a real tie and Mark was forced to admit that he did not believe Lyndon would be making such obvious passes at Sally if she were his, Mark's wife. Besides, there was no real need to be jealous. Sally had assured him over and over again that she loved him; even that she disliked Lyndon. Sally was young and lighthearted and she would have to settle down soon enough. If she wanted to amuse herself with a mild flirtation during dances with the fellow, was he to stop her?

Deep down inside, Mark began to wonder if it were, after all, Sally of whom he was jealous. Suppose it was simply that Lyndon possessed a lot of things he knew he lacked. Social charm, for instance; money; the ability to hold a number of people interested by his witty conversation; his ability to dance, play all the right games, ride, shoot, fence. There seemed to be nothing the fellow couldn't do! And always with any amount of self-assurance, decisiveness, and ability.

For the hundredth time of late, Mark wondered that Sally could still love him when Lyndon was around. It seemed to him, in his lack of conceit, that he measured up very poorly beside the American.

I suppose I must just accept the fact that she does love me, and be eternally grateful to her, Mark thought, with a loving glance at Sally who was chattering away to Shane and Lee. I must just accept the fact, too, that with her laughter and her provocative, impulsive, generous nature, Sally will always be the flame to draw the moths. I must at least do her the honour of trusting her.

It was part of Mark's nature to give everyone he knew the benefit of the doubt. He looked back at Clare and felt that he was being unfair to her, too. There was something behind all this – something he could not quite fathom but which he intended to get to the bottom of sooner or later. The expression on her face now was one of complete and unmistakable sadness. That wasn't the face of a girl who was radiantly in love; nor was it the face of a girl who had set out to trap Shane for her own ends and achieved her aim.

With an unusual impulsiveness, Mark decided that he would talk to Clare. Perhaps she was in some difficulty – there could be something he could do to help. Maybe getting engaged to Shane was a rebound from an unhappy love affair and inwardly she was regretting it. Not that it was his business, but he would try to get her alone some time today and give her the chance to talk. After all, she would become his sister-in-law by marriage and if that were to be so, they should get to know and like one another.

His chance came sooner than he had anticipated. Sally – her hangover, as she chose to call her dispiritedness of half an hour ago having vanished – was suggesting that they all went riding. Shane, as energetic and sport-loving as his twin, readily agreed. Lee admitted that she hadn't been on a horse for years but that she was game to try if Shane chose her a really 'tame horse', which sent the twins off into gales of laughter.

"What about you, Clare?" Shane asked gently.

"I'm afraid I don't ride," Clare said, coming out of her day-dream with a start. "But please don't put off your ride on my account. Really, I'd far rather sit in the garden in the sunshine, or go for a walk and see the countryside. Honestly, Shane, I'd rather. I'm still a little tired from last night."

"I'm none too keen to go," Mark said, to Sally's surprise. "As a matter of fact, I've got a dreadful head from mixing champagne with beer last night. Jolting around on a horse would finish me."

This last statement was only partially true. He had a slight headache, but it came from lack of sleep, too much smoke and a certain amount of heady meditation when he finally got to bed. A little fresh air would put him right for lunch and at the same time give him that opportunity of speaking to Clare alone.

After a great deal of argument, Sally and Shane finally agreed to go without them, and Lee, with a quick glance at Clare's agonized expression, said she would stay behind with Clare. Clare looked back at her gratefully, but Mark was insistent.

"Nonsense, Lee. I'll keep Clare company," he said. "We'll go for a nice long tramp together and get up an appetite for lunch. You go and have your riding lesson."

Unable to refuse without being too pointed, Lee allowed Sally to drag her off to borrow some riding breeches. What was meant to be would happen eventually, come what might. Clare, after all, had admitted that it was best to face up to things, to Mark. Perhaps she would be bored by him if she saw enough of him. Mark, it seemed, was a very quiet person with a great deal of charm and decency, but he was not the leading light of the party. Shane, or that American film star chap, were much more scintillating companions. Still, Clare was rather a different person with different tastes. Perhaps Mark . . .

Lee gave it up, and prepared to be as light-hearted as the twins.

The room seemed strangely silent when the other three had gone. A little uncertain of himself now, Mark felt annoyed for landing himself in what promised to be rather an awkward situation. Clare, it seemed, had nothing to say. Nor, for that matter, could he find words.

At length, unable to bear the silence, Mark said, "Well, shall we go for that walk, Clare? There are some lovely parts of the country round here."

"Yes, of course. I'll go and put on some heavy shoes," Clare said, and escaped from the room as quickly as she could.

Mark waited impatiently for her return. She seemed to have been gone a long while and he was starting to wonder if perhaps she had thought better of it, when at last she came down the stairs and said quietly, "I'm ready. Shall we go?"

They set off side by side, Mark finding to his surprise that he had no need to shorten his stride for Clare. She stepped out at length and unlike Sally, who tripped along beside him chattering ten to the dozen, Clare walked as if it were for some other purpose than talking. In fact, he soon found himself hurrying to keep up with her and at last pulled up short, and said with a smile, "Anybody would think you were running away from something, Clare!"

He knew immediately that for some reason his remark had been tactless. Clare stopped dead in her tracks and stared at him. Her grey eyes were enormous, and the pallor of her cheeks was so white that he wondered if she were not well.

They stood there, facing each other, for a long minute. Then Clare relaxed slightly and started to walk again, more slowly.

"I'm sorry!" she said. "I'm used to walking alone at home – up in the hills. I do walk rather fast."

"Tell me about your home." Mark said. "It's in Scotland, isn't it?"

Clare, glad of a topic of conversation that was impersonal, talked freely about her relations, her home life and the beautiful countryside around.

"It's lovely here, too," she said, "but it's a different type of beauty. Up there, it's wild and gaunt and a little

73

frightening in its starkness and majesty. Here it is more warm and friendly with little fields and trees everywhere. The same amount of difference, I suppose, as there is between summer and winter . . . both lovely but in such different ways. I think I belong up there. I know I always feel a sense of being confined when I'm in the south for long. I get a kind of claustrophobia and want to rush back to the hills and breathe in their solitariness. Do you understand?"

"Yes, I think I do!" Mark said suddenly. "You see, Clare, I had four years in a Jap prisoner of war camp. I didn't suffer too badly," he added, seeing the expression on her face. "But it was the confinement that bothered me, and still does at times. I have that same longing to rush away where there are no people, no sounds other than those of nature itself – only great open spaces and a sense of freedom."

"You'd love Scotland, then," Clare said before she stopped to think of her words. "You should come up there sometime. Where we live there are hardly any people – just a few villagers about a mile away from the house, and you can walk for days and days without seeing anyone – unless it is an occasional shepherd."

"I once went up there for a holiday," Mark told her. "That was before the war. It's strange, you know, but I did think about the hills and the lochs I had seen more than anything else when I imagined myself free again. I always promised myself another holiday up there but by the time I got home, I suppose I'd forgotten my longing to be there. And then I met Sally and I forgot everything else!" he ended with a laugh.

"You must find Sally a wonderful tonic," Clare said with gravity. "She's always so full of fun and laughter. I expect you soon forgot those awful days in prison."

"Yes, you're right," Mark agreed, his brown eyes lighting up. "I never thought of it quite that way before but I think you are right. I do know that more than

74

anything else in the world, I wanted to put the past right out of my mind. Sally had helped me to do that and I remember it now only as a bad dream."

Clare remained silent and Mark thought suddenly that he had given himself an opening to fulfil the purpose of this walk and that he should take advantage of it.

"Don't you agree with me, Clare?" he asked. "About putting unpleasant things out of one's mind, I mean. I'm certain that is the only way to regain happiness."

"Wh-what do you mean?" Clare faltered, unsure if there were a double meaning behind Mark's words. Had he meant to be personal?

Mark took his courage in both hands and said, "You aren't happy, are you, Clare? Perhaps I'm wrong but I had that impression. Can't you forget the past?"

Clare quickened her pace unconsciously and kept her face away from Mark's gaze. The colour had mounted her cheeks again and she did not wish him to see it.

"I've – not been unhappy – not really unhappy," she said in answer to his question.

"Then why do you look so sad sometimes?" Mark countered.

"Do I? I don't know. Nobody is happy always. I expect I have my share of unhappiness like everyone else."

"Clare, forgive me if I'm being too personal and don't answer me if you'd rather not, but are you marrying Shane to escape from something?"

Clare turned and stared at him aghast. Could Mark have guessed? Had he guessed last night in the summer-house after all?

"Don't look so terrified, Clare!" Mark said gently, seeing the fear in her eyes. "You don't have to be afraid of me. There's nothing wrong in it, anyway. If Shane can bring you happiness and help you to forget, why not give him that opportunity, as long as you are prepared to give him something in return. You know, Clare, if you do marry him, you will be my sister by marriage, and I'd like to feel you felt me your friend."

Oh, God! Clare prayed silently, help me to stand this. Mark, as a brother! Funny that I should never have thought of that.

She had a dreadful desire to laugh hysterically, but managed to control it.

"That's the trouble," she said with difficulty. "I don't know what I can give him in exchange. Shane seems to think that he finds some inspiration for his work in having me around. I know that isn't enough, but he says it will do for a start. But I'm not sure. You see, there's so much else involved."

"Care to tell me about it?" Mark asked gently.

"No!" cried Clare. "I can't. No!"

Mark started at the sudden raised tone of her voice. So he had been right! There was something behind her rather odd behaviour and this sudden engagement.

"I see!" he said. "Of course, if there is someone else involved, you are not at liberty to speak."

"There is someone else," Clare cried. "I've told Shane. He seems to think it doesn't matter."

Mark was silent for a moment.

"I'm not sure I agree with him," he said. "Unless of course this other fellow doesn't reciprocate your feelings. I assume that's the position."

"Yes!" Clare whispered. "He's in love with someone else."

"I'm sorry!" Mark replied with feeling. "It's rotten when it's that way. Isn't there any hope then?"

"No, none!" Clare forced out. "The girl he loves is a wonderful person and I quite understand his loving her."

"That's darned bad luck, Clare," Mark said. "And, of course, it puts a different construction on things. I mean, I rather agree with Shane. Time makes such a difference and things which seemed to matter desperately, don't matter at all after a little while. I know that. Things I

76

thought I would never get over – things that happened in that camp – I seldom think of them now. Perhaps you'll get over it, too, and then Shane will come into his own."

"But I don't want to forget him!" Clare was unable to prevent the words that rushed through her lips. "I love him. How can I ever marry Shane?"

"Perhaps you won't," Mark said to calm her. "Perhaps there won't be any need. Maybe this man you love isn't really in love with the other girl and will come to you in the end. People often are mistaken."

Clare turned and stared at him.

"*You* haven't any doubts about the way you love Sally?" she asked pointedly.

"Well, no!" Mark admitted. "But that's different."

"No, it isn't!" Clare cried from the depth of her soul. "That's just it. There isn't any difference at all. He's every bit as sure as you are."

Mark strode along in silence for a moment, thinking hard. At last he turned to Clare and said, "In that case, I think I should do just what you are going to do. I should try to forget him by replacing him with somebody else. But Clare, it's the hardest thing in the world to do."

"I know!" Clare whispered. "I don't think I can do it. But at least I'm going to try!"

Chapter Seven

Something in the tone of Clare's voice sent a shiver of apprehension down Mark's back. A minute or two ago, he had advised her to try to find a new happiness with Shane, but now he began to doubt his own judgment. The very determination with which Clare had spoken was in itself a paradox. She did not really believe it would be a success and that cry, wrung from her heart, had been more to convince herself than him.

That, surely, could not be right – to struggle against one's inner convictions. Mark believed more than most people that honesty was all-important, especially that one should be honest with oneself. Clare's engagement to Shane seemed a flagrant denial of her true self. She had, without doubt, let Shane's arguments influence her decision. Did she not know that Shane, like Sally, was a creature of impulsive moods? If she were relying on his firmness of opinion to carry them both along, then Clare was basing her own happiness on something without a real basis of security. Not, Mark hastened to add to himself, that he was trying to belittle Shane's love for Clare. That might well exist, but would it last? Shane's past affairs had seldom survived for long. He was, after all, an artist and there was great need in him for something new as soon as that intense interest that had held him in grip for a short while was beginning to wane. If that should happen in a few months and Clare had allowed herself to rely too much upon his emotions, would she not end by being hurt yet again?

It was so difficult for him to voice an opinion. He had known Clare so short a while and had only his instinct to rely on regarding herself. Secondly, it was not his business to advise her; nor was it altogether fair to Shane. But he felt, also, that it was his duty to speak out, if by doing so he could protect this strange, quiet, intense girl from further unhappiness. What should he say? Had he not already allowed himself to voice an opinion that he no longer considered so wise?

Struggling with himself, Mark at last decided that he should put this, the other side of the picture, to her, so that she would have the facts as he saw them, and then make her own choice.

Clare listened to him in silence. Deep within her, she felt that Mark was right. She was not, herself, convinced of the depth of Shane's feelings. That he had meant what he said last night, she did not doubt; nor that he still meant it this morning. But would it last? Mark knew Shane better than she did, and she, too, felt Shane's interest in her to be an intangible thing, without deep root. If this were so, there was no excuse for their engagement. Not even the hope that she might forget Mark or at least grow indifferent to him and find eventually that she cared for Shane. It was only excusable if she had belief in that hope and belief in Shane's feelings. And being honest with herself, she did not believe in either.

What made me decide to agree to Shane's proposal? she questioned herself. Because of that moment when she had lost courage and had found comfort in his expression of affection for her? That surely was weakness, not strength. Or had it been because inwardly, subconsciously, she wanted the excuse to stay on here, near Mark, able to see him every day, hear his voice? That again was weakness. Real courage pointed to departure, in the determination to put Mark out of her mind and thoughts and heart and resume her hum-drum existence in Scotland; to put away the temptation of allowing Shane to put balm on her wounds by his flattery and obvious interest in her; to fight alone.

Lee had said she thought the engagement a good idea. But did Lee really understand how deep were her emotions, her love for Mark, even though they had come to light with such swiftness and were based on such little knowledge of him? Could any other human being know how convinced she was in her own heart that there never would and never could be anyone else; and that for her it must be a real, deep love like this, or nothing. A marriage based on friendliness and companionship was not for Clare. She could not live on it as perhaps others could. Lee, perhaps, would find it enough because she had other interests in life. But love meant everything to Clare, and in this moment of honesty, she knew she could never succeed in making her marriage a success if it were not founded on true love. She would, in time, grow to hate the man who stood for second best. Then life would be wretched for them both, and even if she were prepared to face an existence herself, she had no right to ask Shane to share it with her. He did not know her well enough to suspect such results. If he did, he, too, would realise that their engagement was a farce; that it could only be made to be broken, and that was something, she could not tolerate.

"Mark," she said suddenly. "I don't think I ought to go through with it. It isn't because of what you just said. It's because you have voiced my own fears and doubts. I think I mistook the direction of the road courage was pointing to me. If I am really honest, I must have the courage to go home."

"Is – is the man you love living in Scotland?" Mark asked.

Clare shook her head.

"Then why not follow your inner convictions, Clare, and go home. Perhaps up there everything will regain its right perspective. Shane will understand. After all, it could not hurt him terribly losing you now when he has known you so short a while. It is surprising how quickly one forgets pain when there is nothing left to remind you of it."

Clare knew that he was thinking about that prison camp again and yet she could not but adapt his words to herself. Perhaps, with nothing to remind her of Mark and these few days of love, she would forget, too.

"I think I *will* go home," she said, almost inaudibly. "Mark, how can I tell Shane? Sally? What will they think?"

"It doesn't matter what they think, Clare. All that matters is that you should do what *you* think right. I'll help you if your mind is really made up. If you like, I'll tell Shane myself; there's no need for you to tell Sal. I'll tell her after you've gone. You can go on Lee's train after tea and I'll see you have an opportunity of speaking to Shane alone before then."

The kindness in his voice, his interest in her problems and his consideration for her feelings, all touched Clare deeply. She could not help but think how wonderful her life might have been. Supposing Mark had been just one of Sally's friends and that Sally had been getting engaged to somebody else – Lyndon perhaps; that Mark had turned to her and eventually loved her!

She stared ahead of her, the tears blinding her eyes to the gentle, sloping fields; the peace of an English countryside on a summer morning. Life was so beautiful, and so uselessly so when one's heart was breaking with a hopeless love. She stumbled and Mark's hand caught her arm to steady her. As he did so, her face was turned towards him and he saw her tears.

Shocked at the sight of such open misery in the eyes of anyone as young and pretty as Clare, he felt a rush of pity for her flooding through him, and instinctively as he would have behaved with a hurt child, his arms went round her. He felt the sudden tautening of her body and

81

thinking it to be caused by an inward fight to control her tears, he said:

"You don't have to pretend with me, Clare. I want to be your friend. Cry all you want to. I shan't mind. Look, here's my handkerchief. Let me wipe the tears away."

Mark, oh, Mark! Clare cried inwardly. If only you knew! If only you realised what this is doing to me. How you would hate me if you knew. I don't *want* your pity. I want your love!

She pulled away from him and forced a laugh which even to her own ears, sounded a little despairing.

"I'm all right now," she said. "Please forgive me. I think the sooner I get home the better! Everyone is so reasonable and unemotional at home. I don't know what has come over me lately. The family would be horrified at such lack of control."

"Emotions always run high in this family," Mark said with a smile. "Sally and Shane have far too much of the Irish in them to live on a smooth plane. It's up one minute and down the next. Even I find it hard to keep up with them, and I'll admit I find it a bit exhausting sometimes. You have nothing to be sorry for, Clare. I do hope, though that you *will* be happier when you get home. I'm sure you will. I shall think about you and hope you will find time to drop me a line and let me know how things go. It's odd," he mused, "but I don't easily make friends with girls. I don't think I understand them very well . . . except Sally, of course. But with you it's been different. Just our walk and our conversation this morning, has established a strong bond of friendship between us – or at any rate, I feel it. Do you, too, Clare?"

"Yes!" Clare said, but it was not friendship she felt had been strengthened in her own heart – only the certainty of her love for him with all that it implied.

"Well, I suppose we'd better get back to lunch," Mark said easily. "I expect the others will be back by now."

But when he and Clare reached the house an hour later, it was to find a message from Sally, saying:

We're staying to lunch with Lyndon. He wants you and Clare to join us by car. Lunch at one-thirty. Sal.

Mark, reading Sally's almost illegible scrawl, crumpled the note in his hand with a moment's annoyance. Sally, he supposed, had purposefully chosen the ride over to the cottage Lyndon had taken for a few months, so that she would see him. Then he thrust the thought from him, knowing that he was judging her unfairly. It was more than probable that they had met Lyndon out riding and that he had issued the invitation to lunch. Well, Mark also would accept the invitation which no doubt Sally had forced on the American. If he didn't like it, it was just too bad! He turned to Clare.

"My car's outside," he said. "Have you anything you wish to do before we go? We're invited to lunch with Lyndon and are to join the others there."

Clare disappeared to repair the disorder her tears had caused to her face. A few minutes later, she rejoined Mark and they set off together in his car.

Last night's party spirit appeared to have been revived. Mark and Clare went into the cottage to find Sally, Lee, Shane and the American drinking cocktails, all of them in high fettle.

"Nice of you to ask us to lunch," Mark said to the American as they took off their coats.

"Delighted to have you," Lyndon rejoined easily. "Have a cocktail?"

"I'd rather have a beer, if you don't mind," Mark said, wondering anew at the suaveness of his host. It seemed so unlikely, face to face with him, that he was really out to take Sally from him. And yet he had no doubt about the fact.

Clare had a sherry and Shane came across and toasted her.

"To my fiancée," he said loudly. Lyndon turned with a look of surprise on his face.

"Say, that's news!" he remarked. "Congratulations Shane – and to you, Clare."

Clare felt a sudden annoyance with Shane. He had agreed to keep their engagement unofficial. The American wasn't included in the family who were permitted to know. This only made it more difficult to say later that she was going back on her word. It would be harder on Shane himself.

Then her anger melted away. Shane wasn't to know what was in her mind. She had no right to be cross with him. Besides which, it was clear that the cocktails had turned his head a little. Not a heavy drinker as a rule, two or three could raise his spirits considerably, and Lyndon had seen to it that his highballs were pretty strong.

Sally, too, was just the slightest bit out of control. She giggled consistently, and although she had joined Mark immediately and called him 'darling' with every second word, she seemed to be throwing endearments in Lyndon's direction. Mark tried to cool his rising anger.

"Don't you think that's enough, Sal?" he asked her quietly, as Lyndon took away her glass to refill it.

"Don't be such an old stupid, Mark!" Sally said, pouting at him. "Just because you prefer beer, it doesn't mean I have to do without a cocktail."

"I know, Sally, but—"

"Oh, darling, do stop being a wet-blanket!" Sally cried, her cheeks flushed and her eyes sparkling. "I'm perfectly sober."

"You won't be soon, Sally," Lee said, interrupting the conversation. "Besides, I'm hungry. Isn't it time for lunch?"

"Yes, I think I'm hungry, too," Sally cried, forgetting

her annoyance of a few moments ago. "Lyndon, let's have something to eat. I'm starving."

Immediately, the American acquiesced, and took his guests through to the dining-room.

It was an extravagant meal. Iced melon, followed by roast pheasant, although it was out of season for game shooting, and red wine. Then icecream and later port.

Lyndon had put Sally on his right, Shane beside her, Lee opposite him, and Clare and Mark on the other side of the table. It was difficult for Mark to address Sally, and impossible to do so privately. As the meal ensued, he felt his anger returning. Lyndon was plying Sally with wine, refilling her glass whenever it appeared to be empty. Sally, chattering away to everyone in general, eating, laughing, was unaware of what was going on, and feeling a little hot, would drink down her glass unconscious of Mark's disapproving gaze, or of the fact that she had had more to drink than was good for her.

Shane was doing the same. Mark, furious by the end of the meal, determined to see that neither of the twins should ride home. They were in no condition to do so. As soon as coffee had been served and finished, he said, "I'll drive you home in my car, I suggest we send one of the grooms for the horses, Sal. It's much too hot this afternoon to ride back."

"Oh, no, Mark!" Sally objected. "I want to cool down. Besides, Shane and I have promised to give Lee a jumping lesson on the way back. She did terribly well this morning."

"But Sally—" Mark began when Lyndon interrupted him, saying, "If you're worried about Sally, Mark, I'll go with them."

For a second Mark lost control. So that was his game! Then his clenched fist fell to his side, and he said in icy undertones, "Look here, Lyndon, Sally and Shane have both had more to drink than is good for them.

They are neither of them in a condition to go home on horseback."

"Say, you aren't imagining they're not sober enough to ride, are you?" Lyndon remarked in his usual friendly tone.

Was his surprise feigned, Mark wondered, or did he really think the twins could consume that amount of drink without any effect?

"I don't think they are," Mark replied in a quiet voice.

"Gee, I just don't see how any folks can get screwy on so little," Lyndon remarked, his surprise genuine.

"Perhaps in the film world, people are used to drinking a good deal and have stronger heads," Mark said evenly. "I think I know my fiancée's capacity for drink, and this is the first time I've seen her so – so out of control."

"Gee, I'm sorry!" Lyndon apologized. "I guess I didn't think. Look, I'll get my car out and we can all go back in two cars."

But neither Sally nor Shane were to be deterred from their purpose.

"We're going to have our race, aren't we, Shane?" Sally said, laughing. "If Lee doesn't want to ride any more, then Mark can ride her horse back."

"Sally, I insist on you coming in the car with me," Mark said desperately. But his words only made up her mind more firmly.

"If I want to go, I'll go, Mark!" she said with finality.

"Look here, old fellow, you don't have to spoil Sal's fun," Shane put in, rising to his feet somewhat unsteadily.

Lyndon, realising that Mark was right and that the cocktails, which had been strong, together with the wine and the port, had without doubt affected the twins more than he had dreamed possible, took Mark's side.

"Come on, honey, you can race another time," he said. "I want you to have a run in my car. You haven't been in yet, you know."

"I'll go another time," Sally said doggedly. "Lee, are you coming, or is Mark going to have your horse?"

Lee looked at Mark and Mark said, "I'll ride your horse home, Lee."

Realising that he wanted to go with the twins in order to look after them, Lee consented immediately and offered to drive Mark's car home.

Worried now at the result of his own actions, Lyndon said to Mark, "Shall I come too?"

"Yes, I think you'd better," Mark said. "It'll take our combined efforts to prevent the twins breaking their necks."

Mark's annoyance had given way, now, to a deep concern. Sally and Shane were both excellent riders, but they were always a bit wild and took innumerable risks just for the fun of it. Heaven alone knew what would happen on the ride home with Shane hardly able to stand up straight and Sally not much better. It mattered no longer who was to blame for their condition. The whole of his mind was concentrated on determination to prevent eventual mishap.

As soon as they were in their saddles, Lee and Clare drove home in Mark's car.

"Lee, you don't think anything awful will happen, do you?" Clare asked anxiously. She had seen all too clearly the anxiety on Mark's face and felt that it would not be there without good cause.

"I hope not!" was Lee's comment. "I'm afraid I shall be partly to blame. But I never realised how strong those cocktails were. I don't think Lyndon knew what effect it would have on the twins, either. Neither of them seem to have much head for drinking. I'm afraid I have, and not being affected myself, it just didn't occur to me until Mark mentioned it, that Sally or Shane were a bit – well, excited."

They drove the next mile in silence, then Clare said abruptly, "I've decided to go home with you tonight, Lee. I talked it over with Mark this morning – not how I feel about him, of course – and I think I know what I ought to do. I must go home and fight this out alone."

Lee shook her head.

"Shane will be very upset. He was talking about you most of the morning," she said. "Still, you know what's best, Clare, and anything you say is OK by me. Why not stay in town with me a day or two longer? We'll get about a bit and see some shows and flicks – take your mind off things."

"All right, Lee. I'd like your company in the next few days. It would be a bit difficult at home where no one knows what has happened."

"Yes, and you don't want to bottle it all up inside you," Lee said. "You can talk your head off about Mark or anything else and I shan't mind."

"Lee, you're a good friend," Clare said. "I'm glad we met again that day in the Harrington tea-shop – in spite of everything else it brought about. I shan't regret having known Mark, either. At least I know now what it is to have loved."

Lee said, "I hope Shane will have sobered up a bit by tea-time. You'll want to talk to him before you go and explain."

"Yes!" said Clare. "You know, Lee, Mark was most awfully kind to me this morning . . . and very understanding.

"He doesn't suspect the truth?" Lee asked.

Clare shook her head.

"No, thank heaven. I couldn't bear that. He'd be so dreadfully embarrassed. Besides, if he ever did know, I couldn't face him again. Nor Sally."

Lee drove the car up to the front door and climbed out, and the two girls went inside and up to their room to pack. Half an hour later, Lee looked at her watch and said anxiously, "The others should be here by now. It's only an hour's ride, if that. Clare, I hope. . . ."

Her voice trailed away as she heard the sound of a horse's hooves on the gravel drive.

She and Clare rushed to the window and looked down. Below, they saw Lyndon's figure as he flung himself off his horse and ran up the steps to the door.

With sudden nameless fear, Lee and Clare turned by mutual consent and hurried downstairs. Lyndon was talking breathlessly to the twins' parents.

"In heaven's name, get a doctor – quickly," they heard his voice, no longer suave and controlled, but frantic with anxiety. "I hate to break it like this, but Shane's had an accident – hit a tree and was flung from his horse. Mark and Sally are with him and Mark says it's imperative the Doc should get there quickly."

Shane's parents seemed unable to comprehend the situation, or the necessity for quick action. They were both numbed by shock.

Lee said quickly, "Can you get to them by car?"

"No!" Lyndon turned to her, realising subconsciously that here he would find help. "Only part of the way. They're in the wood about a mile from Copse Lane."

"Then saddle an extra horse and take it back to the lane." Lee ordered quietly. "I'll fetch the Doc and take him there in Mark's car. We'll see you at the end of the lane."

She turned and gently forced the doctor's number out of Shane's mother. Then she rushed to the telephone.

While she was waiting to speak to the doctor, she turned to Clare and said, "See if there's a first-aid kit in the bathroom, Clare. If there is, take it down to Lyndon and tell him to give it to Mark first and then go back to the lane to meet the Doc."

Obediently, Clare did as she was requested. The first-aid kit was where Lee, in her cool intelligence, had thought it. She hurried downstairs and caught Lyndon just as he was setting off with the spare horse, and gave it to him with Lee's message.

There was nothing more she could do.

She sat down heavily in an armchair, thinking for the first time of Shane. It sounded as if he were badly hurt. How badly? Poor Shane! Perhaps he would have to go to hospital. Perhaps. . . . No, she put that dreadful thought from her. Then, and then only, she realised the implications of this accident with regard to herself. Now she could not go home tonight. Shane could not be told of her decision . . . and no matter what her private reasons for wishing to go as soon as possible, Fate had decreed that for the time being, at least, she must stay and that her engagement could not for the present be broken.

Chapter Eight

Clare sat in the lounge with Shane's mother and father waiting for the sound of the returning car. It was over half an hour since Lee had left to pick up the doctor, and time seemed to be dragging by on leaden feet. The suspense was ghastly, and not made better for Clare by the older woman's panic. She clung to Clare's hand, saying repeatedly, "I don't know what I would have done without you and your friend, Lee. Oh, I do hope nothing too awful has happened to our darling Shane. How could such an accident have occurred? He and Sally were such *good* riders! Clare, you don't think it's as serious as Lyndon implied, do you?"

Clare tried to calm her by keeping her own voice as unconcerned as possible.

"He will probably be quite all right," she said soothingly. "You mustn't anticipate the worst. Lyndon was no doubt very unnerved by the accident itself and exaggerated the details."

Her words seemed to have the desired effect. Presently her companion turned and said, "You are very brave, my dear! I have thought only of myself and Shane. Loving him as you do, you must be as worried as I am. How selfish of me."

Clare felt a guilty flush rise to her cheeks. Naturally she would be most upset if anything happened to Shane, but no more than over any friend. If it had been Mark, she knew she would be reacting quite differently. She would have wanted to race to him as quickly as possible – stay with him; pray for him; at all costs be near him. She could not wait in comparative calm as she was now doing, to hear if he were – going to live . . .

"Let's talk about more practical things," she said evasively. (She could not, even to salve her own conscience, tell Shane's mother at this moment that she intended to break her engagement.) "Is Shane's room ready? Everything the doctor could want available?"

"Yes, the housekeeper has seen to it all. There's nothing more—" She broke off as the sound of car tyres scrunching in the gravel reached their ears, followed by the steady clopping of horses' hooves.

The car must have been driving terribly slowly, Clare thought instantly, if the horses had been able to keep up. Her heart jumped with nervous apprehension as she followed Shane's mother into the hall.

Mark and Lyndon were carrying an improvised stretcher on which, to Clare's horror, she saw the inert, bandaged form of Shane, unrecognizable through the wad of bandages round his head and face, his arms and even his legs.

The doctor turned, and seeing Shane's mother, said: "I've dealt with the superficial wounds, Lady Sinclair, but your son is badly concussed and I fear there may be some internal damage. I'll telephone for an ambulance to take him straight in to Harrington Hospital for x-rays. Try not to worry too much. These things often look worse than they are and Shane is a very healthy young man. I'm sure he'll come through this given a little time."

Sally, releasing herself from Lee's restraining hold, rushed forward into her mother's arms, sobbing hysterically.

"It was all my fault, Mummy," she cried. "I asked him to race. It was my fault and now he's dying."

Clare, seeing the horrified expression in the older woman's eyes, went forward and gripped Sally's arm.

"You heard what the doctor said, Sally," she told her.

"It doesn't matter whose fault it was now. Get a grip on yourself and see if you can help."

But Sally was past reasoning, and meeting Lee's eyes, Clare went over to the doctor who was by the telephone.

"I think she'd better have a bromide, doctor," she whispered. "If you have some tablets, I'll put her to bed and give her one."

The doctor nodded his head and reaching into his bag, he found a bottle of bromide tablets. Between them Clare and Lee took Sally to her room. Lee went back downstairs and Clare sat down by the bedside. Sally reached for her hand and clung to it like a small child.

"I'm so afraid, Clare!" she whispered. "Supposing Shane dies. It'll be my fault. Mark told me not to go. I disobeyed him just to get my own way. I didn't even mind about the race. He'll never forgive me. I'll never forgive myself."

"Shane isn't going to die, Sally," Clare repeated. "It was just an accident. Go to sleep now. Hopefully by the time you wake up, Shane will be better and you can go and visit him."

As if reassured by Clare's words, Sally lay back on the pillow, the drug sending her suddenly to sleep, the tears still wet on her cheeks.

How child-like and defenceless she looks! Clare thought silently. And how pretty. No wonder Mark loves her. Poor Sally. She knows it was her fault; or perhaps it is the fault of her parents letting her have her own way too much. I hope Shane will be all right. Even Lee looked pretty upset and worried.

She sat with Sally a little longer and then went quietly out of the room closing the door behind her. On the landing, the doctor was talking to Shane's father.

"I suspect compound fracture of the skull and multiple other injuries to the body. I think the best man to operate would be Mr Burrows – he specialises in this kind of thing, Sir Dennis—" he broke off short, biting his lip, "I could be wrong, of course. It's very much guess work at this stage."

The two men disappeared into Shane's room. Immediately Mark came out. He saw Clare and together they sat down on the top stair of the landing.

"How bad do you think it is, Mark?" Clare asked.

"About as bad as it could be!" Mark said through set lips. "God, Clare, it was awful. Shane didn't really want to race. I think all that drink had made him sleepy. But Sally kept egging him on and the more I tried to stop her, the worse she was. I feel partly to blame. If I'd left her alone, perhaps she wouldn't have been so insistent."

"Don't think like that, Mark," Clare said quickly. "I don't believe anyone can alter the course of Fate. If this accident had been meant to happen, nothing could have prevented it – certainly nothing you could say to Sally."

Mark passed a hand over his forehead wearily.

"Where is she?" he asked quietly. "I'm afraid there was so much else to do, I'd forgotten about her. She must be feeling rotten, poor child."

She doesn't deserve your pity, Mark, Clare wanted to cry out. It was her wilfulness more than anything else that could be called the reason for the accident.

But instead she said, "She's asleep. The doctor gave me a bromide to give her. She was distraught."

"I know," Mark agreed. "The shock was dreadful for her. It was a few minutes before she realised what had happened and then when she turned her horse and came back, Shane was lying unconscious, terribly cut about and that huge open wound on his forehead . . . she would go to him. It took both Lyndon and myself to prevent her lifting his head. It might have killed him if she had done so. I was glad when Lee showed up and took her in hand. What a magnificent person Lee is in a crisis."

Clare said, "I wonder if I ought to go down and sit with Shane's mother again. I don't want to. It's so difficult,

94

Mark. She keeps referring to my feelings and . . . well, I feel so mean, as if I were acting a lie. I *am* acting a lie. I meant to go home this evening – to break off my engagement. How can I now? And how can I stay under false pretences?"

Mark turned and stared at her, realising the implications of her words. He had not, so far, thought of this further complication.

"I don't see what else you can do but stay," he said after a moment's thought. "It wouldn't be fair to tell his parents at this moment. They're far too worried and upset. And you can't just go! How damnably awkward. . . ."

"I must stay now until Shane is better – well enough for me to tell him I want to break our engagement. I'll telephone my mother tonight and explain more or less what has happened. She'll understand."

"Perhaps you won't have to stay long," Mark said. "Shane may make a quick recovery. I sincerely hope so, for his sake, yours and even more for Sally's. The twins have always been very close to one another, and to think it was her fault . . . Poor old Shane must get better, Clare, He *must*!"

Clare, seeing the state of Mark's nerves after the dreadful ordeal of the last few hours, suggested that it might be a good thing if they all had a cup of coffee. Shane's parents would no doubt need one, too.

"I'll go down and see the housekeeper," she said. "Don't worry too much, Mark. I have a feeling he'll pull through."

Coffee served as a momentary diversion, but after the ambulance had called to take Shane to the hospital, his parents and the doctor following behind in the car, there was little those remaining in the lounge could do to relieve the tension of waiting for news. The moments lengthened until Clare felt she could bear the tension no longer. The brilliant sunshine streaming into the room was farcical in a way. One could not comprehend that on so beautiful a day, so peaceful a Sunday, a desperate fight was going on for Shane's life. And yet they all realised that this was very probably the case. Suddenly the telephone rang.

It was Shane's father, to say that the specialist, Mr Burrows, had been on holiday in Scotland, but that he had chartered a private plane to fetch him and they were expecting him to arrive at the hospital within the hour. Meanwhile, Shane had been x-rayed and prepared for an operation. He was still unconscious but in no immediate danger.

It was late evening before Sir Dennis arrived home with his wife, both of them looking utterly exhausted. Shane had come through the operation all right but was still unconscious and the surgeon had been unable to guarantee that he would regain the use of both his legs. A lot would depend upon what happened when Shane came out of his coma.

Immediately, Clare volunteered to go and sit by his bedside and Lee echoed her. Mark, too, wished to sit with him and between them, they arranged visits so that there would always be someone with him.

Only Sally would not go. She had come downstairs the morning after the accident, her face pale and her eyes swollen with tears. Mark had come round but she had refused to see him, and to Clare she had said, "I can't face him yet. I can't face his reproaches. I can't even face my own."

"But Sally, Shane's all right. He's going to live. Besides, Mark doesn't blame you. He blames himself."

"Blames himself?" Sally repeated in a strange, sharp little voice. "That's crazy. He knows it was my fault. He must know it. *You* must know it, don't you, Clare?"

"Sally, it doesn't matter whose fault it is," Clare said evasively. "You mustn't upset yourself like this. Shane is going to be all right."

"Oh, yes, he's going to live!" Sally cried in a hard, bitter voice. "But he won't be able to walk, or ride, or swim – or any of the things he loves doing. And all my life I shall know it was I who deprived him of these things."

"Sally, we don't know that." Clare said, anxious at the pallor of Sally's face and this strange hardness. It would be so much better if Sally could break down again. She would get it off her chest and feel less guilty.

"Two specialists have seen Shane now. They hope, they say. Hope! But they don't know. They just evade direct answers. But I know. This is my punishment."

Mark called again, but Sally still refused to see him. She sent Clare with a message saying she was indisposed.

"You mean she's ill?" Mark asked, his face drawn with worry.

"No," Clare said gently. "Just upset. Give her time, Mark. She's strung up like a violin string at the moment. It'll have to snap with the strain she's under. Then she'll want you. You must be patient until then."

"She doesn't think I'm reproaching her, does she?" Mark cried. "Surely she realises that I love her."

Clare bit her lips and forced her voice to stay calm.

"Yes, of course she knows it, Mark, but she's blaming herself and it's preying on her mind. I'll try to get her to see you as soon as possible. I think it would be so much better if she could break down again. She just goes around with that white face and those huge eyes and set expression. Perhaps it will be better when Shane regains consciousness."

He did not do so until the early hours of a Sunday morning fourteen days after the accident.

"He's asking for you, Clare," Lee said on the telephone from the hospital where she had been faithfully observing her four-hour vigil. "Will you tell his parents? And be sure to come with them – it's you he wants to see."

Half an hour later, Clare was hurrying down the corridor to Shane's private room, his parents having opted tactfully to wait to see him after her visit.

97

His face was deathly white and his eyes were shut, but as she sat down beside him, he opened them slowly and said, "Clare, where have you been? I've been wanting to see you."

"Hush, don't talk, Shane," she said, smoothing the fair curls from his forehead. "Just lie quiet and go to sleep."

"I've been ill!" Shane remarked suddenly.

"Yes!" Clare whispered. "But you're better now. Go to sleep, Shane, and I'll stay here with you."

"Stay with me!" Shane repeated, and as if comforted by her presence, he closed his eyes and went to sleep. For a moment Clare panicked. Had he had a relapse? But the nurse quickly reassured her that there was nothing to worry about. Shane was asleep.

Half an hour later, the doctor arrived and sent Clare home.

"Come back in the morning," he told her. "I understand that you are his fiancée?"

"Yes!" Clare whispered.

"Then he will probably ask for you again when he wakes."

"I'll be there," Clare promised.

Sir Dennis drove Clare home, leaving Shane with his mother who refused to leave his bedside.

On her way to her room, Clare stopped dead outside the door. From within she could hear the sound of uncontrolled weeping. Sally! she thought, and then knew that it was not her. That it was Lee. Should she go in? She pushed open the door with sudden determination and went over to the bed on which Lee had flung herself.

"Lee, don't, you mustn't!" Clare whispered. "There's nothing to be so upset about."

"It's – j-just reaction!" Lee said in a muffled voice. "I suppose the strain has been a bit too much . . . sitting there through all those long hours in the darkness, wondering

98

if he was going to die. I'm tired. That's all. I'm all right now."

She sat up and blew noisily into her handkerchief, and then found a cigarette and lit it with hands that still trembled.

"I haven't broken down like that since the war," she said with a wry grin at Clare's worried face. "Silly, wasn't it! But I feel better now so don't look so worried, my poppet. I'm OK."

"You know, Lee, you're the most inexplicable person," Clare said as she started to run a hot bath. "One would think you never suffered from nerves. You're always so controlled, and, well . . ."

"Hard?" Lee put in for her.

"Not exactly that," Clare said, trying to explain. "But you never seem to let things touch you too deeply. I suppose you do and bottle it all up inside yourself until there's too much there and then the cork pops out."

"Very aptly put!" said Lee with a tremulous laugh. "Now, hurry up with that bath, Clare, and I'll have one after you."

While Clare was in the bath, Lee sat on the bed finishing her cigarette while she tried a little self-analysis on herself.

Nerves! my girl, she reproved herself. But why? I've been through far worse ordeals than this and come out untouched. The last time I gave way like that was when I was saying goodbye to Jim and knew it was the last time I'd see him. It had nothing to do with being over-tired. Is it simply strain and lack of sleep that has caused this?

The colour swept into her cheeks as a sudden thought struck her, but she flung her cigarette away furiously as if by such a gesture, she could put her thoughts from her, too.

No! she said. No! That's crazy. I'm not the falling-in-love sort. Shane means nothing to me. He's just a sick boy who needs care and attention. I'll admit he's handsome, she argued with herself, and that he paints beautifully and is good fun. But I don't love him. I know I don't. We're just not the same sort. Besides, he's going to marry Clare – or is he? Would I mind if he did? Of course not. At least, not really. I was only surprised the night of the party when they told me they were engaged. I wasn't hurt or angry. Perhaps I wasn't in love with him then? Perhaps it's only happened through sitting with him alone, watching his face and . . . No, I don't love him. I'm sorry for him and fond of him and I like him, but I don't love him.

She was glad when Clare came out of the bathroom to disturb her reverie. She fully intended to put such silly thoughts right out of her mind. And for the time being she succeeded.

Sally heard the news of Shane's progress at breakfast. Clare, watching her, saw the colour come back to her cheeks and the light to her eyes. "I shall go and see him immediately after breakfast. Mark can drive me—" but her mother put a hand on her arm and said gently, "The doctor says no one but Clare is to go to him, Sally. He mustn't be excited."

"But I'll be quiet, Mummy," Sally cried.

"He said no one else, darling," her mother insisted.

"But Clare has been!" Sally began, and then, as if after some inner thought had struck her, the light went from her eyes and her face became pale again. The hard controlled lines returned to her mouth.

"I see!" she said quietly. "You're punishing me!"

Clare realised immediately that Sally thought her mother blamed her for the accident and was not prepared to risk Shane's health again. Impulsively, she said to Sally's mother, "I'm sure the doctor wouldn't object if Sally just peeped in while Shane was asleep."

But before the reply came, Sally burst out, "I don't want to see him asleep. I want to see him well, don't you understand? I want to talk to him. To tell him I'm sorry."

Her voice broke and she rushed out of the room.

Her mother said nervously, "I'm so worried about Sally, but I'm sure the doctor was right when he said she was in far too nervy a state to see Shane. On the other hand, I hate to see her suffering so. Isn't there anything we can do?"

"Perhaps if Mark were to talk to her?" Clare suggested. "I know Sally has refused to see him, but I feel that if he just walked in she could turn to him and – and everything will be all right."

"I think Clare's right," said Lee.

"Then will you telephone him, dear?" asked Sally's mother. "Tell him we need him here."

But before Mark could come, while Lee was still trying to reach him on the telephone, there was a knock on the door and Lyndon walked in.

Chapter Nine

"Hi, everyone!" Lyndon said to the room in general. "I'm mighty glad to hear Shane is better. Where's Sally?"

Sally's mother looked at Lee as if for guidance. Lee nodded her head imperceptibly as if to say that perhaps the American boy could bring Sally to her senses, and said aloud, "She's just left the room. I'm sure she'd like to see you. I'll see if I can find her."

"No matter, I'll look around for her," he said, with a cheerful smile. "Thanks!"

The American went out through the french windows and straight down to the stables. Had anyone seen the direct route he had taken they would have been surprised to know how he had guessed so easily Sally's hide-out.

But Lyndon had not guessed. Sally had telephoned him to meet her in the stables. She had given him no reason for this strange rendezvous, but he had surmised that something was seriously wrong by the tone of her voice.

He found her in the fodder shed, stretched full length on the clean-smelling hay, sobbing as if her heart were breaking.

With an odd expression in his eyes, Lyndon flung himself down beside her and put a hand gently under her chin, turning her tear-stained face up to his.

"Oh, it's you!" she gulped.

"It sure is, honey!" he said with a grin. "Now dry those tears this instant and tell me what it's all about. Has Mark—?"

"It's nothing to do with Mark," Sally interrupted. "It's everyone else in the house. They won't let me see Shane."

Lyndon cocked an eyebrow at her.

"Is he conscious then, Sally?"

"Yes!" she cried wildly. "And Mother and Father have seen him, and Clare . . . everyone except me. They won't let me near him. They think I want to harm him again."

"That's stuff and nonsense, Sally. They don't think you want to harm him. They're just afraid you'll excite him, I've no doubt."

Sally stared at him with angry eyes.

"So they *are* keeping me from him – from my own twin brother."

Lyndon pushed the dark hair from his forehead and pulled a packet of cigarettes from his pocket.

"Camels," he said briefly. "Like one?"

She nodded her head and he lit two together and handed her one. Sally puffed furiously, the tears still falling from her blue eyes.

"Now see here, Sally," Lyndon said firmly. "You'd better get this straight. You know very well you were responsible for the accident, don't you? You and I together. I gave Shane and you too much to drink, and you made Shane race. That makes us both guilty. You admit that, don't you?"

Sally nodded.

"I wish everyone else would be as honest about it," she said in a muffled voice. "They all try to pretend they don't think I'm responsible."

"Surely Mark could see for himself – he was with us—" Lyndon began when Sally checked him.

"I haven't seen Mark since the night of the accident. I can't face him, Lyndon. He's sure to reproach me and if he does, I can't bear it. If he doesn't, I can't bear it either."

Lyndon grinned again.

"You can't have it all ways, kid," he told her. "And I

103

think you're probably misjudging the fellow. I doubt if he'll mention the subject at all."

"Don't you think he will?" Sally asked, perking up a little.

"Maybe not!" the American said. "But that mightn't be so good either. There would always be constraint between you then."

Sally's face puckered a little as if she were going to cry again. Lyndon bent over her, taking her cigarette away with sudden swiftness and folding his arms round her.

"Look, Sally, I know how you feel. I feel the same way myself. We've no need to pretend to each other. You just get it all off your chest. I don't mind, you know."

Sally looked up at him, her blue eyes meeting his dark brown ones with question in them.

"You're such a strange person," she said after a moment's contemplation of the man at her side. "Sometimes I positively hate you and other times I like you – now, for instance."

"You love me, you mean," Lyndon replied calmly.

Sally tried to pull away from him, but he kept his arms round her, saying, "Physical distance won't separate us, Sally; we're two of a kind. Besides, if you weren't secretly afraid of me, you wouldn't be trying to run away now."

Sally's blue eyes flashed in sudden anger.

"I'm not afraid of you!" she stormed at him. "You seem to forget I'm Mark's fiancée!"

"You seemed to forget it when you asked me to meet you here," Lyndon returned suavely. "Is it really Mark, you need, Sally, or me? If you want Mark, I'll go fetch him for you."

"Oh, don't be stupid, Lyndon," Sally retorted, her eyes not so angry now. "Of course I wanted you and not Mark. I knew you'd understand and I wanted to talk to you about Shane. I certainly didn't ask you here to make love to me."

"I hadn't thought of doing so to date," was the cool rejoinder. "But now you've brought up the subject, I think I might kiss you. You know I find it very hard holding you close like this, seeing those beautiful red lips of yours so near and your eyes shining into mine. You're very beautiful, Sally."

Sally eyed him nervously, but despite his words, he did not try to kiss her. Somehow it piqued her. She had made up her mind to slap his face if he tried.

He had been watching her face closely and now he gave a quick amused laugh.

"Sally, honey, you're woman all over," he said. "I just don't know what to do about you."

Annoyed by his supercilious laughter, Sally gave vent to a burst of Irish temper and her hand flashed up and hit the American across the cheeks. For one long minute, he said nothing, did nothing – only stared at her with narrowed eyes. Then he pulled her roughly against him and before she could cry out, was kissing her on the lips, bruising her, hurting her, and then, as she ceased to struggle against him, with more gentleness and tenderness until she was giving him back kiss for kiss.

At last she drew away from him, her face flushed, her eyes angry, puzzled, star-like.

"Mark would kill you if he knew about that," she gasped.

"And you? What have you to say about it?"

"I think you're mean, despicable, underhand!" Sally flung at him. "Every time Mark is out of sight, you take advantage of his absence to make love to me. You know I love him. You know I'm engaged to him but—"

"But I love you, Sally," Lyndon interrupted. "You know as well as I do that you like it that way . . . oh, don't deny it, Sally. You're far too feminine not to be flattered by my attentions. But it goes deeper than that. I think you love me, too. I wouldn't be sticking around the place if I didn't believe it myself. I wouldn't want a girl who didn't love me. That's why I count Mark out. If you were married to him, it would be different. But I think I can save both him and you a lot of unnecessary pain in the future. So I reckon my motives are all right. Why don't you admit I'm right, Sally? It'd save us so much time and bother!"

"Because you aren't right," Sally said furiously. "I love Mark, and even if I didn't, I wouldn't marry you for anything on earth. I positively hate you sometimes. I couldn't ever love a man I disliked so much."

"Love and hate are akin," the American said in his slow drawl. "Think about it, Sally. You'll find I'm right. Until then I'm sticking around. You see, I'm certain I'll be needed one of these days."

Sally brushed the fair curls from her forehead with a quick gesture of annoyance.

"I do wish you'd stop talking such nonsense," she said. "You know very well that I only kissed you back just now – because, well, because only a cold-blooded girl would not react to that sort of kissing. You're terribly sure of yourself, Lyndon, but this time you are mistaken. I don't love you and I never will. And I only asked you down here this afternoon because I wanted a friend. So if you don't want to be *just* a friend, we'd better go back to the house."

"Sure I'll be friendly!" Lyndon returned easily. "But you haven't changed my mind about anything, Sally. Now let's talk about Shane?"

Sally said, "There's not a great deal to say. The doctor thinks he's very much better. But the specialist won't give us anything definite in the way of promises about his legs. Oh, Lyndon, supposing they are paralysed? That he never walks again! I'll kill myself if it's true. Shane couldn't bear it."

"I'm not so sure of that, Sally. He's got his painting. He can paint from a sitting position, you know."

"But he couldn't play tennis or cricket or golf or dance

or – ride again," Sally whispered, her voice breaking on the last words.

"Now look here, honey, it's no good getting yourself all worried about it until you know it's true," Lyndon said reassuringly. "Your father won't spare any expense to see Shane gets all the best attention the world can give him. Nowadays surgery can perform miracles. It may take time, but he'll get better. You'll see!"

"Oh, I hope so, I hope so!" Sally whispered. "I'd give anything I had in the world to make him well again. Shane is the person I love most in the world – even more than I love Mark. That I, of all people, should have done this to him!"

"Sally, don't torture yourself like that," Lyndon said. "It may all be so unnecessary. Let's go back up to the house now and see if there's any news of him."

"All right," Sally agreed chokily, "and Lyndon, don't tell the others where we've been. It might get gack to Mark and I wouldn't want him to misconstrue what has happened."

"Sure I won't!" Lyndon said, and Sally, already half out of the shed, did not see the strange little light in the American's eyes. Sally, it seemed, had a guilty conscience. So perhaps that kiss had meant something to her after all.

But although neither he nor Sally mentioned the fact that they had been down in the stables together, Mark, driving round to the house in answer to Lee's telephone call, drew up by the front door in time to see Sally's and the American's unmistakable forms as they emerged from the stables some twenty-five yards away. He took a step towards them and then, changing his mind, went into the house instead. A few minutes later, Sally, looking flushed and dishevelled, appeared with Lyndon at her side.

The colour flooded her cheeks as she saw Mark and she felt a sudden annoyance with herself. Why should she blush as if she had been up to some mischief! Now Mark would think. . . .

"Hullo, Sal," he said evenly. "Where have you been?"

"We went down to see the horses," Lyndon put in quickly. "Thought we'd take a look at Shane's mare to see if that leg of hers was improving."

"I see!" said Mark quietly. "And was it?"

"Anyone would think you were more interested in the horse than in Shane!" Sally said nervously. "Aren't you even going to ask how he is, Mark?"

"I know how he is," Mark replied quietly, a faint reproach in his voice as he added, "Lee telephoned me. She thought I might be worried."

Sally flushed a deeper pink and turned away from Mark. How annoying he could be at times, putting her in the wrong. After all, she'd been worried too, and upset. Mark couldn't expect her . . . and yet Sally knew deep in her heart that she ought to have kept in touch with Mark. He had probably been worried about her, too.

She turned to him with sudden compunction.

"I'm sorry, Mark. I would have telephoned. But I've been terribly worried and upset and . . ."

"I know, Sally. I understand," Mark said, his look tender and loving. "Care to come and tell me about it?"

"I guess I'd better be getting along, Sally," Lyndon interrupted.

"Won't you stay to tea?" Sally asked quickly. She didn't know if she were ready, yet, to face Mark's questions.

"Haven't yet gotten into the habit of tea!" Lyndon said smoothly. "Thanks all the same, Sally. So long, Mark. Be seeing you both," and he went out of the door.

Sally watched him go and then, squaring her shoulders, she turned back to Mark, saying, "We'll go on to the porch, shall we? I'll ask them to bring tea out there."

*   *   *

108

Shane lay in the darkened room, half-way between sleep and waking. He couldn't for the moment, remember where he was. His own room was never dark when he woke in the morning. He always drew the curtain wide at night so that he could see the stars from his bed, and could wake to blue sky and sunshine.

Presently he began to distinguish objects in the room and knew that he was not in his own bed.

Then he heard a voice – a cool, feminine voice saying, "Are you thirsty, Shane? Would you like a drink?"

He turned his head and was aware of a sharp pain. He closed his eyes quickly, then opened them again, and Lee's face came into focus.

"Terrible head," he murmured. "Hangover from the party!"

He heard Lee's soft voice with its faint amused tone.

"No, Shane. You had an accident. You're better now."

"Accident?" Shane asked. His lips seemed very swollen and he found it difficult to articulate. "Thirsty," he said.

Lee bent over him and put a glass to his lips. The liquid – some kind of lemon-barley stuff – was cool and soothing as it ran down his throat.

"There!" said Lee. "Now don't talk, Shane. I'll do the talking. You're to rest. I'll guess all your questions and you can tell me if I'm right by blinking your eyes, once for yes and twice for no. Understand?"

Shane nodded his head and then, feeling the sharp pain again, grinned and blinked his eyes once.

"First you want to know about the accident?" Lee questioned, and seeing Shane's reply, went on, "You were racing Sally back after lunch at Lyndon's cottage. Your horse stumbled and you were flung off and hit a tree. You've been unconscious since then. You are in hospital. You were operated on successfully after you were brought back here. Now you are getting better. But you've been very ill and you must rest a great deal and not worry. If you do this, you will get well all the sooner."

She saw his lips form a word and said, "Clare? She's gone down to the canteen for a cup of tea. Would you like me to fetch her?"

He blinked his eyes, and Lee, seeing that his pillows were comfortably arranged, went out of the room and down to the canteen to find Clare.

"He's awake again and asking questions. I told him the bare facts about the accident, nothing else," she whispered. "He's asking for you again."

Clare went up to Shane's room and sat down by his bed. He opened his eyes and looked at her, and she felt a rush of pity for him flooding through her. What would he feel if he knew the doctors were afraid he was paralysed for life? That he would never walk again? Poor Shane! Impulsively, she reached out and took his unbandaged hand in her own.

"How long ago?" he asked with difficulty.

Clare understood his question, and said quickly, "Ten days, Shane. Don't talk any more. You must rest. I'll stay with you and you go to sleep."

Obediently, Shane closed his eyes and Clare thought he had fallen asleep when suddenly he said, "Sally – all right?"

"Yes, Shane. She's fine. She'll be in to see you soon."

Clare left him and went back to the house to find Sally. She was on the porch with Mark and as soon as Clare had delivered her message, she sprang up from her chair and said, "He wants to see me! Oh, Clare, you darling. I'll be very quiet. I won't let him talk, or anything. I'll ask the doc if I can go tomorrow."

"He doesn't know – about his legs, Sally," Clare reminded her. "Talk about other things to him if you can."

Sally raced away to telephone the doctor and Clare stood there awkwardly, uncertain whether she should stay or go. Mark said, "Would you like some tea, Clare?"

She nodded her head, and he immediately drew up a chair for her.

"I'll pour out for you," he said smiling. "Milk and sugar?"

Clare sat on the sunlit porch, listening to the sound of Mark's voice. She was tired, and his deep, rather slow enunciation was immensely soothing. She felt a drowsy contentment steal over her and despite her intentions, her eyes closed.

Receiving no reply to his question, Mark looked up and saw that Clare had fallen asleep. He smiled, and leaning over, put the cushion from Sally's chair behind Clare's head. She did not wake.

Poor Clare! thought Mark. Worn out with worry and long hours of watching Shane's bedside.

He saw the dark, purply-blue shadows beneath her eyes, the long, dark lashes lying on the pale cheeks, and a sudden protective emotion rushed over him. She was so defenceless – even more so asleep than awake. How could any man have hurt her as the fellow she loved seemed to have done? It did not seem possible.

Mark wondered idly what the fellow was like. What sort of man would this quiet, self-effacing girl fall for? It was hard to say. Shane, anyway, was not her type. The trend of Mark's thoughts changed as he considered the problem of the engagement. With Shane so seriously injured, it did not look as if Clare would have her chance to break it off quite so soon as at first expected. It might be months, or longer, before Shane was on his feet again – if at all. Supposing Shane were paralysed for life? What then? Would Clare decide it was her duty to stay with him if he wanted her to? That would be a ghastly mistake. It would mean a life of constant self-denial for Clare; a life devoid of love by the sick-bed of a man she was only sorry for.

And yet there was Shane to think of, too. Supposing he, Mark, were in Shane's position and Sally left him. Then he

111

would no longer wish to go on living. To lose one's legs and everything else one treasured as well – what would life have left? But Shane had his art, Mark argued. Could he not be content with that? Or must he have Clare, too?

Somehow the idea of Clare in such a position was abhorrent to him. She had suffered enough for her years. Somehow or other, he must help her to obtain her freedom again. It did not seem to him as if she had enough strength of mind to help herself. Clare was utterly unselfish. She would sacrifice herself for others no matter at what cost to herself.

Strange, thought Mark, how one always liked people for different things. Lee, now, had qualities different from Clare's but just as likeable. Underneath that rather hard shell, she was immensely kind and considerate and generous. And her sophistication was mostly a pose. Yet she did seem older than the other two. Of course, she was older than Sally by a year, or was it two? It seemed a great deal more. Sally was a child by comparison.

As Mark's thoughts turned to his fiancée, that slight frown of worry returned to his forehead. Ever since the accident, Sally had been behaving most oddly. She had been nervy and difficult and reticent. Mark had not been able to get near her this afternoon. She had talked a tremendous amount about everything – talked too much, in fact, as if she were trying to cover up something.

He sighed.

Of course, he told himself, Shane's accident must have upset her thoroughly. But she acts as if it were my fault, as if, in some way, I were to blame. Perhaps I am. Perhaps she knows she would never have insisted on that race if I had not been so adamant about them going home by car.

And then there was this business of Lyndon. Mark was quite convinced that they had not been down to the stables to see the horses. Sally's blush had assured him of that. She was usually so very straightforward – sometimes to the point of embarrassment. No, there had been something else going on. Sally, for one thing, had been crying. Had the American been upsetting her? If so. . . .

Mark clenched his hands and then uncurled them again.

There I go again – always jealous without any real cause, he told himself reproachfully. How difficult it was to control one's emotions, and how difficult to persuade them into the right path when one was so hopelessly in the dark about everything. Sooner or later, this feeling of constraint between himself and Sally must break. It *must*. He could not bear to be at loggerheads with Sally over anything, still more so when he did not know the reason.

Perhaps after she had seen Shane, she'll be better, he told himself. She must not be allowed to excite him too much, and if she breaks down . . .

As he pushed his chair back it made a sharp noise against the stone-paved floor and Clare woke with a start.

"I've been asleep!" she said stupidly, still half in her dreams.

"I know. I'm sorry I woke you," Mark said with a smile. "I was going in to find Sally."

Clare jumped to her feet.

"I'll go and find her for you, shall I?"

"Will you, please?" Mark said.

"I'll tell her you're waiting," Clare said.

But when she went up to Sally's room, Sally was not there, and the only person she could find was Lee sitting in Shane's room by his empty bed.

Chapter Ten

Three months had passed since Shane's accident. He was now at home convalescing and Clare, after a brief visit home, had returned with Lee to Sally's home, partly to keep Sally company but also because Shane's parents thought the two girls' presence in the house would help to cheer him up. As had become her custom, she was spending the afternoon with him while he sketched pencil portraits of her from his bed.

She had posed, at his request, facing the window so that her profile was towards him. The sun was streaming through the casements and lay warm upon her cheeks. Out in the garden, someone was mowing the lawn and the scent of fresh-cut grass blew in on the slight summer breeze. It was on just such a Sunday of peace and beauty that Shane had been thrown from his horse. . . .

Next week, he was to go back to hospital for an operation on his spine. The specialists were fairly hopeful of its success but they would not say definitely. If things went wrong, they did not want Shane to be too bitterly disappointed. But Clare, and everyone else in the house except Shane, knew that although he might walk again, he would never have the full use of his legs; he could never ride or play fast games like tennis. Golf, perhaps, and swimming – quiet exercise. That was all. It had been kept from Shane, of course. The doctors did not want his progress retarded by useless brooding. There would be time enough to tell him later, they said.

Clare could not help wondering as she sat beside his

114

bed, whether they were being entirely fair to him. The blow would be all the more severe if in the meantime he was hoping. . . .

"What's wrong with Sally, Clare?" Shane interrupted her thoughts. "I can't make her out. And Mark, when I saw him last night, was as fidgety as the devil. Has anything gone wrong between those two?"

Clare was thankful that her pose kept her face turned half away from him.

"I don't know, Shane," she prevaricated. "I think it is only a temporary misunderstanding."

"So there is something wrong?" Shane said astutely. "Clare, don't you, of all people, pretend to me. Everyone else in the house is bright and cheerful for my benefit, but lying here listening, I can sense an undercurrent. I want to know why everyone is so nervy and ill at ease underneath their smiling faces. Mark, Sally, Mother, Father, Lee – even you."

Clare felt the tell-tale colour flooding into her cheeks again. How could she tell Shane that her nerves were terribly on edge? Day after day she lived in this house, seeing Sally laughing and rushing around the place with Lyndon. Day after day, she had to sit quiet and see Mark, his face a mask of silent suffering, as he watched Sally amusing herself at his expense. Night after night she lay awake praying for Mark's happiness in finding Sally again, for they seemed to be growing daily farther and farther apart. And deep within her, torturing her like an evil snake, lay the not-to-be-subdued thought of what might happen if Sally and Mark finally broke apart. And as if this were not enough to make her fidgety, then there was Shane, himself. Daily he became more attentive, more observing. Once or twice lately she had been sure she had seen a question in his eyes when she had sat day-dreaming and had missed some remark he had made. Soon it would become all too apparent to him that the long afternoon hours were torture to her. For Clare

115

wanted to be outside in the garden with Sally and Lyndon and Mark. She wanted to be there to prevent Mark seeing too clearly that he was odd man out. Occasionally she had been able to distract Lyndon's attention for a little while, enabling Mark to talk to Sally alone. Every time he had awarded her with a grateful smile of understanding.

As for Sally, Clare did not feel she could speak of her to Shane and yet maintain a fair opinion. Try as she might, she could not stop herself hating Sally at times – those times when Sally hurt Mark so deeply. Probably she didn't know she had done so. Perhaps she did know and didn't care. No one could understand Sally any longer. Gone was the light-hearted, impulsive little girl. In her place was a young woman, bright enough maybe, but her laughter was hard and unnatural; and her actions and words were all carefully calculated; and if they concerned Mark, were calculated, it seemed, to hurt. On the other hand, she encouraged Lyndon's attentions but as soon as he took too much advantage of it, withdrew her interest as quickly. No wonder Shane thought her changed.

"Well, what is wrong?" Shane repeated forcefully. "Has Mark upset her, or is it Lyndon who has come between them?"

"Shane, I honestly don't know," Clare told him. "As far as I do know, Mark feels exactly the same towards Sally. It is she who has changed towards him. But I don't know the real reason. Sally never confides in me. Why don't you ask her yourself, Shane? She is far more likely to tell you."

"I have asked her and the reply is always the same. 'Of course there's nothing wrong, Shane. Why should there be?' And when I asked her if she was still going to marry Mark, she just said 'Why ever not?' and changed the subject. I can't get any closer to her than you, Clare, and I'm worried. Something has hurt her, hurt her very deeply, and this is her way of hitting back. I suppose she knows that Mark, more than any of us, is vulnerable, and that's why she's behaving as she does towards him."

"I didn't say anything about her behaviour to Mark—" Clare began, when Shane interrupted her with a smile.

"I know, my sweet little innocent; but Lee is more forthcoming, or perhaps more observant." He paused, busying himself shading in a line near her cheek. "You know, Clare, I don't think you are very happy here, are you?"

Clare forgot her pose and forced herself to meet Shane's gaze.

"Of course I am," she said quickly – too quickly. "I enjoy these afternoons with you, Shane, and—"

"And yet you are never at ease, Clare. I watch your hands in your lap. They are never still. Your eyelashes, too. They flutter on your cheeks constantly. Your mind is not at rest. Clare, tell me truthfully, have you regretted our engagement?"

For one brief minute, Clare thought that this was the moment to tell him she wished to break it off. Then she remembered that Shane's operation would be next week; that the doctors had said he was not to be upset in any way. And so she said quietly, "Nothing has altered, Shane. Why should I have regretted it?"

"Perhaps because of the way things seem to be working out between Sally and Mark. Or perhaps because you have found out that you can't stop loving him. Perhaps because you have discovered you could never love me."

Silence followed his words. Shane was so near to the truth. What could she say that would reassure him now of all times when he was asking for reassurance?

"How can I convince you, Shane, that I still want to go on with it?" she asked then. "Don't you believe that I do?"

"I don't know, Clare," Shane answered seriously. "I have sometimes wondered, lying here, what I would do if this operation were not a success. As it was even before the accident, our engagement was a difficult arrangement. We knew then that we would need every weapon we had to make a go of our marriage. There was so much against it in some ways. And now there is even more. I'm afraid, you see, Clare, that what you feel for me is pity."

Clare bit her lip. Had Shane some inner second sight this afternoon that he was hitting so near the mark with every word he spoke?

"Why should I pity you, Shane?" she countered. "As far as we all know, the operation has every chance of success. You will be up and about again very soon."

"But I shall only be a cripple!"

Clare gasped at his words.

"What do you mean, Shane?" she cried nervously.

"I shall be able to walk – stagger along. But no riding, no sports—"

"Who told you?" Clare asked without thinking. She heard Shane's quick intake of breath. Then in an odd toneless voice he said, "So that's true too! Oh, Clare, how easily you let yourself be trapped. I tried it on Lee, but she was too careful. And of course, I knew I'd get nothing out of Father and Mother. But I've known something was wrong. They've all been so nice – so terribly nice in a pitying sort of way. So it *is* true . . . don't look so upset, Clare. I tricked you into saying it. Besides, I'd rather know the worst. Truly I would. Did they think I wasn't man enough to take it?"

"*Well* enough, Shane," Clare corrected him quickly. "But it may not even be true, Shane. It seemed so silly to worry you, perhaps for nothing."

"And let me go on dreaming about the day I should sit a horse again until I'm rudely awakened to the truth? No, I'd rather do without the dreaming."

Clare heard the bitterness in his voice and her heart filled with pity. She jumped up from her chair by the window and went to him impulsively, her arms held out to him. With sudden swiftness, he pulled her down across the bed and crushed her against him, kissing her full on the lips for a breathless hurtful moment. Then he released her with a short, dry laugh.

"For heaven's sake, Clare, don't stare at me like that," he said, his tone mocking. "You look as if I'd assaulted you or something. Did you think kisses weren't included in an engagement?"

Hating him, and yet knowing she had no right to do so, Clare turned away from him, her eyes filling with painful tears, her hand pressed against her lips. How could she pretend any longer? She had not wanted to kiss Shane, be kissed by him. Her lips, like her heart, were Mark's, and if he did not want them, they could still be withheld from other men. If only she could tell Shane the truth!

"I'm sorry, Clare," she heard Shane's voice, gentle now and without its mocking tone. "Honestly, I should have done that. It wasn't playing fair. Especially when you have been so marvellous to me. I'm sorry, darling, really I am. Do forgive me. You seemed so – so out-of-reach, somehow. I wanted just for that moment, to turn you into a real flesh and blood creature. I wanted you to – to want to kiss me. Of course you don't. You're still in love with Mark. I can see it in your face every time I mention his name. I hear it in your voice every time you speak to him. I wonder he hasn't seen it, too."

"Oh, no, Shane. No, he can't have done. I couldn't bear it."

Shane, hearing the panic in her voice, stared at the back of her head with eyes that were both pitying and a little bitter.

"Come here, Clare," he said. "Here, on the edge of my bed. Give me your hand. Now listen, my dear, it's no earthly use pretending. You love Mark. Our little experiment has failed. That's true, isn't it?"

Clare nodded her head.

"Then what is the use of keeping on our engagement?"

119

he asked quietly. "You don't want to marry me, do you, Clare?"

"Perhaps later when—" Clare began, but Shane interrupted her.

"If you are really honest, Clare, you will admit that you don't think anything will change – later. If it did, I should never be sure that you were not influenced by my accident. Besides, I realise now that Mark's shadow will always be between us. You'll never be able to look at me without thinking of him. You see, my dear, I am being more truthful than you are. I am facing facts."

Clare looked up and her grey eyes met his in a long steady gaze. Then she said brokenly, "Shane, I'm sorry, dreadfully sorry."

"It isn't your fault, Clare," Shane said at once. "I don't think it can be called anyone's fault. It was a mad idea in the first place, I suppose. I just hoped . . . well, anyway, now that we are being honest with each other, would you like to go home?"

"No!" Clare said. "And I am being honest, Shane. I want to stay until you are well again. Not because of what people would say if I were to leave you now, but because I am truly fond of you. The only reason I ever wanted to leave was because I hated living a lie; pretending."

"Then I'm glad we've had this all out," Shane said. "I have lain here for hours and hours wondering and searching for the truth. I feel better now I know it. Besides, I would prefer to have you staying here of your own free will as a friend, than kept against your will by a sense of duty. Suppose we tell the others, Clare, that we have decided to break off our engagement by mutual consent? Or should we wait until the op is over? I don't want them saying things about you. If you are agreeable, let's wait until after next week."

"Very well, Shane!" Clare said, grateful for his thoughtfulness. Perhaps this was the beginning of a new understanding with Shane; a better one based on real friendship instead of one based on impossible dreams.

Shane said suddenly, "Look, Clare, now some things at least are beginning to make sense. Your behaviour, for instance, and Mother's and Father's I can see are prompted by worry about the outcome of the op. Sally's I don't understand. Nor Lee's."

"What is wrong with Lee?" Clare asked. "I haven't noticed anything. She seems just the same to me – a little pale and tired, perhaps, but that's all."

"Hadn't you noticed?" Shane replied. "Lee is suffering badly from nerves. She is usually so self-assured, confident, efficient. Lately she has broken a thermometer, knocked over the barley water, dropped her book – all sorts of little things like that. And her hands fidget the whole time. Why, she's nearly as bad as you've been, Clare!"

There was a sudden knock on the door and as Shane said, "Come in!" the subject of their recent discussion pushed through the doorway.

"Hullo, Lee!" Shane said cheerfully. "Have you brought my tea?"

Lee put the tray down on the bedside table, and Clare, watching her, saw that her hands were trembling slightly as she poured the tea into the cups. She handed one each to Clare and Shane, and then sitting down on the chair Clare had vacated, said casually:

"Shane, I wonder if you would mind terribly if I went back to town? I really ought to get back to my work. I've been away so long . . ." Her voice trailed away into an unhappy silence.

Clare stared at Lee aghast.

Only a night or two ago, as they were preparing for bed, Lee had said, "Nothing in the world could drag me away now, Clare. I had thought of going back to town but I want to be with him when he's told the truth. I think in a way he turns to me for assurance – because of my being a nurse, I mean – and I might be able to help. I'll ring up and explain I can't go back for at least another two or three weeks."

And now this! Something must be wrong.

Shane put her thoughts into words.

"I shall hate your going, Lee, but of course if there's anything wrong—"

"It's just work!" Lee broke in quickly.

"But I thought you'd fixed it with the publishers that they were to find someone else to do those illustrations," Clare said, and then regretted her words instantly. Lee's face was suddenly flushed.

"Lee, do you really have to go?" Shane asked. "I know it's selfish of me and all that, but you've been so splendid. I've got used to having you around. Couldn't you do some of your painting here? We could spend the afternoons painting together. That would be fun. All three of us with Clare as a model! Lee, do try and stay. Supposing Father were to ring up your publishers and explain?"

"It isn't the publishers," Lee said, her tone nearly inaudible. "It's just that I felt I ought to be getting back to work. I'll soon be getting out of practice."

"Then why not take my suggestion and work here?" Shane asked bluntly.

Clare, watching Lee's face in an effort to surmise the reason for her sudden incredible change of attitude, saw the colour recede slowly from her cheeks until they were deathly pale. She seemed to be undergoing some inner fight with herself, as if she were arguing silently whether to go or stay. Then she said, "All right, Shane. But I can't promise I'll stay for any length of time. We'll see how it goes."

"Splendid!" said Shane. "You know, Lee, I'm going to need you more than ever now my best girl's broken our engagement."

His expression was teasing, happy, but Lee stared first at him than at Clare, aghast.

"You mean—?"

"I mean Clare and I have decided that it was useless to go on as we were. We'll be far more use to each other as friends. I should never have made that crazy suggestion in the first place. I think the idea of Sally getting engaged without me was partly responsible. We'd always done everything together and I suppose subconsciously I had that in mind. And then I liked Clare the moment I first saw her . . ." He turned and gave Clare an affectionate smile. "But all along I knew underneath that it wouldn't work and I just didn't want to admit it. Seeing Clare so miserable forced me to face up to it, and now, strangely enough, I don't feel as badly as I expected I might. It's strange, but I feel so much closer to her now."

Clare said with complete sincerity, "I feel that way, too, Shane. We can be absolutely honest with one another now. I meant to tell you I had thought better of the idea the day afterwards, but then the accident happened and . . ."

"And you were much too nice to hurt me," Shane finished for her. "Naturally, Lee, we aren't telling anybody just yet. People might jump to conclusions and say Clare was deserting me in my hour of need!" He gave an amused laugh. "So we're letting things be for a little while. Clare has promised to stay and keep me company until the operation. It's been so wonderful for me having you both here, you know. Sally seems to find it so difficult being with me these days. . . ."

Despite his intentions, Shane's voice became a little bitter. Lee said quickly, "It's a guilt complex, Shane. She feels so horribly responsible for everything that has happened to you. That is at the root of her strange behaviour, I know. I think this – this affair with Lyndon is prompted by the same thing. He keeps her amused – makes her forget for a little while what has happened. With Mark, she can't forget. She no doubt feels that he is silently reproaching her – which may be true, but it is not on account of the accident, only because of her attitude to him. If only someone could tell her – make her see that Mark loves her and is desperately unhappy. But she's so wrapped up in her own feelings that she hasn't given any real depth of thought or understanding to Mark's point of view. She can't see what she's doing to him."

"If she's behaving so badly towards him, I'm surprised Mark takes it," Shane said.

"It's surprising what one will take when one is in love as deeply as Mark," Lee returned quietly. "One can suffer and go on suffering and lay one's heart and soul open to pain and unhappiness, but one has no alternative. For a few brief moments of sanity, one can struggle against it with the aid of common sense and reason, and then the loved one holds out a hand, makes a gesture, and you're back where you started. Clare will understand."

And Clare did. She saw beyond Lee's words to the deep emotion that had prompted them. She saw that behind her description of Mark's actions, Lee had been describing her own – not feelings she had once held for some other man, but feelings that were new and painful and not to be denied. She knew now that despite all her intentions, Lee had fallen in love with Shane.

Chapter Eleven

Mark lay full length on the soft green grass, his weight on one elbow as he watched Sally and Lyndon playing out a singles match at tennis.

Sally wore white shorts with a linen shirt open at the neck. She was very sunburnt and her arms, neck and face glowed golden against the startling whiteness. Her fair hair seemed to have bleached in the sunshine to a real platinum. Watching her, Mark thought that she had never seemed more desirable and yet at the same time, further from his reach.

His gaze went idly to the American who looked cool and debonair in his spotless tennis kit. He was under-hitting, Mark could see, in order to give Sally a chance to win. As in every other sport, Lyndon excelled, playing a game far above the average.

He heard Sally's triumphant laugh ring out as Lyndon let an easy ball pass him.

"Game and set!" she cried.

The two white-clad figures ran towards the net and shook hands. Then Sally's head turned towards Mark and she appeared to be hesitating. After a moment's conversation which he could not hear, they turned and walked towards him.

At the same time, Lee strolled across the lawn to join them.

"Hullo!" she said cheerfully. "I've been sent down by Shane to have some sunshine and exercise. Care to give me a game, Sally?"

Sally curled herself up on the lawn and gave a little sigh.

"Oh, Lee, I really couldn't – not just for a minute or two. I've only just finished playing three sets with Lyndon. I won, too. Now I'm totally and utterly exhausted."

"Perhaps Mark would give you a game?" came Lyndon's smooth, slow drawl.

Mark looked up furiously. He knew he was being childish and selfish, but he didn't intend to let Lyndon have Sally to himself for another hour.

"I'm not dressed for tennis, as you can see," he said curtly.

"But you can play in grey flannels," Sally cried. "Don't be so lazy, Mark."

Mark ignored her remark. He turned to Lee and said, "Will you excuse me, Lee, if I don't play now? I'd really rather not."

"Of course!" Lee replied with a smile. "Come along, then, Lyndon. I'm sure you're not exhausted."

Mark saw Lyndon's glance go to Sally, but she was busy pouring herself out a glass of lemonade. He shrugged his shoulders almost imperceptibly, and said, "Sure, I'll give you a game or two, Lee."

They wandered off together and Mark sat down again beside Sally. His heart was beating furiously – partly from anger but mostly from nerves. This was the first moment in the last ten days that he had had Sally to himself, and he meant to make the most of it. Sally had been blatantly avoiding him. The whole situation was absurd. This time, come what may, he was going to get to the bottom of it.

"Sally—" he began, when her voice interrupted him.

"Isn't it hot?" she asked. And then, "I wonder where Clare is?"

"She's no doubt with Shane!" Mark said curtly. "So there's no good hoping she will turn up to spoil our *tête-à-tête*, Sally. This time you're going to listen to what I have to say."

Sally's colour deepened. She kept her eyes averted from Mark's gaze.

"Mark, must you be so intense?" she asked coldly. "This isn't the time or the place for serious discussions."

"You have chosen this time and this place by making any other time and any other place quite impossible," Mark replied, his hands clenching at his sides. "I've been wanting to talk to you for a long while, Sally, and you've known it. Also you have avoided it. This time, you'll stay and listen to me."

Something in the cool, determined, angry tones of his voice prevented her jumping to her feet and stalking off to the house as she would have liked to do.

"Well, for goodness' sake get it off your chest then," she retorted rudely.

She knew immediately that she had gone too far. Mark's face had become deathly white, and from the corner of her eye she could see his lips pressed together in that thin, stubborn line she knew so well.

How difficult Mark was these days, she thought. He was always trying to get her into corners to talk to her. Why couldn't he be amusing and sociable like Lyndon? There was enough seriousness in the house with Shane's coming operation without Mark going round like a thundercloud and spoiling everyone else's fun.

She felt Mark's hand on her arm and tried to shake herself free. His grip tightened until she cried out, "You're hurting me, Mark!"

He loosened his grip but kept his hand on her arm.

"Listen to me, Sally," he said, the words coming in slow, sharp syllables. "I'm not going to ask for reasons. I am only interested now in facts. Answer me truthfully, Sal, do you want to break our engagement?"

Sally blinked nervously. The sound of Mark's special pet name for her had touched her to an unexpected emotion. She did not want to feel emotions like that any more. 'If you care too much about anyone, you become vulnerable yourself,' Lyndon had told her once, and she had learnt it to her own cost with Shane. The sentimental moment of weakening passed and she felt annoyed with Mark for bringing up serious issues before she was ready to cope with them. She wasn't sure any more whether she did want to stay engaged to him. She wasn't sure if she loved him any more. And there was Lyndon. He kept asking her to put the past behind her and go to America with him and start life again.

'It would be such fun, honey – the two of us together. You'd love Hollywood and they'd sure cotton on to you. We'll get ourselves a bran' new house and car and perhaps if I do well next year, a plane so's we can go visiting Niagara Falls and Mexico and places. Gee, Sally, you don't know what you're turning down. I can show you a new world, and you wouldn't have to forego any of the luxuries you have here. Why, you'd have half as many more again. No restrictions, no rationing, no coupons. You can reach out your little hand for anything you take a fancy to, and it'll be yours.'

It all sounded such fun! And Lyndon was such fun too. What was it that kept her to Mark? Memories of the times they had been so happy together? Sentimental memories? Or was it because deep down inside her she knew that Mark was the better man and she didn't want to be married to second best. But that didn't make sense, either. Lyndon was much more attractive than Mark – to look at and to listen to. He could beat Mark at most of the sports and was tremendously popular. Not that Mark was unpopular, but he was slow to make friends whereas Lyndon could make a friend of anybody at a moment's notice. Was it merely sentiment that kept her from breaking her engagement to Mark?

"Sally, I'm waiting for your answer!"

She looked up and met Mark's gaze. The brown eyes were staring into hers and she knew that she couldn't dissemble, couldn't lie to him.

She said, "I don't know, Mark. I'm not sure any longer."

She heard his quick intake of breath as if he had received a blow. She felt a moment's pang of guilt, and then annoyance. It wasn't fair of Mark to make her feel guilty. It wasn't her fault she had hurt him. He'd asked for the truth. Then Mark said quietly, "I suppose I was expecting that reply, Sally. I've known for some time that you had ceased to love me."

"I never said—" Sally began, when Mark cut her short.

"I know you too well, Sally. Something changed your mind about me after the accident. I don't know what it was and I don't want to know. Ever since then you've been trying to make up your mind whether you loved Lyndon or me. That proves one thing first – that you don't love me. Secondly, it proves you don't love Lyndon, either."

"Those are both sweeping statements, Mark," Sally cried. "How *can* you know my mind when I don't even know it myself?"

"Because, Sally, if you're in love, you always know it. You can fight against it, argue against it, but deep down inside you know it's there. Since that is so, you couldn't toy with the idea of marrying me. You would know you wanted to do so. Nor could you toy with the idea of marrying Lyndon. You'd know you wanted to. So if what you say is true and you really can't make up your mind, then you don't love either of us."

"That's not true. I'm very fond of you both."

Mark gave a short, hard laugh.

"Fond!" he echoed. "My God, Sally, do you think being fond of someone is necessarily loving them? You should ask Clare what it means to be in love. She's in love with some fellow and nothing he nor anyone else can do or say will ever change it. That's why she is breaking her engagement to Shane. Shane knows it's the only thing

129

and he's quite happy about it. He knows he didn't really love Clare."

For a moment, Sally was silent. The news that Clare and Shane were breaking their engagement was a complete surprise to her. Once again, she seemed to have been kept in the dark . . . she, Shane's twin! Well, then she'd tell Mark something he seemed to be in the dark about – who the man was Clare loved so deeply, so passionately. Lyndon had opened her eyes to that all right.

"Do you really mean you don't know Clare's in love with you, Mark?" she asked with a mocking laugh.

Mark swung round and faced her, his eyes blazing.

"You don't know what you're saying, Sally. For heaven's sake, don't make up lies about Clare . . . stupid, impossible lies."

"So you don't believe it?" Sally asked. "Then why not ask her yourself. Ask Lee, if you prefer, or Shane, or Lyndon. You're the only person who doesn't know."

Something in the tone of her voice convinced him that she was speaking the truth. For a moment, he was completely thunderstruck. Then, flashing through his mind, came the thought that perhaps this was the reason for Sally's odd behaviour. Perhaps she had been jealous! But sickeningly came the return of reason. Sally had not denied that she had been contemplating marriage to Lyndon. Clare had nothing to do with it . . . Clare! In love with him! It couldn't be true . . . and yet now he thought about it, it explained so much. Her intense shyness in his presence; the colour that always rushed to her cheeks when he spoke to her; hundreds of little things made sense. And he . . . he had thought he could advise her, help her! Now what in heaven's name was he to do?

"Sally, are you sure?" he asked desperately.

"As sure as everybody else seems to be," Sally told him. "And I shouldn't be a bit surprised if you didn't fall for her. She'd probably suit you far better than—"

"Sally!" his voice cut like a whip and she knew once

again that she dare not go further with her taunting. Why was it she always wanted to hurt Mark? Because he laid himself open to it so easily? Why couldn't he fight back like a real man – like Lyndon would, for instance? He'd have put her across his knee and spanked her if she had dared to mock him or tease him as she had done Mark in the past. Perhaps there was something in her nature that liked to be bullied. When any man became so completely her slave as Mark was, she only grew to despise him.

Her thoughts frightened her for a moment. Did she despise Mark? It was a very hard word. And they had had such good times together once. What had come between them? Mark was right when he had said the accident was the beginning. But had it been the cause? Or had Lyndon been the cause? Was it really that she had only started to compare them after the accident? Found Mark over-serious, too intense, beside the light-hearted American?

Supposing she were to break her engagement to Mark and go with Lyndon, what would Mark do? Would he turn to Clare and marry her instead?

The idea piqued her. If Mark really loved her as he seemed to think only he knew how – then he ought to break his heart, or jump into a river, or something! Still, she didn't really want Mark to be unhappy. And anyway, she couldn't possibly leave now just before Shane's operation. She'd put off the decision a little longer . . .

"Mark," she said, her tone pleading and gentle, "must I make up my mind just yet? I'm really not at all sure . . . after Shane being so ill and I don't seem to know what I do want. Couldn't we leave things as they are for a little while?"

"For how long, Sally?" Mark asked pointedly.

"I'll make up my mind by the end of the month," Sally said. "Shane will be over his operation by then."

Mark was silent for a moment. Then he said quietly,

"All right, Sally. We'll wait until then."

And he drew himself up and without looking at her again he walked slowly away from her towards the house.

*   *   *

Shane said, "You're a wonderful model, Clare. You sit as still as a mouse. What do you think about all the time?"

Clare smiled.

"Oh, just things and people and life!" she said vaguely. She and Shane were very happy companions these days. It seemed hardly possible that a bare six days had passed since they had agreed to break their engagement, and yet in so short a time, they had grown close together and genuinely fond of one another. They talked of everything – when Clare wasn't lost in thought . . . even of Mark.

Shane had said, "You know, Clare, I'm not sorry we became engaged when we did. If you'd gone to Scotland, you wouldn't be here with me now, keeping a petulant, bed-ridden patient amused. Nor would you have been here when . . . I mean, if anything goes wrong."

She had asked his meaning and he had replied frankly, "Personally I think Sally will end up with that American fellow. She's crazy, of course, because Mark is the better fellow every time. But there it is. Lyndon's probably more her type, and he's really quite a nice chap for an American! That leaves Mark with a broken heart and you on the spot to mend it."

She ought not to have taken his words so seriously and yet they returned again and again. Supposing it were true? But deep down inside her, she did not believe it could be true. Sally might well break her engagement to Mark and go to America with Lyndon, but what reason was there to suppose Mark would turn to her? He treated her as a sister. In fact he was on far better terms with Lee. He never teased Clare, or joked with her. And mostly, he

132

talked of Sally – certainly whenever she gave him an opening . . .

Shane said, "If perseverance and complete and utter self-effacement could win the battle, you'll wake up one morning and find yourself married to Mark!"

She smiled at him, but her eyes were serious as she replied, "Don't say things like that, Shane. I'm superstitious. Such things shouldn't be joked about."

"I'm sorry, Clare," Shane grinned. "I'm afraid I'm in far too good spirits. I don't know why I feel so absurdly light-hearted when I'm going into that beastly hospital the day after tomorrow."

"What's made you so happy?" Clare asked.

"I don't know!" Shane answered vaguely. "But every-one seems to be happier. Lee, for instance. She's lost all that nerviness we spoke of last week, and she's on top form. I think she's great fun. I like her tremendously."

"She likes you, Shane."

"Does she? I'm glad. I like nice people like you and Lee to like me," Shane said boyishly. "I shall miss you terribly when you've gone."

"Perhaps Lee will stay on a little while," Clare suggested. "You could always ask her."

"I don't really feel I can," Shane said. "I know she wants to get back to her work."

"It isn't so much a question of 'wanting to' as 'must'," Clare explained. "You see, Lee's parents are dead and she supports herself financially."

"Oh, Lord!" Shane said. "I never thought of that. You know, Clare, I've come to the conclusion that it's high time I put my own life to some use. Now I think about it seriously, I see that I've been living like a first-class spiv."

Clare laughed.

"What nonsense, Shane. You've no need to work. And you certainly don't live on other people's earnings like the spivs!"

"I'm not sure I don't," was Shane's reply. "I live on Father. I know he's got packets, but still, at my age, I ought to be independent. Supposing I wanted to get married, for instance. I couldn't let Father keep my wife for me. I'd feel . . . well, frightful, if I did. No, I think if I get through this operation in any kind of shape, I'll get a job."

"What sort of job, Shane?"

"I don't know. I'd like to do something to help the country, but I don't see that I'm trained. Even if I wanted to, I doubt if I'll be fit enough for physical work!"

"I'm afraid you won't!" Clare answered truthfully.

"Lee was talking about her job this morning," Shane mused. "You know, I wouldn't mind doing something like that. But I'd rather have a regular job than be a free lancer. I'm much too lazy to force myself to work when I don't feel inclined. Now if I had to be in an office from nine to six, I'd really get something done."

"Then why not get a job in one of the art departments in a publishing firm?" Clare suggested. "You're very talented, Shane. I'm sure you'd get a job easily enough."

"I'll ask Lee if she thinks she could get me an introduction," Shane said eagerly. "Then I'd get a flat in London and paint my own pictures in the evenings."

Clare smiled at his enthusiasm. It was good to see Shane so happy and hopeful. He had made a wonderful recovery and perhaps, in this frame of mind with the determination to get well so that he could really do a job of work, he would come through the operation even more successfully than he had hoped.

"I'm sure Lee will do all she can to help," she said. "It would be fun for her having you in town, too. She leads rather a lonely life in that flat of hers."

"But she must have a tremendous number of friends," Shane said. "An attractive girl like Lee would be much in demand I should imagine."

"She's popular enough," Clare said. "But Lee's a

strange girl. She takes very violent likes and dislikes, and nothing will make her behave even civilly towards the people she doesn't care for. She's rather hard to please."

"I'd hardly have thought so," Shane said. "She seems happy enough with even my company."

"Perhaps she really likes you very much," Clare said carefully. Lee would never forgive her if she were to let Shane know her secret. Not that Lee knew Clare had guessed. No, Shane must find out for himself. In the meantime, she would set his feet in the right direction!

"I think she does, you know!" Shane said with a laugh. "I'm rather flattered when I think about it. She's a very clever person, is Lee . . . in fact one of the best women artists I've seen."

"Perhaps that is because she lives life so thoroughly." Clare suggested. "She once said to me that artists couldn't create anything unless they had lived it themselves. I think she meant that one could not portray sorrow in a face, for instance, unless one had known sorrow, and so on."

"She's right, of course," Shane cried. "And I believe that's why my own work seems so . . . well, lifeless. The movement is there, I know, but not the human emotions. Clare, it's high time I started to live – really to live."

"You have started, Shane," Clare said. "You've suffered a lot of pain recently for one thing. And disappointment, and now you know what it is to hope with every part of you. You are feeling all the time."

"I suppose I am," Shane admitted. "But I haven't known love, yet, Clare; not love such as you know it. I wonder if I ever will? Perhaps men don't fall in love the same way as women."

"I think Mark loves Sally as much as I love him," Clare said thoughtfully.

"I'm not so sure," Shane told her. "Men are very easily swayed by the physical. Sally's a pretty enough kid to turn any man's head, and you know, she was the first girl he met after he came out of that prison camp. I think he loves her in a way, but it's more habit now than anything else. And of course, Sally's behaviour with Lyndon, judging from what I've ben told, would only make him jealous and therefore more ardent. I wonder if Mark could be really and truly honest with himself, what he would find in his heart."

"I believe he loves her," Clare said. "And I think she loves him. I think Lyndon attracts her but underneath she admires, respects and loves Mark. She'll tease him and taunt him and make him jealous, but she'll never leave him. I'm sure of it, Shane. She couldn't compare the two and prefer Lyndon."

"You say that because you don't know Sal as well as I do, and because you love Mark," Shane retorted. "That makes you biased in Mark's favour, but it doesn't necessarily make Sally feel the same way."

Their conversation was interrupted by Lee's arrival with tea. She smiled at Shane and then turned to Clare.

"Mark's on the porch, Clare. He says he would like to speak to you if you can spare him a few moments."

The colour rushed to Clare's cheeks and then receded slowly.

"What about, Lee?" she asked. "Sally?"

"I don't know!" Lee replied. "But he seemed a little upset."

"I'll go down," Clare said quietly. But inside her heart was racing at twice its normal speed.

136

Chapter Twelve

Mark was pacing up and down the porth when Clare joined him. She stood for a moment watching him before he became aware of her presence, then stepped towards her as if he were going to say something urgently, hesitated, and finally said nothing.

Seeing his obvious confusion, Clare said the first thing that came into her mind – anything, in fact, to break the silence.

"Is anything wrong, Mark?"

Mark sat down heavily in one of the wicker chairs and motioned to her to do likewise. After a moment, he said, "I don't know, Clare. I'm utterly confused. All of a sudden I don't seem able to understand anything any more. Life has turned upside down."

Clare looked at him anxiously. She had never seen Mark so upset, nor heard him speak so personally of himself. He was like a small boy who has suddenly found himself lost. Her heart cried out to comfort him and her arms ached with the longing to wind themselves round him and draw his head down to her; to give him the comfort he needed. But the right to do so was not hers. He was Sally's. And even if Sally did not exist, Mark would no doubt still have no need of her, except as a friend.

Trying to keep her tone merely friendly, Clare asked gently, "Is it – Sally?"

Mark struggled with himself, trying to find words – words he had not, for all intentions, the courage to say.

How to say to Clare 'Is it true that you are in love with me?' What right had he to ask such a question? What good would it do? It might only embarrass her and put constraint between them where hitherto there had been such a calm and complacent friendship. But could that friendship continue to exist if Sally was right? Mark argued with himself. Surely the question and his desire to know the answer would lie between them and make companionship in the true sense of the word an impossibility.

No, he could not repeat the suggestions. Sally had made. It would do no good in any case. What had possessed him to come striding up here and ask to see Clare without giving proper consideration to the outcome of such a discussion? He must have been crazy!

Desperately, Mark sought for something to say, and remembering Clare's last question, he seized on this as an excuse and said, "Sally is no longer sure she wants to marry me, Clare. It seems that Lyndon has entered into the picture."

Clare stared at him, her heart jumping swiftly as his words sank into her mind.

"She's not – broken her engagement?" she faltered.

Mark gave a rueful smile.

"Not quite! But I think she will. I've given her until the end of the month to make the decision. Somehow I know what it will be. I've tried to ignore it for a long time – ever since Shane's accident, in fact, but now it's out and I'm trying to face up to the truth."

"Oh, Mark!" Clare whispered. "I'm sorry. Perhaps—"

"I'm not thinking of perhaps any more," Mark broke in. "I'm facing facts, Clare. I've known ever since I first met Sally that I wasn't worthy of her – that she deserved a far better man than myself. Lyndon can give her everything that I can only take from her. It's probably best this way."

Without thinking, Clare cried from the depth of her soul, "That's not true, Mark. You can give her far,

138

far more. You can give her something so much more worthwhile than money and the things money can buy. You can give her your love and that is the most any girl could ask – and the best. Sally must be mad to turn you down."

"Lyndon loves her. She will have his love," Mark said.

Again impulsive, Clare spoke from her heart.

"But what is his love compared with yours, Mark?"

"What is any man's love worth compared with another's?" Mark said gently. "It is only worth something to the person who loves that man, Clare. If Sally loves Lyndon, then his love for her is worth more than mine."

Silence fell between them – a meaningful silence as the import of Mark's words was made clear to them both. Believing what he had just said to be true, and remembering Clare's last remark, he could no longer doubt that she loved him. To her, his love meant everything, as he would have had it mean everything to Sally. Life was indeed a strange mix-up. And yet it softened the blow of Sally's change of feelings to think that someone at least felt that he was a decent sort of fellow – worthy of being loved. And Clare, whom he respected and liked was not the kind of person whose affection was lightly dismissed to be as of no consequence.

Clare, meanwhile, was undergoing the most strenuous need for self-control that had ever been required of her. She knew that through her own unpremeditated remarks that she had given herself away. Mark *must* know now that she loved him. Whatever must he be thinking of her? How could she look him in the eyes again without feeling utterly ashamed?

And yet, she argued with herself, was there need to be ashamed of her love for him? There was no harm in that love and none intended to him or to Sally. It could not hurt either of them – only herself. Why should she feel ashamed of the most wonderful, most perfect feeling in the whole world? To be in love – to demand nothing from the object of one's affections, to love from a distance as she had done for so long – was it not, for all the pain and hurt to herself – still a source of pleasure to her? Mark was so utterly worthy of her love and she was, therefore, fulfilled even in her unfulfillment. She would, after all, prefer it this way than to be in love with all the hope in the world, to a man who deep within her she did not really respect.

With sudden pride, she raised her head and met the intense gaze of Mark's brown eyes. With unexpected courage, she heard herself say, "You know that I am in love with you, don't you, Mark?"

The expression on his face became at once gentle and confused. He said, "Sally told me. I think perhaps I knew, anyway. I'm sorry, Clare. I did not realise before."

"There is nothing to be sorry about, Mark," Clare told him. "It's not your fault. It's not really mine. I am not sorry and therefore you must not be. While you did not know the truth, I could stay here, happy to be near you. But now our friendship is spoiled. I have spoiled it. So I shall go home, and you must forget about this afternoon and remember me only as Clare, your friend."

Mark put his hand suddenly over hers and his voice was rough and almost husky as he said, "Nothing is spoiled, Clare. I shall think of you often and remember with gratitude all that you have done for me. Often you have selflessly put yourself out to give me a chance to see Sally alone for a few minutes. You have always been ready with your company if I asked you for it. You have been a very wonderful friend, Clare. I'm proud that you should – should feel as you do about me. I know I don't deserve it. So you see, I shall not want to forget this afternoon, shall I?"

Clare released her hand and rose to her feet. Mark's words had touched her very deeply and she knew that this was their good-bye. It was best that it should all end this way. She would not see him again and tonight she would go back to Scotland and resume her old life. She could look back on this afternoon and remember a moment of real happiness . . . more than she had ever anticipated.

With tears in her grey eyes, she said:

"I'm going home tonight, Mark, so I probably won't be seeing you again. I – I hope everything will work out all right with you and Sally. I'm sure it will. Anyway, I'll pray for you and trust that there will soon be good news for Lee to give me. She's sure to write to me if I ask her to. Good-bye, Mark, and . . . good luck!"

"Good-bye, Clare!"

He did not try to stop her as she went. He knew that it was not fair of him to do so, even though the loss of her friendship and company at such a time would be a large one. Life, it seemed, was determined to take everything from him in one stroke – Sally, and then his friend, Clare.

He gave a sudden laugh.

I'm jumping my fences before I reach them, he told himself wryly. Sally hasn't given me up yet. I wonder why I'm so sure she will. Am I being unduly pessimistic?

It did not occur to him that perhaps he, himself, no longer was certain of what *he* wanted and that was why he took the pessimistic view. He had loved and wanted to marry Sally for so long now, that any other emotion was utterly foreign to him. He was still Sally's – still ready to marry her – if she still wanted him.

The tennis match was over and Lee had returned to the house to wash and change before taking Shane his tea. Sally and Lyndon lay side by side on the grass, faces turned to the warm sun, their heads on their arms.

"What did Mark have to say for himself?" Lyndon asked suddenly. "He seemed to be having a very ardent

141

conversation with you. What's more, you seem a little upset by it, honey."

"So would you be!" Sally said indignantly. "Oh, Lyn, I don't know what to do about him. He's still terribly in love with me and I couldn't hurt him. I just couldn't."

"Are you so sure it would hurt him?" came Lyndon's drawl.

"What do you mean?"

"Just what I say, Sally. After all, it won't be the first time a fellow lost his girl. He'll get over it."

"But it means more to Mark than – than just losing me," Sally said. "You see, he had such a rotten time in some Jap prisoner of war camp. He talked about it once. It must have been awful. And afterwards he said that I'd done more to help him forget it all than anyone else in the world; that if ever he lost me, he'd be desperate . . ." Her voice trailed off into an unhappy silence.

"Sally, it's no good just feeling sorry for him. If he does love you, he'll want more than that. I know I should."

"I don't feel sorry for him," Sally argued. "At least, I don't think I do. I'm really terribly fond of Mark. In fact, I still love him in a way. The trouble is, I'm in love with you, too."

"So you admit it at last!" came the American's triumphant voice.

"I suppose so," Sally acknowledged. "Mark says if I think I love you both, then I can't be in love with either of you. I don't know. It's all such a muddle!"

"There's no muddle, honey. You just love Mark from habit. It's seeing him around all the time and memories keep cropping up. You'd forget him soon enough if you went away."

"Leave my own home?" Sally asked, looking at him in surprise.

Lyndon gave an amused laugh.

"Come away with me, my sweet. Come back to America with me. We'll get married on the boat, if

142

you like, or by special licence. We'll leave tonight. What say, Sally?"

Sally stared at him, perplexity in her eyes.

"It sounds so easy when you put it like that. But I don't think I want to be married – at least, not yet. I want to be quite sure first. I promised Mark a decision by the end of the month."

Lyndon sat up and pulled Sally over to him. He held her very close and stared down into her eyes with unusual seriousness and determination.

"Sally, don't go on procrastinating," he said urgently. "It isn't fair to Mark and it isn't fair to me. Nor is it doing you any good. You're looking like a pale little ghost these days."

The tears started to Sally's eyes and her head fell forward onto his shoulder.

"I'm so miserable, Lyndon," she choked. "I hate not knowing my own mind. I've always known before what I wanted in life. And I know it's not fair to you or Mark. But now I don't know. I just don't know."

Lyndon looked down at the fair head and his hand stroked the curls with clumsy tenderness.

"Look, Sally, how'd it be if I went away? Perhaps it's all my fault. Things were all right between you and Mark before I turned up. Maybe I should have left them that way. I guess if I disappeared, you'd make up your mind easily enough. Either you'd settle down again with Mark, or else you'd miss me so much you'd have to send for me – or come to me."

Sally raised her head and stared at him aghast.

"You can't go away!" she cried wildly. "What would I do if you went? It's gloomy enough round here with Shane ill and – and everything. Lyn, you *can't* go!" Her voice rose hysterically.

Lyndon gripped her arms.

"You can't have it both ways, Sally. You've had Mark and myself dancing attendance for a long while now.

143

You've got to let one or other of us go. Mark wants it that way, and to be honest, I guess I do, too. I don't want to share you with him any longer. If you won't come with me, then I'll go alone."

Realising that Lyndon meant what he had said, Sally burst into tears.

With an imperceptible little smile, Lyndon tightened his hold on her and kissed the top of her head.

"There now, Sally, don't cry, honey. You've nothing to cry about. You can have either man, you know. You should be the happiest girl in the world with two males at your pretty little feet. All you've got to do is to make up your mind which one you want."

"B-but I d-don't k-know which one I w-want!" Sally sobbed.

Lyndon said, "Suppose Mark were to say he was going away tonight, how would you feel about that?"

"I don't know!"

"Would you feel as bad as if I were to go?"

"I d-don't think so," Sally admitted. "Mark is so – well, gloomy these days. At least you make me laugh." Lyndon smiled.

"Well, that's one thing in my favour. Sally, why *don't* you come away with me? Is it just Mark you don't want to leave, or has Shane something to do with it?"

"Of course I couldn't leave Shane before his operation," Sally said definitely.

"And afterwards?"

"If – if he were all right, I might."

"Sally, 'might' isn't good enough. I want a definite answer. Can't you let me have it?"

Sally drew away from him and blew her nose noisily with the handkerchief he handed to her. It seemed that she wasn't, after all, to be allowed to wait a little longer. Mark was prepared to wait, but not Lyndon. He was going away if she didn't give him a reply, and she knew that she did not want him to go. He was far too much part of her life now, for her to be able to have any fun without him. And America – California – Hollywood! She had always wanted to travel and especially to the States. And with Lyndon, it would be an amusing and exciting adventure. She would meet all the film stars, see all the famous places like Coney Island and New York, and she would travel on the *Queen Mary* or a Clipper. . . .

The alternative was a quiet domestic life in a little house with Mark; financial restrictions because Mark would not allow her to spend her allowance on them both; no travelling for at least a year or more because they could not afford it; and only the local people to meet – nobody new or exciting or famous. . . .

What then, kept her to Mark? There was never an answer to this question. It must, she decided, now be habit, as Lyndon had said. Once away from Mark, she would soon forget him and all the things they had done together. There would be so much to do, so much to see, that she would have no time for the past, only for the present. And Mark, no doubt, would soon forget her. Or would he?

Her mind was still not made up. She turned to Lyndon, and said desperately, "Please won't you wait until after Shane's operation? Please, Lyndon, give me until then."

Shane looked up from his sketching board as Lee came into the room. Her face was unusually flushed from her strenuous game of tennis, and she looked very young and cheerful.

"Hi, Shane!" she said. "How's the painting?"

"I don't seem to be getting along very well!" Shane said with a smile. "Inspiration lacking, I suppose."

"Let's have a look-see," Lee said, moving over to the bed and looking at Shane's pencil portrait of Clare.

"That line is wrong!" she remarked. "And this isn't right, either."

145

Shane sighed.

"I know! But Clare moved and when she came back, she didn't seem to get the same position. I'm not trying to blame her for my bad work, Lee," he added with a laugh. "But she's not a very helpful model for all she tries so hard."

Lee put the tea tray down and poured out two cups of tea.

"Why not try another subject?" she asked. "Get Sally to sit for you again. You've done some lovely sketches of her."

"That was easy," Shane said quietly. "We were so much part of one another that I knew her expressions by heart. I didn't have to try to get inside her soul because I knew it. We're out of touch now."

"Do you always have to know a person's soul before you can draw them?" Lee asked curiously. "It's very unusual."

"I suppose so," Shane admitted. "Of course, I can draw from a strange model, but all my best work is from – from someone I feel very deeply about."

"I see!"

There was an uncustomary note to her voice and Shane looked up, but Lee did not meet his look.

"Lee!" he said suddenly. "Have you ever been in love?"

Lee smiled.

"Once I thought I was – during the war. But now I know I wasn't."

"How do you know?" Sahne asked astutely.

"I just know!" Lee replied. "The same way you know you aren't in love with Clare, I suppose,"

"It's funny how one can mislead oneself and then suddenly wake up to the truth, isn't it?" Shane admitted.

"Very odd!" Lee agreed.

"I wonder if I shall ever fall in love – really deeply in love the way people fall in books!" Shane said with a smile. "Somehow I don't think I'm the deep-feeling type!"

Lee laughed.

"You'll surprise yourself one day, Shane. I think you will fall in love. But not the way people do in books, as you put it. It's always so wildly dramatic and emotional in stories."

"Then how do you think it will be for me?" Shane asked boyishly.

"I think you'll just quietly wake up to it one day," she told him. "It'll be quite simple and quite clear and quite wonderful, and you'll know it's there and that it's true and that she loves you and you'll go quietly off together and get married and live happily ever after."

Shane gave a shout of laughter.

"I do believe you're a romantic at heart, Lee," he said. "You try and appear to be cool and independent and devoid of deep feelings but underneath you're as bad as Clare – just romantic schoolgirls."

"Perhaps all women are like that at heart," Lee said quietly. "They may try to pretend they are different; they may even think they are. But sooner or later the truth comes out. It's natural, I suppose. No doubt we all long for a husband and a home and children – just as Clare does."

"Don't you think men want the same things?" Shane asked curiously.

"I don't know!" Lee replied. "Perhaps. Only it isn't so important to them. They have their work as well."

"You have your work, Lee."

"But it would come second to love," was Lee's quick reply.

"Would it?" Shane asked. "You know, you are a most perplexing creature, Lee. One gets quite a wrong first impression of you. Either that or you've changed."

"Changed?" Lee echoed.

"Yes! You're different, or you seem to be, from the

Lee I met at the party. You were terribly sophisticated then and a little frightening. But attractive."

"And I'm not attractive now?" Lee teased.

Shane laughed.

"I didn't mean that, Lee. I meant – well, that you're softer – I don't know. Words sound so silly sometimes. All I do know is that the longer I know you, the better I like you."

"That goes for me, too, Shane," was Lee's quiet comment.

"Then we must be sure to see plenty of each other in the future," said Shane. "You know, Lee, I'm serious about that job. I really want to settle down and work. I'm absolutely determined to get through this operation successfully. So much depends on it now. I want to get that flat in town and meet all your friends and become a decent member of the community. I'm sick of lying here surrounded by luxury and the knowledge that I haven't done a single thing to warrant it. The more I think about it, the more ashamed of myself I become."

"You're going to come out of the op A1, Shane," Lee told him. "You know, even the specialists are saying you've a good chance of doing so now and you know how gloomy they were a few weeks ago. You've made such a splendid recovery."

Shane smiled. "Promise to come and hold my hand, nurse, when I'm coming round from the anaesthetic."

"I'll be there," Lee promised, "provided I'm allowed."

Two days later, Shane was operated upon for the recovery of the use of his legs. Lee, as she had promised was there when Shane came out of the recovery ward. She was there when he smiled up at her saying, "Gosh, my legs hurt, Lee," and the two of them realised that there was feeling in the nerves and that there was no longer any doubt that he would walk again.

She was with him for those happy moments. She was with him, too, when the day after he returned home, he

148

opened the note Sally had written to him, saying:

'Darling Shane,
   Don't think too harshly of me for leaving you
before you are really well again, but Lyndon won't
wait and I'm going to America to marry him. When
you are fit you must come out for a holiday to
California. I'll write to you often, and forgive me
for leaving Mark. Always your Sal.'

And Lee was the only one to hear Shane's comment, "It
isn't I who should forgive you, Sal. It's poor old Mark."

Chapter Thirteen

Twilight merged into darkness and one by one the stars appeared in the velvet sky until it became a carpet of myriad lights. Mark sat in his room staring out through the window with bitter eyes and a hard-drawn line round his mouth.

Sally's note lay on the blotter before him, her hasty, almost illegible handwriting staring back at him in complete and unanswerable finality.

She had gone – gone with Lyndon. And even now, five hours after he had found her note on the hall table at her home, he could not fully believe what reason told him was now fact. Sally had left him. She had broken her engagement. She had left for America with Lyndon whom she had finally chosen to replace him.

In the darkness of his unlit room, Mark tried to imagine Sally at that precise moment. She might be boarding the Atlantic Clipper at London Airport. Or she might already be airborne, sitting back in the comfortable seat, her face turned happily towards the American's, her eyes smiling and excited. Or she might be walking up the gangplank of the *Queen Mary*, her little high-heeled shoes tapping on the deck as she went towards the luxurious cabin Lyndon would no doubt have reserved for her. She might be already on the seas . . .

It's strange, he told himself without emotion, that I cannot imagine her in any of these places. Perhaps that is because she didn't tell me how she was going to travel. What does it really matter, anyway? All that matters is the bare fact that she has gone – gone for good and I may never see her again.

And yet even this could produce no deeper emotion in him than surprise.

I feel just exactly the same as I felt when I woke up in that Jap prisoner-of-war camp, he mused. Shock, I suppose. Couldn't believe it at first, and then it took me a day or two to realise fully what my life would be like. It's the same now. I can't believe Sally's gone. I can't start imagining tomorrow and what it will be like without her . . . that will sink in when tomorrow comes.

Wearily, he got to his feet and went to switch on the light. His room started to life and he stared around it with sudden curiosity. This was his room – his most personal and private domain. In here he had dreamed all his dreams . . . lived all his hopes for the future . . . argued with himself what life was really all about – life and love. There – on the table, was a snapshot of Sally taken last summer in the garden by the tennis court.

He looked away quickly. The tennis court reminded him with a stab of unhappiness, of Lyndon; of the man who had taken Sally from him.

He wandered back to the window and stared out into the night. Did he really blame the American? Had he any right to blame him? The choice after all lay with Sally herself. Or perhaps it lay with Fate. Perhaps Fate had known all along that she would take Sally from him, destroy his life so carefully built up since his return home at the end of the war, with just this one crushing blow.

Mark turned away from the beauty of the night and sat down heavily on his bed. With steady hands, he reached for his pipe and once it was going, lay back against the cushions, biting the stem and blowing smoke into the room. It became at once more masculine and more his own. The room, in fact, assumed a sudden importance. This was at least his, had always been his since he was a little boy; was part of him.

Downstairs the telephone shrilled. Mark started to his feet, thinking automatically that it must be Sally. Then something inside him told him it was not. He sat down again but the telephone continued ringing and at last he went down to answer it. It was Shane's voice and Mark's hands clenched the receiver with sudden feeling. He hoped that Shane was not going to talk of Sally. He couldn't bear it – not yet.

But Shane was saying, "I say, old fellow, Lee and I wondered if you'd be an 'absolute angel', to use Lee's expression, and drive us down to the local. Mother and Father have gone out in the Daimler and I'm not up to the walk yet. We're dying for a good honest glass of beer."

Mark let out his breath and relaxed. It was late – nearly closing time, but come to think of it, a pint in the local wouldn't do him any harm either. He knew suddenly that he didn't want to stay here by himself any longer, thinking, remembering, brooding.

"All right, Shane. I'll pick you up in three or four minutes. Don't keep me waiting or we won't get in."

He heard Shane's cheerful laugh and then the telephone clicked and Mark went quickly out of the house towards the garage to fetch his old Ford.

With his usual foresight and aplomb, Lyndon had managed to get himself and Sally through the formalities at the airport with the minimum of difficulty and waiting. They had been through the customs, emigration authorities, money exchange and were now sitting in the lounge drinking a cup of coffee. Sally stirred vigorously with her spoon and kept her eyes on the dark liquid as it swirled round the white cup.

"You'll be drinking real coffee soon," Lyndon remarked. "Excited, Sally?"

She did not look up and her voice was almost inaudible.

"I suppose so!"

"Not regretting anything are you, Sal?"

She did not reply for a moment. Then she said slowly, "I don't know, Lyndon. I'm – I'm worried."

"About Shane?"

"Yes, a little. I'm afraid of what he'll think of me for not having the courage to tell him I was going."

"He's your twin, Sally. He'll understand you couldn't face saying good-bye to him. Is that the only thing eating you, honey?"

She shook her head.

"No, there's Mark. I'm so afraid he'll . . . oh, Lyndon, I've never felt so mean and guilty in my whole life. I know this will hurt him dreadfully. I don't know how I could have done it."

"There's still time to call it off, Sally," Lyndon said quietly. "Do you want me to take you back to town and put you on a train?"

"N-no," Sally said. "No, I don't think so. But I wish – I wish I could see them all at home now. Mother and Father and Shane and Mark – see their faces, know what they are feeling."

"Suppose you telephone?" Lyndon suggested. "There's still time. Take-off isn't for another half-hour, I think. Hi! Stewardess!"

He beckoned to one of the smartly dressed girls in her pale blue Pan-American uniform. She came up to them smiling.

"Yes, sir?"

"How long before we have to board the plane?"

"About fifteen minutes, sir. Your baggage is going aboard now."

"Thanks!" Lyndon said. He turned back to Sally.

"Fifteen minutes, Sally. Do you want to make the call?"

The stewardess said, "Could I get the number for you, madam?"

Sally looked from her to Lyndon and made up her mind.

"Yes, please," she said. "It'll be a trunk, I think. Huntingdon 103."

"I'll call you when I get through," said the girl.

Sally and Lyndon sat in silence. Sally's heart was beating with nervous swiftness. She was suddenly as uncertain as to whether she wanted to go with Lyndon after all, as she had been finally convinced that she did after Shane's operation had proved so successful. She was more than a little worried about Mark. Lyndon did not – could not begin to realise what Mark and she had once meant to each other, nor how much Mark depended on her. And it had been terribly wrong and cowardly of her to leave without telling any of them she was going. She had not even said good-bye to Mother and Father. Nor even Lee. Clare, of course, was back in Scotland now. . . .

"Your call, madam!"

Sally jumped to her feet and ran towards the phone booth.

With trembling hands, she lifted the receiver and said, "Who is speaking, please?"

"It's Mrs Martin, the housekeeper. Is that you, Miss Sally?"

"Yes! I'm in a great hurry, Mrs Martin. Is – is Master Shane in?"

"I'm sorry, he's not, Miss Sally. He went out about ten minutes ago. Miss Lee went with him."

Sally drew in her breath sharply.

"Oh! Then is – is Mister Mark there?"

"I'm afraid not, Miss Sally," came the reply. "He went with them. He came to fetch them in his car. I think they were all going down to the Hannington Arms. You could probably get them there if it's urgent."

"No – no, it's not urgent. Mrs Martin. Thank you, good-bye."

She hung up the receiver and stood there for a moment,

staring unseeingly out of the glass windows into the reception hall where people were standing around in groups waiting for the tannoy to tell them to go out to the plane.

So Shane, Lee and Mark have gone down to the pub, she thought with sudden misery. They had not, after all, taken the news of her departure very much to heart. In fact, they had done the opposite and were celebrating. And she had been wondering whether to back out of the whole show and go home. It was funny . . . very funny.

She gave a little laugh and angrily brushed the tears away from her eyes.

I'm quite mad, she told herself severely. First I want them to be miserable, then I don't. I suppose I should be glad it's happened this way. Now my mind is really and truly made up. It would be absurd to go back for their sakes when they don't seem to care if I'm going or not!

She turned and walked out of the phone booth with sudden resolution and a lifting of her spirits. Lyndon jumped to his feet, looking at her anxiously. His face relaxed as he saw the smile in her eyes.

"Everything all right, honey?"

"Yes," said Sally. "Everything's all right."

The tannoy blared out suddenly.

"Will passengers travelling on the Atlantic Clipper to New York kindly take their seats please. Will passengers . . ."

Lyndon linked his arm through Sally's and pressed it gently against his side.

"Is the future Mrs Rea quite ready to take her seat?" he asked, looking into her eyes.

She smiled back at him and returned the pressure of his arm.

"Quite ready, Lyn," she said softly. "Shall we go?"

They walked out into the starlit night, hand in hand.

"Two pints and one shandy, please," said Shane.

The barmaid handed them to him with a cheerful smile.

"It's good to see you up and about again, Mister Shane. We've all been that worried about you."

"I'm fine now, thank you," Shane said.

He carried the glasses back to Lee and Mark and sat down with them.

"Well," he said. "We just made it. In fact, if we drink up quickly, we might make another round."

Lee laughed.

"I certainly can't drink two shandies in a minute," she said.

Mark raised his glass to them both and drank it down in one draught. Shane followed suit and the two men went back to the bar together. Lee watched them, or rather she watched Mark's face, wondering what lay beneath that expressionless mask.

She and Shane had worried themselves stiff ever since Sally's note had been brought to them. At first they had expected Mark to come round to the house to see if he could stop Sally going. Then they decided that he had no doubt realised she would already be gone. Finally, they resolved to ring him on some pretext to see if he was all right.

Shane had decided on the visit to the pub.

"We can always go there if he says he'll come," he said to Lee. "If he won't come, then we'll go round to his house. I don't think he ought to stay alone brooding."

So here they were. Mark, it seemed, had not yet fully understood that Sally had left him. He certainly did not seem suicidal. He seemed, in fact, to be his normal self.

Shane came back with him to the table, and Lee looked up sharply as Shane said in a matter-of-fact tone of voice:

"So our Sal finally deserted us for an American, Mark. Now what have those fellows got that we haven't?"

"A great deal of charm, I suppose," Mark replied evenly.

Lee said, "I don't think they have any more than Englishmen. It's just that it's all on the surface, whereas with you two, for instance, one finds another quota underneath."

"Thank you, fair lady," said Shane. "Let's drink to her, Mark. She deserves a toast after that compliment."

Mark smiled and raised his glass to Lee.

"I feel very privileged," she said, "having two such handsome men to escort me."

Shane said suddenly, "What a pity Clare isn't here. She'd have loved this little pub with all this pewter and oak. We never came down here while she was with us, did we? You know, Lee, I miss her."

"I do, too," said Lee. "Clare is one of those people you don't notice while they are there but miss tremendously when they have gone. She's a wonderful person."

"Have you heard from her since she got home?" Mark asked.

Lee nodded.

"A postcard yesterday saying she'd had a tiring journey up but that it felt wonderful to be back in the Highlands again. I think I've got her postcard here in my bag."

While she searched in her handbag, Mark was thinking of that conversation he had had with Clare about her home in the wilds of Scotland. He remembered the light in her grey eyes and the eagerness in her cool voice as she spoke of her native country, and knew suddenly that he was anxious to see the card; to see Clare's home surroundings.

Lee found the card and handed it to Mark. He looked at in intently and, deep within him, something began to stir – some emotion he could not explain. The same feeling, perhaps, that he had once felt in that prison camp when his heart was locked – as his body had been imprisoned – behind bars; the same longing to transport himself into exactly the sort of place this picture postcard portrayed – a wild, barren, granite-rocked hill with heather growing in abandon among the crags, and a grey mist encircling the summit.

There lay peace – and comfort. Peace through the great and wonderful simplicity of the landscape. Comfort from the knowledge that self was, after all, of so little importance among the imposing majesty of nature.

Up there, I could forget Sally, he thought. None of it would matter. I should be free and happy and young and strong. And there would be Clare, with her grey eyes like the grey Highland mists, and her cool, soft voice like the mountain burns, and her cheeks aglow and rosy like the heather. Clare . . . even her name is strangely comforting. It is so simple, so easy, so fresh and quiet and unspoiled. Clare . . .

"I wonder if Clare would renew that invitation?" he said aloud. "She asked me to go up there once for a holiday. I think I'd like to take a holiday now."

Lee said gently, "Clare would love to have you, Mark. Why don't you write to her? Or if you prefer, I will. Then you needn't feel that she could not refuse to have you. But I'm sure she won't refuse."

"Would you write, Lee?" Mark asked. "I'd rather you did."

He didn't want to impose on Clare. She might be busy with her family, or just not want to see him.

"I'll write," Lee said. "How soon would you go, Mark, if she will have you?"

"As soon as possible!" Mark said, the idea forming slowly in his mind. "Yes, I'd like to go soon – as soon as I can."

Lee sent a telegram by phone that night. The reply came next day and Mark left by the night train from London. Twenty-four hours later, he arrived at Clare's home.

She came to the little station to meet him in a pony trap. Her eyes were shy but smiling with welcome, and Mark, tired after his journey and not a little dubious as to whether he had been crazy to make the trip after all, knew suddenly that he had done the right thing.

Driving home, Clare asked him about Lee, and about Shane and his mother and father. She did not ask about Sally, and Mark surmised correctly that Lee had written and told her of Sally's departure. She had not wanted to know any more than that. Reasons did not matter. All that mattered was that Mark was here – that he had come to her in his unhappiness; to find comfort and peace among the beautiful surroundings of her home.

"You shall find them!" she whispered softly. "All you need from life is here – among these hills, Mark."

He glanced sideways at her serious, flushed face. "Clare, are you happier up here?" he said urgently.

She turned to look at him from those grey eyes of hers and she felt suddenly that she could not keep from him all that was in her heart. She said simply, "Now that you are here, too, I have everything I want in the world, Mark."

"Thank you, Clare. You have a way of making a fellow feel really important. Tell me, what do your family say about my visit?"

"Mother and Father never ask questions," Clare said. "It is enough for them that you are a friend of mine. The children, of course, are agog with curiosity. They so seldom see a foreigner."

"I don't know that I like being called a foreigner," Mark said, smiling.

"Perhaps if you stay long enough, they will call you a friend," Clare replied. "Will you stay long, Mark?"

"I don't know, Clare. I'd like to stay a little while, if it's not inconvenient. I've come to find something here, among your hills. I'm not quite sure what it is. Perhaps I just want to forget the past. Perhaps I want peace of mind. Perhaps I've just come for a holiday. I don't know."

Three days later, Mark was still uncertain of what he had come to the Highlands to find. He was surprised by the fact that the expected anticlimax of the shock of Sally's note, had still not hit him very seriously. No doubt this was due to the fact that he had had so little time for thinking. Clare's little nephew and two nieces were constantly round him, asking him questions, making him tell them stories about 'England', teasing him about his 'accent' and laughing when he tried to imitate their brogue. Clare, too, kept him busy. There were a hundred and one little things to do around the house. And in the evenings when her father and brother-in-law, brother and sister came home, they would all sit around the peat fire talking of the day's work. When at last he retired to bed, it was to fall into instant sleep. The mountain air was exhilarating while one was in it, but it took its toll at night when one sat by the fire.

It was, he decided, a simple life – different in every way from the luxury here, and the struggle to keep up a fair standard of existence was a hard one and a challenging one. It seemed to him that this was the way life was meant to be lived – not with many luxuries and comforts and time to waste, but filled every hour with good honest work and at night, family companionship and children playing at one's feet; good wholesome food and early hours to bed and early hours to rise to the fresh mist-shrouded dawn.

Would he in time grow tired of it? Mark was not sure.

Two weeks later, he knew that he had not tired of it. He knew, too, that he was going to find it difficult to go home. He did not want to go back to his own village – to the village filled with so many memories of Sally. Up here he could forget her. Indeed he seldom thought of her. No, he did not want to go home. He did not want to leave the children who openly adored him. He did not want, either, to leave Clare. Had he then, in finding so fulfilling an existence, also found what he had come in search of?

'All you need from life is here, Mark, among these hills,' he recalled Clare's words.

160

Quite suddenly, he knew the answer to it all. He knew what it was that had made him come up here when Sally left him. He knew what must have lain buried in his heart ever since Fate had sent Clare across his path. He knew, without any shadow of doubt, that he had found love among these Highland mountains. Love of life, and love of Clare. Tonight he knew he would ask her to become his wife; and Clare would – she must say 'yes' because Fate had meant them for one another.

Later, when the children were in bed and Clare bent over them to kiss them good-night, they looked at her with serious questioning eyes and said, "Aunty Clare, why don't you and Uncle Mark have some little girls and boys like us?"

Clare, conscious of Mark's presence in the room, felt the colour rush to her cheeks. She sought desperately for words and then she heard Mark's voice saying, "Perhaps we will, one day!"

She felt his arms lifting her gently to her feet, his hands turning her face tenderly towards his.

"Clare!" he said. And in his eyes she saw all her hopes and dreams fulfilled. "Clare!" he said again. "Will you be my wife?"

She closed her eyes and the nursery changed slowly into a little summer-house. And perhaps, Mark, too, was remembering, for his arms went round her, and with a strange new light burning in his brown eyes, his lips found hers in a gentle pledge of love.

Chapter Fourteen

A week had passed since Mark had asked Clare to marry him. It had been a week filled with pleasant memories and on this, the last day before he returned home, he reflected that all was well with his world.

Clare's family had been delighted with the news. That evening they had sat round the fire making plans for the future and Mark had felt that his life had been like a jigsaw puzzle, broken up and suddenly fitted together again. The future had become, instead of a lonely forbidding stretch of time filled with reminiscences of Sally, a happy eventful prospect which he could view with a calm, contented mind.

Because it had been Clare's wish, they were to be engaged a full six months before their marriage.

"You see, Mark, I want to be absolutely certain in my own mind that this isn't just – just rebound."

"You know that isn't so," Mark had said, holding her long, slim hand tightly in his own. "Why, the first thing I did when I knew Sally had left me, was to come to you."

Clare had surveyed him from serious grey eyes.

"Yes, darling, but that could still have been rebound. You didn't give yourself time to miss Sally, and perhaps you were right. But when you go home, I want you to think about her and try to get everything absolutely clear in your mind."

"But everything is clear," he had argued, and then knew immediately that it was not. He still did not quite realise how all this had happened. One day he had thought his life was ruined, his heart broken, and a few weeks later, he was in love with Clare. Could that make sense?

"If you had never really been in love with Sally, then it would be different, Mark," Clare had pointed out. "But you were in love with her, and we both know it. That is why I want you to have time to reconsider what you are doing. You may feel differently when you get home. If you do, you must promise me faithfully upon your solemn word of honour that you will tell me."

"I should never go back on what I have said," Mark replied with conviction.

But Clare gripped his arm with such unusual perturbation, that he could not ignore her words.

"You must give me that promise, Mark. It is for my sake. Loving you as I do, I could not bear to live with you day in and day out, knowing that you were in love with someone else. It would hurt less if you were at a distance. Do not forget, Mark, that I am speaking from experience. I know how I felt seeing you and Sally together, knowing you loved her and wanted to be with her every moment you spent with me. I was far happier when I came home. Being parted from you hurt less. It is for my sake, Mark," she repeated urgently. "Please promise me."

For answer, he had held her close in his arms and kissed her soft red lips with great tenderness.

"I promise, my darling," he had whispered, knowing that she was right, and that she had already suffered enough on his account. But he did not believe in his heart that it would be necessary to keep that promise. He felt that Sally had already gone out of his life and his heart, and the empty space she had left was so utterly and completely filled by Clare that he was no longer certain if his love for Sally had been as deep-rooted as he had always imagined.

After all, he argued with himself, if I really loved her so much, I could not be so contented now. Clare could not replace her so easily, so perfectly. I seldom think of Sally, and then without any real hurt – only the hurt to my pride.

Could it be, then, that he had anticipated Sally's departure so often and with such painful misgivings, that the realisation when it had come, had been by contrast less painful?

Or had Sally been just a habit? She had meant so much to him in those early days after his return from the prison camp. She had symbolised his dreams and helped him to forget the past. That might not have been love – true love, such as he believed now existed between himself and Clare.

Clare was such a wonderful person. He had liked her right from that first meeting and more every time he saw her again. He respected her and admired her and she was to him the perfect companion, intelligent, thoughtful, utterly selfless, and he could not but realise the fact that he meant all the world to her. He had never been so important a part of Sally's life. Sally had had so many friends, so many other interests. And Sally's way of life was fundamentally different from his own. The financial background, for instance, had been a constant source of contention. With Clare, that did not exist. Her standard of living complied exactly with his own. Her needs were no more extravagant than his and it seemed that he had so much more to give Clare than he had had to offer Sally who already had everything money and love could give her.

It was, too, a relief to be with someone as cool and calm as Clare. He had not realised until now what a strain it had been to keep up with Sally's endless energy and constant change of ideas. She had never been able to sit still for more than a moment or two and such unpretentious occupations as walking or merely sitting and discussing life and politics and people, did not appeal to her. He had forgotten how much these things had meant to him until he found himself doing them again with Clare. In fact, he decided, he had not really been himself with Sally. He had slowly become the sort of person Sally wanted him to be. With Clare he could be himself and still feel that his best was good enough.

Now, tomorrow, he was going home and Clare would stay here in Scotland for a month and join him for a visit if, at the end of that time, he still wanted her. It would be without doubt a lonely month. He would miss Clare abominably, and the children, too. He had taken a long holiday following Shane's accident with his employer's agreement, but it was time now for him to return to work. He knew that now, with a clear and happy mind, he would settle down again to his job the better for his prolonged absence.

Clare interrupted his reverie as she came into the sitting-room which was only half lit as darkness seemed to fall more quickly in the Highlands, and he had not noticed the sun's disappearance.

"Shall I put the light on, Mark?" she asked.

"I don't think so, Clare. Come and sit here beside me for a moment or two before the others come in to tea."

Here, in Clare's home, the Scotch habit of high tea was still maintained, principally because the other members of the family came home from work tired and hungry, and it was found simpler to give them a tea and supper together and so leave the remainder of the evening free for rest and relaxation.

Clare sat down at his feet and leant her head against his knees. Gently, he ran his fingers through her smooth dark hair, thinking how fine it was, how silky and beautiful to the touch.

"What were you thinking about, Mark?" she asked, turning her head a little and rubbing her cheek against his hand.

"About you, darling, and us, and the future."

165

She seemed contented with his reply and in the twilight he saw a smile come into her eyes.

"I'm so happy, Mark. I can still hardly believe it is all true. I'm a little afraid, too."

"Afraid, Clare? Why?"

"You're going tomorrow and supposing I never see you again!"

He laughed.

"You will, my sweetheart. What could prevent it?"

Clare smiled up at him.

"I don't know. Nothing, I suppose. Perhaps I'm just feeling 'fey'. Suppose you just disappeared and I came to London and couldn't find you?"

"Supposing you never came to London!" Mark returned, teasing her. "Supposing I came up to Scotland to find you and you had disappeared – spirited away like Barrie's Mary Rose by the Highland fairies."

"I love that play," Clare said dreamily. "It's very sentimental but I like it all the same. Sad and lovely."

"But sadness is not for us any more, Clare. We are going to be so happy, aren't we, darling?"

She looked up at him, the smile gone from her eyes.

"Do you want me to reassure you, or are you reassuring me, Mark?" she asked.

Mark put his two hands to her cheeks and bent forward and kissed her gently on the lips. Passion flared suddenly into life, and as her arms went round him, he drew her closer to him and kissed her hungrily.

"Clare!" he said huskily. "I love you. Don't you believe that? Don't you believe this?" And he kissed her again until they were both breathless and trembling.

Clare drew away from him and gave a shaky little laugh.

"I believe you, darling, darling, Mark," she said. "I must believe you for I don't think I could bear to lose you now."

Mark drew out his pipe and lit it with unsteady hands.

166

"Do you *really* want us to wait six months before we are married, Clare? I'd like us to be married now – today. I want to prove to you that I mean what I say. Once you are my wife, you cannot say such things any more; you cannot torture yourself with doubts as you are doing now."

For a long moment, Clare hesitated. Mark was right in a sense. Once they were married, Mark would never go back on his word and no matter what happened, he would be hers, her husband until death alone should part them. It would mean, too, that she could go with him tomorrow. For the past few days, his impending departure had cast a cloud over her happiness. It would be so wonderful to go to London with him, to be married and go home with him and be with him always. And she needed him physically too. For the last week when Mark had held her in his arms and kissed her more and more passionately and demandingly, her whole heart, mind and body had ached with longing to give herself to him as completely as any woman could. It had become daily more difficult for them to keep reign on their feelings and that Mark was finding it a strain, too, she knew very well. It only needed a glance between them in a crowded room for each to be drawn to the other, longing to be near. And when Mark moved across the room to sit by her and hold her hand, for a moment the slight contact would satisfy them both until his fingers pressed more tightly round her own and her heart would leap into her throat and the colour to her cheeks and, looking into his eyes, she could see the little lights of passion burning there in answer to her own . . .

But slowly reason reasserted itself and Clare remembered the circumstances under which Mark had come to her. Sally's sudden departure had been a shock to Mark – it must have been. That he had not yet realised it, she alone knew to be true. He must, sooner or later, undergo a reaction. From all he had told her, this moment had not yet occurred. And it must not occur after they were married.

Mark must be utterly and completely unbiased and then make his decision finally and for ever; hard though the waiting would be for her.

"Darling," she said very softly. "I love you – terribly. You know that's true. My life won't be complete until we are married. But I don't want to rush things. You know why. I feel convinced in my own mind that we will both be so much happier one day if we wait a little while now. But it isn't that I don't want to marry you. You know I do. I'm so utterly sure that I have no doubts at all – in any way – that I should never regret it if we were married immediately. No doubts about myself. But I should doubt you, even if you did not doubt yourself. I cannot forget in a day all Sally meant to you, Mark. I saw you with her too often. I heard you speak of her so much. You were so sure – and now . . . Mark, believe me, it's better to wait."

Mark bit on the stem of his pipe. It worried him to hear Clare talk this way. He knew that to her way of thinking she was, without question, right. But he was sure that he would not change and six months was a long while. He did not really want to go back to Hannington alone. He did not want to go back to an empty house and remember. He did not want to be parted from Clare; to be four hundred miles away from the comfort of her arms and the loveliness of her grey eyes and the softness of her lips. He wanted to have her near always, in his arms, close to his heart.

He realised that he was looking upon it selfishly and instantly his mood changed and he said, "It shall be as you want it, darling. From now on everything is to be as you want it. But you must write to me often. I shall be lonely without you."

Clare thrilled to his words and with rare impulsiveness, flung her arms round him and held him to her.

"I shall be lonely without you," she said. "I shall miss you every hour of every day. I shall think of you all the time and see you in everything I do. At least having you here, walking on the moors with me, sitting in this chair, sitting at table, seeing you light your pipe, playing with the children, talking to the family – I shall be able to imagine you doing these things and in that way you will remain part of my daily life. I shall write to you every day."

Mark smiled.

"I shall keep you to that, Clare, and in return I will write to you every day, too. Which reminds me, sweetheart, I suppose you haven't heard from Lee, or Shane?"

"No," said Clare. "Not a word. I'm sure Lee would have written if anything had been wrong so I assume Shane is better. You could call in on Lee on your way through London. I think she was going back to town this week."

"I wonder if Shane and Lee will make a go of it," Mark mused. "They seemed very fond of one another."

"Lee is in love with Shane," Clare said softly. "But I think Shane only looks on her as a companion. Perhaps one day . . ."

"I hope so," Mark broke in. "I like them both. And Shane will miss Sally a good deal. Not as much as he might have done had he seen more of her those last few months. But they used to be such constant companions, you know."

"I think Shane was a little hurt at her neglect," Clare said thoughtfully. "He didn't understand that she was going through a very difficult time – what with feeling guilty about his accident and being so uncertain what to do about you and Lyndon."

"Yes!" said Mark. "I think for the first time in her life, Sally was undergoing some strain. I hope she'll be happy with Lyndon, Clare. I think she will be. He can give her so much. Sally's rather like a hothouse plant. She thrives on luxury and attention. She will have all that in America."

Clare would not have been human if the thought did not flash through her mind that Mark still cared enough for Sally to worry as to her happiness. Then she chided herself quickly for the meanness of such petty jealousy. Any friend would feel the same way and she, too, would hate to think that Sally was not happy in America. And Lyndon, too. She had much for which to be grateful to them both – Sally for being the cause of her meeting Mark; Lyndon for taking Sally away and leaving Mark free to fall in love with her.

For the hundredth time of late, Clare thanked God for His goodness in sending Mark to her. It seemed that her happiness had been held by such a thin thread. What could have put the idea of coming north into Mark's mind at that critical moment? Was it Fate? Or was it the natural outcome of her conversation that day with Mark when they had talked of Scotland and his longing for it when he had been in the Japanese camp? Whatever the reason, he had come and God alone must be responsible for his falling in love with her. For Mark did love her. He must surely do so! He could not pretend the sincerity of his voice. He could not pretend the light in his eyes; his physical response when she was near him. No, there could be no doubt that he loved her, but was it the kind of love that would last? Or might it die away as quickly as it had kindled and his feelings change with his surroundings? At Hannington there would be a hundred memories of Sally to haunt him, a hundred reminders of her as he went around his usual daily occupations. There would be Shane, too – Sally's identical twin. To look into Shane's laughing blue eyes was to look into Sally's. To see the fair, cropped, curly head was to see the simile of Sally's. Was Mark proof against such ghosts? Was he proof against the habit of his old love? Could any new love really replace the old?

She restrained the impulse to put her thoughts into words and hear Mark's reassurance. He must not be worried by her emotions for she wanted him, above everything, to think this out for himself; to make his own decision unhampered by her opinions or anyone else's. She must leave him as much as was possible, completely free to make his decision, and showing him

170

too clearly her own need of him was not to leave him free. For Mark was essentially kind and unselfish and it would be indeed hard for him to hurt anyone – especially someone of whom he were truly fond. If it were to happen that way, she must do everything in her power to make it easy for him to set himself free.

That she had set herself a hard task, Clare never doubted, but she had belief in her own strength of purpose and she knew she had, if necessary, the courage to carry it out.

A month was, after all, not so very long. And then she would be with Mark again. She would go to London and stay with Lee, and Mark would come up for weekends and occasional evenings. She might even find rooms in the local hotel at Hannington and see him still more often.

Mark, watching the fleeting expressions in her eyes, asked curiously, "What deep thoughts are passing through your mind, Clare? Sometimes I think you wander away into a world of your own. You know, darling, I think I shall call you Mary Rose. You remind me of her so often. She was a Highland lass, too, wasn't she?"

"Yes, I think so," Clare said smiling.

"Then Mary Rose you shall be to me," Mark said. "And yet I am not sure if I dare tempt Fate, or the fairies might still spirit you away from your Simon! Are you superstitious, Clare? You ought to be with your background and yet you always seem so level-headed and sensible."

"I don't think I'm unduly superstitious," Clare said with a laugh. "But there must be some of the Highland blood very strong in my veins. Sometimes I see things."

"Good Lord," Mark said boyishly. "Ghosts?"

"No! I see into the future," she told him. "But not very often. I have premonitions about things."

She was very serious and Mark joked to relieve the tension.

"Then take a peep into the future, Clare, and see if you can see us sitting by our fireside in our own home and a couple of children upstairs asleep in bed!"

"Oh, Mark!" Clare said, her voice almost wistful. "I wish I could see that and know for a certainty that it was to be so."

Mark put his pipe back into his pocket and drew her back into his arms.

"It will be so, my darling," he said, against her hair. "Believe me, Clare, it will be so. I know it as surely as I know it is you I hold in my arms now."

Clare leant against him, weakened as she always was by his proximity. Mark was so strong, so masculine, so very, very dear.

"Tell me more," she said childishly. "What else do you know?"

"That I love you very, very much."

"And that I love you?"

Mark smiled.

"Yes, that you love me. And that we will be very happy always because we will always feel the same way about each other. We shall be the proverbial Darby and Joan and everyone will call us a dull, sentimental, domesticated couple. But we will never feel dull to each other. I could never feel anything but ecstatic when I hold you in my arms like this. You are so lovely, Clare. I'm no good at pretty speeches, but to me you symbolise all that is most beautiful in woman – and all that is best."

Clare sighed contentedly. Mark was, without doubt, the most perfect lover any girl could hope for. For all his lack of 'pretty speeches' as he called them, he still said the most wonderful things. If only emotion did not leave her so tongue-tied what wouldn't she say to him? One day she would try, but not yet – not before Mark had had time to decide once and for all about the future. She resolved yet again that she would avoid saying anything that would make it harder for him to leave her if ever he should wish to do so.

Mark said suddenly, "Clare, give me something of yours, something you wear or which is close to you. I want it to keep with me so that I shall feel you are near when I'm away."

Smiling, she slipped a thin gold chain from her neck and put it over his head.

"I've worn that ever since I was two years old," she said. "It has never been off since then."

"Now you must wear this," Mark said, taking the gold signet ring from his finger. "It will have to do until we can choose you a real engagement ring in London next month."

He put it over the third finger of her left hand but it was too large and slipped off again. Mark laughed and said, "Oh, well, it'll have to go on the middle one. Now, darling, kiss me and tell me you are as happy as I am."

Clare kissed him but she could not tell him with any truth that she was happy. Although she had just denied that she was superstitious – although common-sense told her that Mark's ring would obviously be too big for her third finger, she could not but feel it was a bad omen. It seemed that Fate was warning her that it was not time for her engagement to Mark – yet.

Chapter Fifteen

Mark found Lee cooking herself some supper in her little studio flat in Chelsea. She was dressed in a paint-covered, flowered smock and looked much less sophisticated than he had seen her yet – but nevertheless still attractive.

She greeted him with a surprised smile.

"This is an honour, Mark! Come in. I'm having bacon and baked beans on toast! Would you like to share my meagre repast or have you already eaten?"

"I've just come from the station," Mark explained. "And your cooking smells delicious, Lee. Would it be hard on the rations if I stayed?"

"Of course not!" Lee said. "I'd never have eaten a whole tin of beans on my own and they would no doubt have been thrown away tomorrow," she lied easily. She wanted to talk to Mark – to hear about his holiday and Clare.

Mark put his suitcase down in the hall and following Lee's instructions, found a seat in the studio and waited for her to bring the supper in on a tray.

He looked around the room with interest. Lee was a surprisingly tidy artist. He had expected to find a jumble sale and here everything was stacked neatly in its correct place. Only a few pieces of sketching paper were scattered around on the floor and he surmised correctly that this was what she had been working on before supper.

It's strange, he mused, how people's rooms are like themselves – and their surroundings part of them. Lee's studio is as much part of herself as Clare's Scotland is her background. You really know a person's character when you go into their room or their home.

He was reminded suddenly of Sally's house. That, too, was part of Sally, luxurious, attractive, expensive and a little disorganised in its decorations, as though the person buying furniture and ornaments had done so on sudden impulses and without premeditation as to the result of the whole.

Lee brought in the tray and sat down opposite Mark.

"There!" she said. "Eat first and then tell me all the news."

Mark surveyed the huge plate of beans on toast with a grin. He was extraordinarily hungry. He needed no second bidding to get down to his meal.

After they had both finished and were drinking coffee, Lee said, "Now, Mark, tell me about your holiday. Did you have a good time? Is Clare well?"

"Very well indeed and I had a marvellous time," Mark said. "You know, Lee, I shall never understand what prompted me to go to Scotland that evening in the Hannington Arms, but I shall always be thankful from the bottom of my heart that I followed the impulse. You see, I found out in Scotland that I was in love with Clare. I have asked her to marry me."

For one fleeting second, a frown creased Lee's smooth forehead. But it was gone in an instant and Mark could not be certain that it had been there at all. Then she smiled and said, "Mark, I'm so glad. Congratulations. There's no need to ask if Clare accepted you. I know she's been in love with you for ages. She must be very, very happy. When are you going to be married?"

Mark gave a rueful grin.

"Not for at least six months," he said. "Clare wants to wait that long because she thinks I'm on the rebound from Sally."

"Are you, Mark?"

He looked up in surprise.

175

"Good heavens, no! I'm as certain about this as I have been about anything in my life. I love Clare very deeply. I . . . it can't be rebound, Lee. It goes too deep for that."

Lee was silent for a moment and then said, "Of course, you know yourself and your own feelings best, Mark. I'm really awfully pleased to hear your news. I'm so glad, too, for Clare."

Mark, in his turn, was silent for a minute. A slightly puzzled look came into his eyes.

"Lee, you don't doubt that I love her, do you? I'm very much afraid Clare does. It worries me."

"I don't doubt it if you don't, Mark," Lee said gently, "but I will admit that it seems – very sudden. At least, for you, Mark. I mean, you don't very often act on impulse, do you? And it's all happened so soon after . . ."

"After Sally left me," Mark finished for her. "Yes, I know it must seem that way, Lee. But I'm beginning to wonder now if I ever really loved Sally as much as I imagined. I don't think I could have done. Her going was a shock, of course, but for some strange reason, it had none of the expected results. I had anticipated such a thing happening, I suppose, and was, in a way, ready for it. Then when it came, I waited for the effect and nothing happened. Next time I felt anything at all, it was for Clare. The whole time I was in Scotland, I rarely thought of Sally. Clare took all my interest, all my time. Surely if Sally had meant as much to me as I thought, I could not put her out of my mind so easily? That is why I think I was not in love with her towards the end. So if that is so, it cannot be rebound now, can it?"

Lee did not answer his question directly. It was not for her to question Mark's feelings – even if she did so in her heart. Instead she said steadily, "Have you heard from Sally since she left, Mark?"

Mark's head jerked upwards.

"No, nor do I expect to do so. She'll be far too busy to write – and anyway, what would she have to say?"

176

"Perhaps that she was regretting her elopement; that she was coming home. You never know."

She heard Mark draw in his breath sharply.

"She . . . has . . . have you heard from her then, Lee?"

Lee shook her head.

"No! Shane had a letter but it was mostly just news of her journey. She didn't say whether she was happy or not. Apparently she rang up that night we were in the Hannington Arms – to say good-bye, and was very disappointed we were all out."

"I . . . see . . . !"

Somewhere deep inside him, he felt something painful stirring, a return of the old tenderness for Sally. At the back of his mind, he had felt bitter towards her for leaving only that note – for not having the courage to say good-bye. Now, hearing that she had attempted to do so, he could feel more kindly towards her. He wondered suddenly what she would have said to him on the telephone. Just good-bye? Or had she rung to tell him she might still change her mind . . . ?

His mind ran on ahead. Supposing that had been it! Supposing even at the airport Sally had regretted her decision and was ready to come back if he, Mark, would have her? What would he have done? Rushed off in his car to fetch her, or told her it was too late because he was in love with Clare?

But he had not been in love with Clare then. He had not discovered his feelings for Clare until he had been in Scotland a few weeks. Would he then have gone to fetch Sally home? Might he, if they had never gone to the Hannington Arms, still be with Sally now? And if he were, would he be happy?

Questions raced through his mind at tremendous speed, always without answer. Mark suddenly pulled himself up short realising that they were hypothetical questions and that they did not really matter since Sally had gone now anyway. Besides, there was Clare – lovely, grey-eyed, desirable Clare; Clare who loved him and was waiting for him in Scotland. That was the only thing that mattered in his life now. Sally was a memory of the past.

He looked up and found Lee watching him.

"So Sally's memory can still stir up feeling?" she said quietly.

Mark looked at her directly from serious brown eyes.

"I shall always be fond of Sally," he said. "I don't suppose I shall ever forget her. But it's all past and done now, Lee. I'm going to marry Clare. Sally is a memory only," he repeated his own thoughts aloud.

"Suppose she were to return in person?" Lee queried.

Mark took out his pipe and lit it with slow deliberation.

"That's hardly likely, is it, Lee? So it's not much use wondering what would happen if she did."

"No, I suppose not!" Lee replied. But she was not so sure that Sally's return was an impossibility. Mark had not seen her letter. Oh, it had been cheerful enough on the surface, but underneath there was something else – even Shane had noticed it.

"You don't think Sally's regretting it, do you, Lee?" he had asked. "She seems – I don't know – homesick, perhaps."

"That's probably the answer," Lee had replied. And it might well be so. Sally had never been away from home before. She would miss Shane in any case, and no doubt life in America was very strange to her. She would probably settle down once Lyndon took her to California to their home.

"Is – is she married now?" Mark broke in on Lee's thoughts.

"She didn't say, Mark. I suppose she must be – unless they are waiting until they get to California. I believe they are spending a month in New York first so that Sally can see the sights."

"That will be nice for her," Mark said formally. But somehow he could not imagine Sally in New York. He did

178

not know New York for one thing – only from American films. He supposed she was buying a lot of new clothes and going to the well-known night clubs and to heaps of parties. It all seemed very remote and somehow a little jaded after the freshness of the Highlands he had left barely twenty-four hours ago.

He had a sudden longing to be back there, to be with Clare again and see the light in her eyes and feel her slim young body in his arms. He was strangely afraid – of what he could not quite imagine. Of losing her? She seemed so very far away all of a sudden. And yet he had only to close his eyes to picture her as she would be now, sitting by the fire with the family, or perhaps running upstairs to see if the children were asleep.

He wished very ardently that he had not left her behind. He wished she had come with him – that she were not now so inaccessible. He must just wait for her first letter. There might even be one waiting for him in Hannington by the time he got home.

He turned to Lee and said, "I'm afraid I'll have to go. I've got a train to catch, Lee."

"Can't you stay a little longer?" Lee asked. "Shane is dropping in some time this evening. He's just moved into his new flat, you know. He'd love to see you."

"I can't stay, Lee. You know what Hannington is. If I miss this train, I'll have to walk from the station."

"Of course I understand. When will we see you again, Mark? Is Clare coming down soon?"

"In about a month's time," Mark told her as he rose to find his overcoat and suitcase. "I don't suppose I'll be up before then, Lee. I've got to get back to work."

"I'll write to her," Lee said. "And Mark?"

"Yes, Lee?"

"If you really love Clare, don't let anything come between you – nothing at all. Promise?"

"Of course I won't let anything come between us," Mark said.

179

But as he left Lee, he wondered what she had meant. What could come between them now? He forgot Lee as he recalled that he would be home within two hours, and perhaps there would be that letter from Clare . . .

Lee put away the supper tray, deciding to leave the washing up for her 'daily' to do next morning, and went back to her chair to think.

Mark had not, of course, understood her remark. He did not seem to be one whit afraid of what Hannington would do to him – and to Clare. But Lee was afraid and she did not believe she was wrong in surmising that Clare felt likewise.

Mark had not had time to think about Sally before he went to Scotland. His departure had been very sudden and perhaps, in one way, the wisest move. But it had also been in one sense a form of escapism. He had not stayed to face Hannington with all its memories of Sally – without her. He had not given himself time to miss her or to be upset by her jilting him. Nor, it seemed, had he had time to do so in Scotland. He had rushed headlong into another love affair which might be a dangerous and precarious thing if he had done so in order to forget the old unhappy affair of Sally. Rebound! The most dangerous reaction in the world. And the cause of so much unhappiness. In this case, it might result in the wrecking of Clare's life. If Mark fell out of love with her now, Lee did not doubt for a moment that Clare would never fall in love again. She would not allow herself to do so, or give herself the opportunity. She would no doubt remain in Scotland for the rest of her life – among her family, turning slowly with the years into a bitter old spinster.

Lee gave herself a sudden shake.

This was nonsense. Mark seemed quite sure of himself and his feelings. He had not permitted any questioning as to his love for Clare. Why then should she, Lee, question it? Mark was probably right when he said that he had no doubt fallen out of love with Sally some time before her departure. After all, Sally had treated him badly enough those last few weeks. No one would have been surprised to see Mark break the engagement of his own accord. On the contrary they had been amazed at his doggedness in continuing to accept her constant change of face and her open flirtation with Lyndon.

Besides which, Mark was a decent sort of person. He was, in fact, one of the nicest men she had ever met. Did it not stand to reason, therefore, that he should discover in Clare qualities that Sally could never have? Realise Clare's worth and, too, compare her love for him with Sally's philanderings?

Yes, it made sense. Why, therefore, had she these stupid doubts and fears on Clare's behalf?

Lee was still trying to work out an answer when Shane knocked on her door.

She waited a moment before going to open the door – purposefully she waited while her heart beat in quick painful jerks of excitement. She waited until she was outwardly calm and there could be no question of Shane's noticing her inner feelings.

This is frightful! Lee told herself severely. It gets worse every time I see him. But he must not know I love him. If he does he will cease coming to see me. I must just bear it and go on hoping that one day . . .

She rose slowly to her feet and opened the door.

Shane put his arms round her and gave her a brotherly hug.

"Hullo, Lee!" he said with his warm smile. "Am I late?"

"I don't know," Lee answered untruthfully. She had seen by her watch that he was five minutes early. "Come in. I'll get some coffee, or would you rather have a glass of beer?"

"Either!" Shane said, taking off his coat. "Well, Lee, what news?"

"I've just had a visitor," Lee said as she went into the tiny kitchen to find the beer and two glasses.

Shane followed her in and leant against the doorway watching her. She was very conscious of him and even with her back to him, she could imagine him standing there, his blue eyes twinkling, his fair curly hair and lean brown face, one hand, long and slim, resting on the stick he still carried.

"Anyone I know?" he asked.

Lee turned and walked past him into the sitting-room. "Yes!"

"You're being very mysterious. Who was it?" he asked. He followed her into the sitting-room and sniffed suddenly.

"Aha!" he said smiling. "A man! Who was he, Lee?"

She left him guessing for a moment, then she told him it was Mark. Immediately the smile left Shane's face and he became serious.

"Is he all right?" he asked.

"Surprisingly so!" she told him. "In fact, very much so. He's just got himself engaged to Clare."

"Well I'm damned!" was Shane's surprised comment. Then, "I say, Lee, that's one in the eye for Sal! Still, I'm jolly glad. Good for Mark. And very good for Clare. She's always been crazy about him. I'm frightfully pleased, Lee."

"Yes!" said Lee. "I hope they'll be happy."

"You sound doubtful," Shane said. "Why shouldn't they be?"

"I don't know. I'm being silly. I can't help feeling that Mark . . . well, don't you think it's rather odd, Shane? His getting over Sally so quickly, I mean?"

"No, I don't think so," was Shane's reply. "Sal treated him pretty badly, you know. I don't blame him a bit for turning to Clare. After all, Sally's out of his reach now, anyway. Why shouldn't he find someone to replace her?"

"No reason at all," Lee said. She gave a sudden laugh.

"I'm just being pessimistic," she said. "I'm really awfully glad. Clare must be in her seventh heaven."

"Well, that's Sally and Clare successfully married off – or almost," Shane said. "Now it's time we found you a husband, Lee."

She looked down quickly at her glass and her fingers curled round the stem with sudden strength.

"I don't want to get married yet, Shane."

"Nonsense!" Shane said lightly. "You said once that all girls wanted homes and husbands and children. You're no exception."

"Perhaps not. I just haven't met the right man," Lee said, her voice stifled.

"Wonder what sort of a chap it'll be," Shane said. "He'll have to be pretty wonderful to deserve a girl like you, Lee. In fact I'm not sure I won't reserve you for myself. Now *I* really do appreciate you, Lee."

"Do you, Shane?"

Something in her tone caused him to look up at her curiously. Her face was unusually flushed and the thought crossed his mind that perhaps Lee was feeling a bit left out of things. With his usual impulsiveness, he went across to her and touched her cheek lightly with his lips.

"Yes, I do!" he said again. "In fact I'm not sure I'm not a bit in love with you, Lee."

She drew away from him and her tone was controlled and faintly amused as she said, "Can one be 'a bit in love' with someone, Shane? I thought it was always 'all or nothing at all'!"

Shane sat down on the rug at her feet, feeling as he always did, completely at ease with Lee. Lee, to him, was the perfect replacement of his twin, with the added advantage that she was an artist and understood his art, too. He was really tremendously fond of her. In a brotherly sort of way, of course.

He wondered suddenly if it *was* in such a brotherly way. Lee was a very attractive girl and once or twice lately, he had wondered what it would be like to kiss her. But she was so unapproachable somehow. He felt awkward and inexperienced and was afraid to make a fool of himself. Lee might not want to kiss him. He said suddenly, "Lee, do you look on me – as a brother?"

"Do you look on me as a sister?" she countered, her heart beginning to race again at his words. She was glad his face was turned away from her. But he turned suddenly towards her and his blue eyes were serious as he answered, "No, I don't think I do. You're too attractive for any man to feel about you just – well, fraternally."

"That goes for you, too," Lee said as lightly as she could.

Shane stared at her for a moment, his pulses quickening as he realised that Lee found him attractive. He had never thought of her quite this way before. She had just been Lee – his friend, Sally's schoolfriend, and Clare's. Now, suddenly, she was a woman, very lovely, very desirable, and he wanted more than anything in the world to kiss her.

"Lee, do you dislike men who – who try to make love to you?"

She smiled at the boyishness of his question.

"It depends who the man is, Shane."

"Supposing I tried?" Shane asked, his voice husky and suddenly nervous.

"Why not try and see?" Lee suggested.

In those few moments of conversation, Lee had thought, how young and unsophisticated Shane is! And then, as he gathered her quickly into his arms and his lips came down on hers in a swift, passionate embrace, she knew that beneath his boyishness, Shane was a man – a man who desired her – the man she loved.

Her arms went round his neck and her fingers to his fair curls. She felt his arms tightening round her waist and his body pressing against hers with increasing urgency.

"Shane!" she whispered against his lips. "Shane!"

He drew away from her then, his breath coming in quick uneasy jerks. He sat down and drew her on to the sofa beside him. She felt his body taut against her side and knew that she herself was trembling. Her legs felt very weak and her heart and pulses were throbbing wildly. Presently he relaxed and said somewhat shakily, "Well! That proves I don't have any brotherly feelings towards you, Lee. And a moment ago I was thinking perhaps that was what you meant to me – a companion and sister." He reached out and taking one of her hands in his, raised it to his lips.

"You're very lovely, Lee," he whispered. "I think I am a little in love with you, you know."

She drew her hand away gently and her eyes were older and wiser than his and a little sad, "No!" she whispered. "It's just that you're a man, Shane, and I'm a woman – but that doesn't necessarily make us in love."

"I suppose not!" Shane said, his voice still husky and uncertain. "But I would like it to do so. Lee, do you think you could ever love me?"

"Perhaps!" Lee said with forced lightness. "We'll see. Now I think you'd better go home, Shane. It's late."

He rose immediately, but before he left, he drew her into his arms and kissed her with unexpected tenderness.

"Good night, Lee dear!" he said. "When can I see you again? Tomorrow?"

"If you like," Lee told him, her eyes starry. "Ring me when you get back from the office."

His lips touched hers again for a fleeting moment, then he was gone.

For a long time, Lee stood with her back to the door, her eyes closed, her hands cupping her hot cheeks.

"Oh, Shane, Shane!" she whispered. "I've waited so long for that kiss. So very long. Oh, dear God, let him love me. Let this be the beginning, for I can't go back now."

Chapter Sixteen

Mark settled down to work again feeling contented and happy. Hannington had not altered his views about Clare and none of the expected nostalgic memories of Sally had arisen to haunt him and give him doubts. He wrote to Clare regularly and her letters to him were cheerful, affectionate, filled with scraps of news of her everyday doings.

Only one thing was lacking in those almost daily epistles, and that was the undercurrent of passionate feeling which had been so apparent during his stay in the north. He worried a little at first in case Clare, at a distance, was no longer sure of her feelngs for him. And then he decided that Clare was probably one of those people who found it difficult as he did himself to put deep emotion into words, so he left it at that.

The real reason, however, was Clare's promise to herself that as far as possible she would leave Mark free to change his mind if he should find he wished to do so.

She, too, had worried a little at first. But now, nearly a fortnight later, Mark's letters were still coming as regularly as ever and there was no reference to Sally – nor could she find between the lines any trace of a change of heart. Every letter he said he was waiting impatiently for her to come south – that he missed her and wished she were with him; that he loved her very much and could not bear to live without her now that he had found her at last.

She need not have had any qualms. Shane was still in London, his parents away, and Mark did not even go to the big house on the hill where once he had spent so much of his time. Once or twice he thought of going there to see if Sally's mother and father were back; then he had put it off and found out one evening when he dropped into the local for a glass of beer, that they were still away.

So there no longer seemed to be any reason for him to go there.

Another week passed and Mark, walking home from work, thought happily that in seven days, Clare would be coming down. He thought, too, with a warm glow inside him, of the letter he knew would be awaiting him.

He pushed open the front door and went to the hall table. There were three letters for him instead of the usual one. He recognised Clare's handwriting on one of them and then, with a sudden inward shock, saw an American airmail stamp and knew that one of the letters was from Sally. The third he did not bother to pick up. It was only a bill - one he had been expecting for the diamond and sapphire engagement ring he had bought ready to give Clare on her arrival.

He walked through to the sitting-room and sat down in his armchair, holding the two letters in his hand. He stared at them both, knowing that he could not decide which to open first. He really wanted to open Sally's because he did not know what was in it. But he felt it might be in some strange way disloyal to Clare, and with sudden resolution, he put Sally's aside and opened Clare's.

He had come to the bottom of the first page before he knew that he had not taken in a word of what he had read. He forced himself to concentrate and read the whole letter word for word. It was little different from Clare's usual letter – mostly because life ran to routine in her home and nothing changed in the ordinary course of daily arrangements. But perhaps because the time was so nearly here when she would be coming to him, her letter was more outspoken; more loving than any of the previous ones.

I'm so afraid something will happen to prevent my coming to see you, Mark dearest, she wrote. *I know it is silly of me, but I have a feeling that it's all much too good to be true. No doubt a relic from childhood days when it seemed Christmas Day was always tomorrow and tomorrow and never now. Do you understand, darling? And do you feel this way, too?*

It seems a hundred years since you last held me in your arms. Oh, if only Saturday week was here and I was stepping out of the train into your arms . . . will that day ever come?

Mark put the letter down, knowing that he was not in the mood to give it concentrated consideration. First, he *must* know what Sally had to say. Then, when he had read it, he would go back to Clare's letter and read all the wonderful things she said again.

He took the oblong airmail envelope and slit it quickly open, drawing out the pages of Sally's untidy scrawl. He read through them more and more slowly, the colour leaving his face as he did so, the frown creasing his forehead deeply.

"Oh, God!" he murmured once aloud. "Oh, Sally!"

At last he leant back in his chair, his eyes closed, his fingers clenching the letter, his mind trying to take in the fact that Sally was on her way home. She was coming back. She had not married Lyndon after all. Why? Why? Why? It did not make sense.

Darling Mark, she had written, *I have been in New York three whole weeks now and I'm a complete wreck. I enjoyed it at first but I simply can't stand*

188

it any longer. You've no idea what it is like. It's one long round of parties and drinks and meeting people. I'm so tired I can hardly think. All I know is that I want to come home. I don't know what mad idea I had ever to come here with Lyndon. He sees how unhappy and homesick I am and says it will all be different when we get to California, but that he's been away from business so long, he must stay in New York another three weeks before we can go. It's all very well for him. He knows all these people who keep ringing up and asking us out. I don't know them and it's such an effort for me to keep up when I'm feeling so tired. He says we must go or we will hurt their feelings.

Suddenly last night, about two in the morning, I knew I couldn't stand it any more and that I wanted to be home with Mummy and Daddy and Shane and you. I have missed you all so much and will never forgive myself for rushing off the way I did. Often and often I've thought about you all and how wonderful life was at home and how lonely it is here. Everyone tries to be kind and Lyndon has done his best, but how can I feel anything else but a stranger? I'm not an American and I don't think as they do. Nor am I used to their ways.

Of course, some of it's marvellous – the life I mean, and the clothes in the shops, and the food and dancing. Lyndon seems to know hundreds and hundreds of important people. All the women dress beautifully and look like glamorous film stars and I feel like a dowdy country cousin amongst them. Lyndon says I don't need to have an inferiority complex and that as soon as the new clothes I'm having made are ready, I'll be as glamorous as any of them, but I know I won't. I feel so young and silly and they are all so sophisticated.

No, New York isn't my life and I'm not taking any

189

chances on California. What will Hollywood be like, I keep asking myself? It would be worse there. So I am flying home. I haven't dared tell Lyndon yet. I seem to be an awful coward about telling people things. But he's been so kind and tried so hard to make me happy. I've booked a passage on the Clipper next Thursday. I thought I'd surprise the family so don't tell them. But I wanted to tell you so that you could meet me if you can. I'll tell you all about it when I see you . . .

Thursday! Mark thought. Tomorrow! And Clare coming Saturday week. Oh, Lord! What a dreadful mess. What am I going to do? What shall I say to Clare? Shall I meet Sally? Of course, she doesn't know about my engagement to Clare. Why should she? It isn't official yet so Shane won't have told her. What shall I do?

Questions raced through his mind in an incoherent jumble. He did not think any further than what he must do. He knew that he would meet Sally. He could not allow her to arrive back in England with no one there to see her. Nor did it occur to him that he could wire Shane to meet her. He must go himself. Sally had asked him to be there and he had never failed her yet . . . But Clare . . . did he mean to fail her?

Mark shelved the question of his own feelings and tried to sort out facts. He could get away from the office early. He still had enough petrol to run up to London Airport in his car. But what should he do about Sally's parents? They were not due back until next month. If only he could make up his mind what was best done. If there was someone he could ask . . . Lee!

Mark jumped to his feet and went to the telephone.

The moments while he was waiting for the number to be put through dragged interminably. Then at last Lee's clear, cool voice said, "Hullo! Who's speaking?"

"Lee, it's Mark! I – I thought you ought to know that

I've just had a letter from Sally. She's arriving back in London by plane tomorrow."

"Sally! Coming back! But Mark, why? What's wrong? Is she ill?" Lee gasped her surprise.

"I don't think so. She seems to be unhappy out there. I don't altogether understand. The thing is, she hasn't told anyone else she's coming – planned to surprise them. But of course no one is at home. Should I tell Shane to come back? Does he know where to get hold of his parents?"

The line was silent for a moment as if Lee were thinking. At last she said, "I think Shane should be told, Mark. Someone ought to meet Sally."

"She asked me to," Mark said without thinking. "I can run up in my car and bring her back."

"But – the line went dead for a second, and then Lee said: "Mark, I've no right to be personal, but just how do you feel about all this? I mean, will Sally's return change everything?"

It was Mark's turn to hesitate. He said slowly, "No . . . I . . . Lee, I don't know. Of course, I wouldn't do anything to hurt Clare. You know that. But I can't refuse to see Sally, can I? Especially as she is so unhappy. Lee, what do you think I ought to do?"

"It isn't what you ought to do so much as what you feel you want to do," came Lee's reply immediately. "You want to meet her, don't you?"

"Yes!" said Mark without hesitation. "But that doesn't mean I've changed my mind about Clare. How could it? I could never hurt Clare after all she's done for me."

"You could only hurt Clare by keeping the truth from her," Lee said quickly. "Look, Mark, you've asked for my advice. Well, I'll give it to you. I think you're right to go and meet Sally. I think you should see all you can of her and find out just exactly what she does mean to you – if she means anything at all. Pretend Clare doesn't exist – if you can. If you find you still love Sally, then write to Clare and tell her. She'll understand. But for the time being, don't say anything. She's not coming down just yet, is she?"

"Saturday week," Mark told her.

"Then say nothing about it yet. Wait and see how you feel tomorrow when you meet Sally again. You know, Mark, Clare always felt that this would happen – only that it would be Sally's ghost that haunted you and not Sally herself. If you want my honest opinion once more, I think this is the best thing that could happen. It'll clear the air once and for all. And now, to be practical, I'll tell Shane. He'll come down, I'm sure. Then we'll leave it to him to tell his family or not as he thinks fit. And Mark . . ."

"Yes, Lee?"

"Don't get in a state about this. It'll sort itself out. Worrying won't help."

"I can't help worrying a little, Lee. It's all so very unexpected. I'm so afraid . . . well, it seems I'll have to hurt either Sally or Clare. You see, Sally doesn't know about Clare. Judging by her letters, I should imagine she expects . . . well, that she expects me to feel the same way as I once did."

"Sally has no right to expect anything from you, Mark," Lee said firmly. "She left you for another man. If she comes back to you, it is on quite a different footing. It's no longer a question of whether Sally wants you, Mark. It's whether you want Sally."

"Yes, yes I suppose so," Mark said doubtfully.

"Mark, I think I'll come down with Shane," Lee said suddenly. "Things may be a bit awkward one way and another and I might be able to help."

"That would be wonderful!" Mark said enthusiastically. "You're such a good person to have around in a crisis. You keep so calm and level-headed."

"I'm frightfully good at managing everyone else's affairs and very bad at managing my own," came Lee's amused voice. "Well, go and get a good night's sleep,

Mark, and once again, don't worry. We'll talk it all over tomorrow night."

Strangely reassured by Lee's words, Mark had some supper and soon afterwards, went to bed. Unexpectedly, he had a good night's sleep and he did not dream. In fact, when he woke first thing on Thursday morning, it was some minutes before he realised with renewed shock, that Sally was coming home and that in a few hours he would be driving up to London Airport to meet her.

The plane was an hour overdue. Mark's nerves were stretched almost beyond endurance by the wait. He tried to sort out his emotions but could not. He knew that he was excited at the prospect of seeing Sally again; that he was also apprehensive; that he felt acutely disloyal to Clare; but none of these feelings made much sense and he forgot them all when he saw the plane coming in to land, and not long afterwards, the passengers climbing down the gangway and coming across the tarmac towards them.

He caught sight of Sally's unmistakable figure and hurried forward to meet her. As soon as she saw him, she ran forward with a cry of delight.

"Oh, Mark! It *is* good to see you. I feel I've been away years instead of a few weeks. You're looking terribly well!"

He stared down into her upturned face and knew that she was waiting for him to kiss her. Her self-assurance annoyed him although the realisation was only subconscious, and he bent his head and kissed her lightly on the cheek.

"You're looking wonderful, Sal," he said, the nickname coming quite naturally to his lips, his voice genuinely warm with admiration. Sally was wearing a new tailored suit, very smart in a soft blue material which matched her eyes and showed off her golden hair to perfection. His pulses stirred suddenly and he turned away.

Sally tucked her arm through his and as they walked back towards the building, she chattered happily beside him.

"Of course, I'm quite mad to come rushing home like this," she said with a laugh. "And you know, Mark, I didn't get round to telling Lyndon. I just went. He'll be furious when he finds out. In fact, I wouldn't put it past him getting the next plane after me. But it's no good. I won't go back to New York. I hate it. It's so – so big. I felt just a little nobody who didn't matter at all out there. But I must say, it was a wonderful holiday. You should see the clothes, Mark! They're quite beautiful. And the food and the parties—"

"I thought you didn't like it there," Mark said uncertainly.

"Well, I didn't, really," Sally said. "I suppose I was homesick or something. I don't know. Perhaps I missed you, Mark."

She looked up at him and he bit his lip nervously.

"Did you, Sally?" he asked, not knowing whether he was pleased by her remark or annoyed by the laughing tone in which she had made it.

"Of course I did, silly. I missed you and Shane and Mummy and Daddy. I wish you could all have come with me. Then it would have been glorious fun."

Conversation ended as they went through the customs and other formalities. Then at last they were in Mark's car and Sally was saying as he put the key into the ignition, "Aren't you going to kiss me, Mark?"

Reluctantly, he turned towards her and then, seeing the provocative dancing light in her eyes, remembering the old longing for her, he suddenly put his arms round her and his mouth came down to hers in a hard, passionate kiss.

Sally's response was ardent, but Mark drew away, his mind suddenly filled with memories of Clare and the knowledge that she loved and trusted him. He felt

194

mean and rotten, the more so because he knew he was still attracted to Sally and that her kiss had not left him unmoved.

"What's the matter, Mark? Don't you still love me?" Sally asked, her voice faintly puzzled.

"I'd rather not answer that, Sally," Mark heard himself reply.

Then, to his surprise, Sally laughed.

"Oh, well! I suppose I have no right to expect you should," she said lightly. "In fact, I can see I have no right. But I must say, it is a little disappointing. You see, I've been looking forward to this for such ages."

Mark let in the clutch and the car rattled forward.

"Ages?" he repeated. "But you only decided to come home a few days ago."

"Well, it seemed ages," Sally said. "You know, Mark, you've changed. I suppose that's falling out of love. But you are different."

"Am I? In what way?"

Sally shrugged her shoulders.

"I don't know. You seem . . . critical, or something. I suppose you're dreadfully cross with me."

"Cross?" Mark asked. "Why?"

Sally looked at him genuinely surprised.

"Well, me dashing off with Lyndon and then coming back like this."

"I'm not cross, Sally. You had every right to go with Lyndon if you wanted to as long as you loved him. Don't you love him, Sally?"

Sally sighed. "I don't know, Mark," she said. "All I do know is that I couldn't stand the life we were leading out there. I suppose if I'd loved him, I couldn't have left him. I must be in love with you after all."

"But you left me, too," Mark said, bluntly.

A frown crossed Sally's smooth forehead.

"Anybody would think you weren't a bit pleased to see me back," she said petulantly.

195

Mark felt suddenly repentant. Sally had come a long way to be home again. He could hardly be giving her the reception she had anticipated. She must be tired, too.

"Of course we're glad to have you home," he said.

"We? Have you told anybody else then?"

Mark explained that her parents were away and that he had sent for Shane and that Lee was coming down with him.

"They'll be waiting for you at the house now," he said.

Sally brightened up a little.

"Darling Shane!" she cried excitedly. "It'll be wonderful seeing him again. How is Lee? And is Shane quite all right again – his leg, I mean?"

Mark told her the news and felt a sudden inward trepidation that Sally would mention Clare. Somehow or other, he did not want to talk of Clare. He did not know what he should tell Sally.

But his fears were realised as soon as he had exhausted news of the others.

"And what of Clare?" she asked.

"She's in Scotland."

"I suppose she's still in love with you," Sally said, her voice faintly questioning. "Or wasn't I right in assuming she was?"

"Yes, you were right!" Mark answered shortly.

"I suppose I should be flattered that you haven't rushed off to Scotland to mend each other's broken hearts," Sally said, little guessing how near to the truth she was.

Mark's hands gripped the steering wheel. Sooner or later Sally would have to know the truth. She might as well know now. With sudden resolution, he said, "I did go to Scotland, Sally. I ought to tell you that Clare and I are unofficially engaged."

Sally stared at him, completely taken aback. Surprise robbed her of feeling for a second and then emotions crowded through her; so Mark hadn't taken long to get

196

over his broken heart! she thought jealously. And then, perhaps it's rebound and underneath he still loves me. I've come home just in time – if I want him. He's not Clare's property yet. Perhaps, though, he does really love her and he doesn't want me. What a fool I was to come rushing home to him!

It seemed as if she had made a real fool of herself. After all, if it hadn't been for Mark, she would never have come back. New York wasn't much fun but Hannington would be even worse without Mark to take her around and look after her. And Lyn really did love her. There had been no doubt as to that. In fact, if she'd put up with the social round for a few weeks longer they were going to California to get married and then Lyn said she really would have been happy.

No, it was home-sickness that had made life miserable in New York – so many strange faces and strange people and then Lyn having so many business appointments. She had suddenly had a longing for the quiet of the country and Mark's slow, soothing voice and unhurried ways. She had regretted her hasty decision in that moment and made an equally hasty one to return. She ought to have found out first what was happening at home.

Tears of mortification rose to her eyes and fell down her cheeks. She searched blindly for a handkerchief and then Mark turned to look at her and saw that she was crying. Instantly he stopped the car and put a hand on her arm. He couldn't bear to see women cry and Sally – Sally of all people. It was his fault. He had been wretchedly blunt and tactless in his way of telling her about Clare. He had made her cry.

"Sally, don't. Please, Sal!" he said. "It'll all work itself out."

Unconsciously he used Lee's words.

Sally clung to him, sobbing with childish abandon, "Oh, Mark, d-don't l-leave me now. N-not now when I n-need you so badly. Tell me you still love me, Mark."

197

Mark stared down at her tear-stained face, his mind desperately confused. Did he still love her? Or did he love Clare? Could Sally really need him as much as she said or was she just tired and overwrought? Clare needed him, too. And he loved Clare. At least, he had thought he did. Had Sally's homecoming changed all that?

He sought for the truth but could not find it. Knowing that Sally was waiting for his reply, he said, "Sally, don't ask me that now. I want time to think it over. I never expected you would come home like this. I thought you had gone for ever – I thought you were probably married to Lyndon by now."

"So I'm getting my desserts!" Sally said a little bitterly. "I made you wait while I tried to make up my mind about you and Lyndon. Now you are making me wait while you decide about me and Clare."

"Sally, don't talk like that – please," Mark begged. "I don't know what to do. Can't you see how your return has muddled everything up? Why, yesterday I didn't even know you were coming. And Clare is arriving in London Saturday week. I shall have to write to her – to put her off. I must have time to make up my mind."

"I thought you once told me when one was in love one always knew it," Sally reminded him.

It had become all of a sudden a matter of the utmost importance as to whether Mark loved her or not. Now that he no longer was sure of the fact he was a hundred times more desirable. It was part of Sally's nature to want what she couldn't get . . . perhaps because she had always had what she wanted so easily.

"I did say that. I thought it was true," Mark said. "But I suppose it can't be. I did love you. I know that's true. Perhaps I still do. But there's Clare now and . . ." he could not go on. He could not say 'I love her, too' any more than he could put her in the past and say 'I did love her'. What then was the truth? He could not be in love with them both.

"Sally, it's no good trying to sort this out now. You're tired and we're both upset. Let's get home now. The others will be worried about you. Your plane was over an hour late, you know."

Sally did not answer, but sat in silence while he restarted the engine and drove her towards home. But her mind was working busily and she was completely sure of one thing now – that without Mark, she could not tolerate being at home. And since she had burned her boats and left America and Lyndon, she must win Mark back or else fall between two stones; and she certainly did not mean to do that.

Chapter Seventeen

Sally seemed to recover her usual good spirits as soon as they reached home. She flung herself into Shane's arms and gave him a sisterly hug, her eyes shining.

"Oh, it *is* good to see you again, Shane darling," she cried with genuine warmth. "And you look so well, too! Lee, I'm sure it's all your doing."

Mark watched with puzzled eyes as she danced round the room looking at familiar objects with remembered affection as if she had not seen them for years instead of weeks. What a fantastic child Sally was at heart . . . so irresponsible and impulsive. The seriousness of their meeting seemed to have been forgotten and now one would think, to watch her sparkling eyes and laughing little mouth, that she hadn't a care in the world. Could it be that she was sure, with some childlike optimism, that everything would work out all right for her? Could she believe, deep in her heart that he belonged to her and she to him, and that there could be no real need for worry? She must not be allowed to think so, if that were the case. There was Clare to be considered – and Clare's life and happiness which he knew all too well was totally dependent on him.

Lee, watching Mark across the room, saw the varying expressions in his eyes and wondered what was passing through his mind. What, in heaven's name, she thought, will happen now? How could Sally waltz gaily home and with one, no doubt irresponsible decision, upset all the plans that had been made!

Poor Clare! Lee thought. Sally had no right . . . but then had Sally known when she decided to come back, that Clare and Mark were engaged? She could not have known for it had been kept a close secret and that exonerated Sally from blame. But she must keep out of the picture now. She must leave Mark and Clare to their new-found happiness, whatever the cost to herself.

With a sudden sickening of her heart, Lee knew that it was not within the bounds of Sally's nature to do the big thing – to put herself second. If she had returned to Mark, then there was no hope for Clare unless Mark's second love was the real one, and not as Lee supposed the rebound from Sally. Surely, surely Mark must see which of the two girls was the more worthy of him? Surely he must know which one the more capable of true and lasting love such as he needed and could return? Sally was a will-o'-the-wisp! She would dance gaily through life, probably unaware of the hurt she sometimes inflicted on others, urged on by her own selfish desires and quest for happiness.

Perhaps Shane can help, Lee thought. He is the only one with influence over Sally. I can try. Clare, too, must fight for her own happiness. But I'm afraid she won't. She'll stay in Scotland and leave Mark to make up his own mind.

With sudden determination, Lee decided that she would do everything in her power to persuade Clare to come south whatever happened. She must be there, on the scene of the battle – there for Mark to see and hear and touch, so that she was real to him and not just a memory of a few happy weeks in Scotland.

She walked across the room and lightly took Sally's arm.

"Tell us what brought you home, Sally. We're all dying to hear your news. Are you and Lyndon married? Have you come for a holiday or is Lyndon coming over on a new job?"

201

The smile left Sally's face and a petulant pout spoilt the pretty curve of her lips. She pulled away from Lee and went across to Mark, slipping her arm through his with feigned unconcern.

"I'm not married, Lee, and I'm home for good. I decided that I ought never to have left at all. So here I am."

No one spoke and Sally broke the silence with a forced laugh.

"I don't seem very welcome!" she said.

"Of course you're welcome, Sal," Shane broke in quickly. "It's just that . . . well, I suppose you've got to know – Mark and Clare are engaged and—"

"Oh, I know!" Sally broke in. "Mark's already told me. But it's not my fault, is it? Besides, I can't see why my coming home is such a bombshell. If Mark is in love with Clare then that's that. I'll just step quietly out of the picture."

There was a dangerous tone to her voice of which only Lee was aware. Shane, at once reassured, gave Sally a brotherly pat on the back and told her to have some of the sandwiches and coffee which were awaiting her.

With a backward smile at Mark which was clearly an invitation to follow, Sally went with Shane into the dining room. Mark hesitated and was about to move after them when Lee said quickly, "Does Clare know Sally is home, Mark?"

He shook his head.

"Not yet! I don't know how to tell her."

"You could telephone, or is it that you don't know what to say?"

Mark sat down suddenly and pulled out his pipe with nervous hands.

"I ought to telephone," he said. "But I'm in such a confounded muddle, Lee. I don't want to hurt Sally, and I don't want to hurt Clare."

"You'll have to hurt one of them, Mark, my dear,"

202

Lee said gently. "It seems that there's some choice in the matter. I'd hoped that you were sure about Clare. You both seemed so terribly in love and so very happy."

"We were – I mean we are . . . oh, I don't know what I mean. Of course I love Clare. But Sally . . . she told me in the car coming here that I was all she had left; that she'd made a terrible mistake and regretted it. How can I . . ."

"You can do anything if you really want to, Mark. Sally may have said she came home to you, but she has plenty else. She has a lovely home, horses, a car, luxury, doting parents, friends. No man will ever be life and death to Sally – not even you, Mark."

"No, I suppose you're right. All the same, she does need me. Even you will admit that, Lee."

"Oh, yes! I'll admit that all right. What woman doesn't need one man when another has failed her? Lyndon didn't come up to scratch apparently, so she comes home to you, expecting to find the devoted slave you used to be, Mark. Finding you engaged to another girl only makes you more desirable."

Mark looked up and met Lee's gaze, his eyes uncertain.

"Don't you like Sally, Lee? I thought you were such friends. Now you speak as if . . ."

"As if she were about to ruin your life – and Clare's," Lee finished for him. "That's the truth, Mark. I think Sally is young and thoughtless and not altogether to blame, but she's not entirely stupid. She wants you. She'll get you, probably, and there's nothing I can do about it. It's not really my business, anyway. But I'm worried about Clare. She ought to be here to fight her own battle."

"Why are you so sure there is going to be a 'battle' as you put it, Lee? You heard what Sally just said. That she'd step out of the picture if I was in love with Clare."

"Are you?"

"I think . . . of course, you know I am, Lee. Clare's the most wonderful person in the world."

"Are you trying to convince yourself, or me, Mark? If it's the latter, then you're failing. You can't be in love with two people, you know. If it's Sally, and Clare was just rebound, then Clare ought to be told as soon as possible. If it's Clare, then don't stay here, Mark. Go to her, or else send for her. Get married now, as soon as possible. Don't let Sally come between you."

"No, I won't!" Mark said with sudden conviction. "I do love Clare. I know that's the truth. It's just that I've known Sal so long and wanted her so desperately. It's so odd – so fantastic finding her here, waiting on my words, really in love with me. I suppose I wouldn't be human if I wasn't a little pleased and flattered – and worried by it."

"No, you wouldn't be human if you didn't feel all those things, Mark. But remember them for what they are. Don't be confused later and think you still love her."

Mark stood up and took Lee's hand.

"You're a wonderful person, Lee. Shane is going to be a lucky man one of these days as soon as he has sense enough to find out the truth. I suppose he hasn't . . . yet?"

Lee smiled and shook her head.

"Not yet! But I'm still waiting – and hoping."

"I'm going to telephone Clare and tell her to hurry down," Mark said. "I'll have my coffee afterwards. Will you tell them?"

Lee went into the dining room and watched Sally's face as she told them Mark was phoning Clare. Sally bit her lip, frowned, and then said suddenly, "You've no need to crow about it, Lee. Anyone would think you were pleased my whole life is ruined . . ."

She burst into tears and hid her face in her table napkin.

Shane was round the table at her side in an instant.

"Sal, don't say things like that. You know very well Lee is the best friend in the world. How could you think—?"

"She wants Mark to marry Clare. She doesn't want me to be happy again after all these months of misery," Sally sobbed.

Shane looked across at Lee unhappily.

"We were all pleased about Mark and Clare, Sal," he said gently. "We thought you were happily married to Lyndon and it was the best possible thing for Mark. You wouldn't have wanted him to be unhappy and miserable for the rest of his life, would you?"

Sally did not answer but sobbed on. Shane, with the usual masculine discomfiture at the sight of tears, said awkwardly, "You're tired, Sal. Why not run along to bed? It must have been a long day for you."

"So now you're trying to get rid of me," Sally cried fiercely. "I supose you want to be alone with Lee."

Shane's expression changed.

"Don't be so darned silly, Sally. You're acting like a kid of ten. Nobody is going to be very sympathetic while you go around making stupid remarks like that. Now run along to bed and sleep it off. Everything will seem worlds better in the morning."

Sally did not answer but went slowly from the room, the tears still falling, her shoulders bent tragically.

Shane turned to Lee and said, "I'm afraid she's terribly cut up about it, Lee. It's rather a shame old Mark got himself tied up so hurriedly. I wonder what he's really feeling. Bit awkward for him if he is still in love with Sal. Be darned bad luck on Clare, too."

"I think he loves Clare," Lee said quietly. "In fact I'm sure of it, Shane. If only Sally will let things be, I feel sure Mark will marry Clare and be happy and make her happy. You, yourself, never thought Sally and Mark would make a go of it. They're worlds apart. Sally will get over it. She's so attractive and – so young. There'll be plenty of other young men in her life."

"Yes, of course," Shane said, reassured. "You know, Lee, she can be an awful baby at times. That remark just now – about us . . ."

"Was it so ridiculous?" Lee asked with a smile.

Shane reached out and took her hand.

"Perhaps not!" he said. "It seems ages since we were alone together, Lee. There've been so many people and so many parties these last few weeks in town. I've hardly seen you. Where've you been?"

"In the studio, working," Lee said. "You went a bit too social for me, Shane."

"I think I did overdo it. I know I missed our evenings together. Have you?"

She nodded and smiled into his eyes. His own flared with sudden passion and with a swift gesture he caught her into his arms.

"You're the most attractive woman I know, Lee. I don't understand what it is you have that the others haven't, but there's something – something that drives me a little crazy when I'm so close to you. Kiss me, Lee."

She surrendered herself with glowing heart to his embrace.

At the top of the staircase, Sally paused, hearing Mark's voice in the hall below. The desire to eavesdrop became overpowering and she went back to the first landing where she could easily decipher his words, remaining herself unseen.

"Is that you, Clare? Darling, it's Mark. Yes, I've some news for you . . . oh, good news, really . . . Sally's home . . . hullo? Clare? Are you still there? I thought we'd been cut off. Did you hear what I said? Sally's home! Yes, tonight. Yes, it was a surprise . . . no, she left him . . . I don't know. I suppose they didn't hit it off. I don't think she liked America either. Oh, Clare, of course not. You're to come without fail . . . Did you hear, Clare? Yes, Saturday, without fail . . . but darling . . ."

206

There was a long pause and Sally gripped her fingers into the palms of her hands, willing Clare to put off her arrival. If only she had time. She was certain that was all she needed to win Mark back. After all, he'd loved her a long time before he set eyes on Clare. There were all the memories that could be revived. He'd only known Clare a short time and he'd soon forget. He must forget. She wanted him back, and she would have him. If only Clare would put it off a bit . . .

"But Clare, why? I don't understand. It doesn't make any difference at all. You know I love you . . . but darling, if that were so I'd tell you. I don't need time to think it over . . . I made up my mind and I'm not going to change it . . . Clare, you can't mean it. It's crazy. Don't you understand . . . three months! Clare, this is nonsense. We've already waited a month. I'm coming to Scotland to fetch you myself if you won't come here . . ."

Another long silence. Sally felt the tension mounting. It seemed as if Clare were playing into her hands. But would Mark go to Scotland? Could she, Sally, prevent him?

The few remaining words were lost. Then the telephone receiver was replaced and just as she was about to go back upstairs she heard Lee's voice.

"Everything all right, Mark? You look as white as a ghost!"

"Everything's wrong," came Mark's reply. "Clare's refused to come. She says I must have time, or something silly. I'm going to Scotland tomorrow, Lee, to fetch her. This is sheer nonsense. She must be made to see the truth."

"I think you're very wise, Mark. I'm sure when she sees you and sees that you are still in love with her, everything will clear itself up."

"I'll catch the day train. I could be up the day after tomorrow. I'll have to start early tomorrow morning. I wonder if you could ring up the office for me and explain, Lee? Make some excuse for me. I'll have to be in London early to catch that train and I won't have time to see the boss."

"Of course I will, Mark. Don't worry about anything."

"I'll get home and pack," Mark said. "Will you make my apologies to Sally and Shane?"

Sally turned and hurried upstairs and into her room and flung herself onto the bed, thinking furiously. If Mark went tomorrow her last chance would go. Something must be done to prevent it. Something that wouldn't raise suspicion. What could she do? Illness? What illness?

She heard footsteps outside the room and a knock on the door.

"May I come in, Sally?" came Lee's voice.

Sally murmured an assent and lay back quickly on the pillows, her eyes closed.

"What's the matter, Sally? Aren't you feeling well?" Lee asked, seeing Sally's flushed cheeks and closed eyes.

"I'm cold!" Sally said. "And my head hurts."

"You're overtired, Sally," Lee said gently. "Pop into bed and I'll go down and get you a hot-water bottle."

Sally opened her eyes and caught Lee's hand.

"No, don't leave me," she said. "I'm not well. I'm afraid. Oh, Lee, don't leave me."

Lee sat down on the bed, looking at Sally with worried eyes.

"What's the matter, Sally? Have you a pain? Is something wrong?"

"Yes, yes, a pain!" Sally murmured. "In my stomach. I've had it on and off for weeks. I'm afraid, Lee. I think it might be appendicitis. I didn't dare go to a doctor in America. A friend of Lyndon's died two days before we got there from an appendix. I'll be all right. I don't want a doctor. It'll go off."

Lee was really worried. Sally, usually so healthy and very much the kind of person to hate sickness and sick rooms, certainly didn't sound too good. Her voice was hardly decipherable. If she had been having pains it might well be an appendix and if it had been going on for some weeks it could now be acute and was dangerous.

"You must have a doctor, Sally. If you have an early opinion it might mean nothing more than a slight operation. If you leave it, then it may become serious. People don't die from appendix operations, you know," she added reassuringly.

"Lyndon's friend did," said Sally almost inaudibly.

"Then he left it too long. I'm going to get a doctor, Sally."

The younger girl sat up and clutched Lee's arm with a frantic desperation that was not feigned. If Lee got a doctor in now he would pronounce her fit and all would be lost! No, she had started the lie and she must go on with it.

"No, Lee, you mustn't. You don't understand. I lied just now, I didn't mean to tell anyone the truth. You must swear not to tell anyone at all. Promise Lee. On your word of honour?"

Lee stared at Sally in amazement. What on earth could be wrong with the girl.

"All right, Sally. I won't tell anyone, unless it's absolutely necessary. Tell me what's wrong."

Sally lay back on the pillows, closing her eyes and thinking fast. She must be really ill – so ill that Mark could not go to Scotland. Something fatal.

"I did go to a doctor in America," she said. "That's why I came home. Lee, I've only got a little while to live. I've got tuberculosis."

Lee was struck into silence as the full import of Sally's words reached her. The flushed cheeks; the sudden return home; the whole thing made sense now. How ghastly! And the poor child had meant to keep it from everyone so that they should not be worried.

"Sally, my dear child, are you sure?" she asked. "Did

you have a second opinion? It must be curable. It always is these days unless it's left too long.

Sally grabbed at those last words.

"That's the trouble, Lee. I've had it for years. I've always been so well I've never had an x-ray. Else it would have been seen. There wasn't any need for a second opinion. It's both lungs. I haven't a chance. I asked the doctor to tell me the truth and he showed me the x-ray plates."

Lee sat there, holding Sally's hands, her heart filled with horror and pity. It couldn't be true. It just couldn't. People didn't look well and fit and healthy one minute and die the next. Then she recalled a conversation she had heard as a VAD where tubercular patients looked a hundred per cent in the best of health in the later stages.

"Sally, if you went to a sanatorium . . . didn't the doctor suggest it?"

"It might prolong life for a year, a month. I told him I'd rather live my last months happily, in my own home," Sally said, improvising quickly as her belief in her own lie almost began to seem real. "That's why I came home, Lee. I wanted to be here – just like old times, with Shane and Mother and Father – and Mark."

Mark! Lee thought. This really did alter things. He would have to be told. Sally must not be allowed to suffer alone these last months. Clare would understand – and wait.

"Sally dear, you'll have to let me break my promise. There is someone I must tell. Two people. Mark – and Clare."

"No, you mustn't tell Mark!" Sally cried. "I don't want his pity, Lee. I want his love. Let him go to Clare. I want him to be happy."

It sounded, she thought with the half of her that was not acting a part, like a really romantic film. It might almost be true, except she didn't really want to be dying

– at least not once she had Mark back. She would have to recover then . . ."

"Sally, why didn't you tell someone sooner?"

"What difference would it have made?" Sally asked. "I came home as soon as I could. Lyndon understood. Oh, Lee, if only I'd never gone. If only I'd never left Mark. Then it would all have been so much easier. I'd just have died and—"

"Sally, you're not to talk like that. You'll get well again. Wanting to is half the battle. We'll have the best specialists . . . send you to Switzerland . . . anything that can be done. You know they thought Shane's life was lost and he recovered. You will, too. Now promise me, Sally, that you'll do everything to help the doctors. You will try to get well?"

"What is there to live for?" Sally asked inaudibly.

For the first time, Lee felt a little impatient.

"You have everything to live for Sally, your whole life ahead of you. Mark isn't the only person who matters . . ."

"He's the only person who matters to me," Sally whispered. "And I won't see any doctors, Lee. I want to be left alone. I only told you because you promised not to tell anyone . . ." Her voice rose with her anxiety that Lee might, in spite of her promise, ruin everything by calling in a doctor who would soon unmask her ruse. Then she would be made to look stupid and theatrical and Mark would leave her in disgust. Tears of self-pity filled her eyes, bringing Lee once more to pity and sympathy.

"Sally, don't, darling. You're not to worry. I won't tell anyone. You're to rest and get well. That's all that matters. We'll talk it all over tomorrow. Now will you go to sleep like a good girl?"

"I'll try!" Sally whispered. "But only if you promise me again you won't call in the doctors or tell Mark – or anyone?"

"I won't call in any doctor tonight," Lee promised

evasively. For she knew that she could not keep her promise not to tell Mark. He must know. It was only fair that he should, and Clare, too. Mark alone could talk Sally into having a specialist down before it was too late, if it was not too late already. Somehow she could not believe that Sally was really dying. It would be too tragic a fate for a girl as young and lovely as Sally. The American doctor must have frightened her unduly. Or else Sally had talked herself into thinking it worse than he had said by suffering alone and worrying too much.

As she turned out the light and left the room, Sally turned over and snuggled down comfortably into the soft sheets. She was more than certain, judging by Lee's last remark, that she meant to tell Mark, for all her former promise. She could sleep in peace now knowing that Mark – good, kind, gentle Mark – would never go to Scotland while she was so terribly ill – and so desperately in need of him to help her to recover!

Chapter Eighteen

Lee took off her hat and coat and followed Mark into his sitting-room, wondering how she could say to him what must be said. She was so apprehensive about Clare. Mark was the type to be protective, and he might consider it his duty, too, to stay with Sally. Then Clare wouldn't have a chance. And whatever the state of Sally's health, it would be no earthly use Mark living a lie. Sally might want a quick marriage before . . . she could not put it into words. Then Clare would always be in doubt about Mark's true feelings for her, unless Mark went to Scotland and explained.

"It's very late, Lee," Mark said with a smile, adding quickly, "not that I'm not glad to see you. Is everything all right?"

"Not altogether," Lee said hesitantly. "Oh, Mark, life can be terribly cruel sometimes. It worries me. The unexpected always seems to happen and spoil the 'best laid schemes of mice and men'."

Mark poured Lee a drink and sat down opposite her.

"I know you're worried about Clare, Lee. But there is no need. Strangely enough I am quite happy and convinced about the way I feel for her. Seeing Sally again has removed the last doubts I may have had. I love Clare, Lee, and we're going to be married. I'm sorry to hurt Sally but I can't help feeling she will get over it quick enough. Why, I don't believe she is really any more in love with me than she was with Lyndon. I don't think she knows what she wants."

Lee took a deep breath and said as gently as she could, "I'm afraid there won't be time for Sally to look around for someone else, Mark. She told me tonight in strict confidence that she had TB."

A shocked silence followed her words. The colour flared into Mark's face and left it as suddenly.

"Lee, that can't be true. Besides, it's curable . . ." his voice trailed away on a questioning note.

"She appears to have had it some time. The American doctor she saw said it was too late."

"Then how – how long . . . ?"

"A year, perhaps not as much."

"Good God, Lee, I can't believe it. She must be wrong. The doctor must have made a mistake. Sally is so healthy. She always was. I've never known Sally to be ill or have even a day in bed for years."

Lee was silent, understanding Mark's perplexity. It did seem so fantastic, and yet there was no accounting for illness. Often girls in the services had been x-rayed in the periodic overhauls and found to have contracted TB. Why not Sally? And yet she seemed even now, so rosy-cheeked – so bright-eyed!

"I want her to see a London specialist, Mark," Lee said. "I feel sure her parents will, too. But the whole trouble is, Sally has sworn me to secrecy. I don't think she means to tell anyone. I suppose she's afraid of their pity, or something. Or perhaps she wants to spare them. But they are bound to find out sooner or later. When she starts coughing, or something."

"But she must see a doctor. It's absurd," Mark cried. "I don't think your pledge of secrecy should be held in this case, Lee. It's a matter of life and death. Supposing that American doctor had made a mistake! The right treatment now might save her life."

"I agree, Mark," Lee said quietly. "But I don't think Sally will listen to me. I doubt if she would listen to Shane.

214

To be perfectly frank with you, Mark, I don't think she wants to get well. Or I should say that I think she thinks she doesn't want to get better. It may be shock – it may be disappointment at finding you engaged to Clare. That isn't the point. The point is I think you could persuade her to treat this illness sensibly."

"But surely she'd listen to her parents?"

"She might, after weeks of talking to them, but I have a belief that every minute counts, Mark. I'm sure it isn't too late to save her life if she has proper treatment right away."

"I . . . see!" said Mark. "Do you think I ought to put off my trip to Scotland – to Clare – and stay with Sally?"

Lee looked at him compassionately.

"It's not for me to tell you, Mark. Personally, I want you and Clare to be happy – to be married as soon as you want. But I must be honest and say that I think it might mean an immense amount of risk as regards Sally."

"Lee, do you think I ought to pretend to Sally – that I still care?"

"No, I don't think it is any good pretending, Mark – not to a woman. She can always sense the truth. But she needs hope – something to live for."

"But she has so much to live for. I can't believe I have suddenly assumed such importance to her. Sally isn't the type to feel so desperately about any one person. If it had been Clare . . ."

"Mark, listen to me. It's your life – yours and Clare's happiness at stake. It's for you to do whatever you feel is best for you both. I thought you ought to know about Sally because I feel that a word from you might persuade her to see a specialist. If he confirms the other doctor's opinion, then I know Clare, for one, will want to put off the wedding. She could not go through with it knowing how Sally felt about you now and what was to happen to her. It might be kinder to try and pretend just for a little while. But Clare must be told

215

the truth so that she understands. She will understand, Mark."

"I'm so afraid she will doubt my feelings for her," Mark said almost in an undertone. "Quite naturally, she has been worried about my quick change of heart. I don't blame her. But I have no doubts now, Lee. Seeing Sally again has only made me realise how much Clare means to me."

"Clare loves you, Mark. You have only to tell her what you have just told me and she will believe you."

"But how can I tell her? She won't come to me and I can't go to her."

Lee bit her lip. Clare's desire to make certain of Mark's real feeling was very obviously the reason for her refusal to come when Mark had asked her to do so on the telephone that evening. But if she, Lee, were to telephone her and explain – explain that Mark needed her and *must* talk to her. She could stay at the flat in London and Mark could get there easily enough in a day to talk to her and tell her what had happened.

"Leave it to me, Mark," she said suddenly. "I know Clare will trust me if I tell her the truth. I'll have her down at my flat in forty-eight hours, so there's no need for you to worry. Are you sure that it is what you really want?"

"As long as I can see her – talk to her," Mark said softly.

"And you think you can persuade Sally to see that specialist?"

"I'll certainly try," Mark said. "Poor little Sal. What a ghastly thing to have happened, Lee. She's so young – so very young. I don't think I realised before tonight just how childlike she still is."

"Mark, do you think I have the right to tell Shane?"

"I don't know. Perhaps if you wait a little I can persuade her to tell him herself – to stop trying to keep this a dreadful secret. I suppose this is the real reason for her return home. It all makes sense now. Naturally she would become homesick and afraid in a strange country.

I cannot understand why Lyndon didn't bring her back. One would have thought the man had sufficient affection for her not to let her travel alone in such a condition. She presumably did tell him?"

"I think so. I don't quite understand what has happened yet. Sally was so upset herself tonight that I didn't like to question her too deeply. I left her going to sleep. I didn't want to cause a rise of temperature or anything."

"No, of course not. I'll go along first thing tomorrow morning, Lee, and have a talk to her. Don't worry. I'm sure she will see things the sensible way."

"I'll ring Clare tomorrow. It's too late now. I ought to get back. Shane will be wondering where I am. I didn't tell him I was coming. I was so upset I just flung on my clothes and rushed down here."

"I'm glad you told me, Lee. I should hate to think that anything I did might hasten – retard—" he stumbled over the words neither of them cared to say aloud. Sally's death was a subject both felt too deeply about and, indeed, it still seemed so unbelievable a possibility that it was better left unsaid.

"Lee, where on earth have you been? Do you realise it's nearly midnight?"

"I'm sorry, Shane. After putting Sally to bed, I went down for a quick word with Mark. I thought he might be worried. I should have told you where I was going but I didn't think I'd be so long."

Shane looked at her with puzzled eyes, his expression faintly annoyed.

"You're an odd girl, Lee. Didn't it occur to you I was waiting? I thought something might have happened to you when I went upstairs and couldn't find you."

"You went in to Sally?"

"Yes! She was fast asleep. I darned nearly woke her up to ask where you'd got to but I thought it was hardly fair on the poor kid. She's had a long day."

217

Lee relaxed and moved over to Shane, standing with her arms at her sides, looking up at him with a smile in her eyes.

"I didn't think you'd get so worked up about my absence, Shane," she said softly. "I'm flattered."

She was unprepared for the sudden movement of his arms as he pulled her roughly against him, straining her against his heart.

"Lee, I love you," he whispered, his voice urgent. "I suppose I have done for a long while and never realised it before. Quite suddenly – tonight, I knew. Lee, tell me it's not hopeless. Tell me you love me, too."

She closed her eyes and leant her cheek against his, happiness flooding through her in a long, warm wave. At last, at last . . . it had seemed so long.

"Oh, Shane, Shane!" she cried. "I've loved you ever since we first met, I think. I'll always love you. Darling!"

He put his hand gently beneath her chin and raised her face to his; the kiss he gave her was surprisingly gentle, filled with tenderness and wonder. Then as she wound her arms round his neck, drawing him closer, passion flared between them and when they drew apart both were starry-eyed and breathless.

"Lee, I love you," he said again. "Will you marry me, dearest? Tomorrow?"

She drew away from him, her eyes clouding quickly as she remembered Sally and her illness. If only she could tell Shane now. But Mark had wanted her to wait. It would be better if Sally told him herself.

"Shane, I do love you. I will marry you, but give me a little time," she said.

"How long? Why do you need time, Lee, if you are sure? Are you not sure, after all, that you want to marry me?"

"Yes, I'm certain," Lee said. "But I want to wait a little while, Shane. I can't tell you why. You must trust me. You'll know why – soon. Don't force it from me yet."

Shane sat down and pulled Lee down beside him, his expression grave and thoughtful.

"Is something wrong, Lee?"

For a moment she hesitated. Then she nodded her head.

"I can't tell you, yet, Shane. Believe me, I have a good reason. But you mustn't worry. We'll be married soon. I promise you."

"How soon?"

"A year – perhaps a little longer."

"A year!" Shane cried. "But Lee, that's not soon. That's a lifetime. Don't you realise I love you? I'm not inhuman, Lee. I've wanted you as every man wants the woman he loves and now that I know you love me, too, what reason can there be for putting off our marriage?"

"Shane, don't ask me, I beg of you. It has nothing to do with the way we feel about each other, but it affects our marriage. That's all I can say. Perhaps tomorrow you will understand better. Please trust me, darling. Maybe it won't be a year. Perhaps things will come right much sooner. I'm hoping so."

Perhaps, she thought silently, Sally will find that doctor was wrong. Then Clare, too, can have her happiness, and Mark, and Shane and myself, and Sally will find happiness for herself, too.

Shane made an effort and curtailed his questions. Lee was looking tired and worried and a new feeling of protectiveness and tenderness was uppermost in him when he said, "All right, sweetheart, I'll leave it in your hands. But tell me again that you do love me – that you'll marry me as soon as it is possible."

* * *

Lee took Sally's breakfast upstairs herself, wishing to be the first to go in to her.

Sally was awake and sitting up in bed, her cheeks rosy and her eyes bright. Seeing her again after the doubts and worries of the previous evening, Lee found it harder than ever to believe she was really ill.

"How are you feeling, Sally?" she asked. "I brought up your breakfast so that you could have a long lie in this morning."

"Oh, but I don't want to stay in bed," Sally cried, her lips pouting. "Besides, it's bad for me. The doctor said I ought to get all the fresh air I can."

"But surely you must rest, too?"

Sally gave an angry little jerk to her head. She did not want Lee questioning her too much – not until she had a chance to read up the symptoms and treatment of tuberculosis.

"Oh, why can't you leave the subject alone, Lee," she said. "Can't you understand that I want to forget it?"

Lee was immediately contrite and the impulse to try again to persuade Sally to see a doctor faded quickly. Mark would be along shortly and it was to be hoped Sally would listen to him.

"Well, you do as you want, my dear," she said more gently. "Mark is coming in this morning to see you. I think he wants to talk to you."

Sally kept her eyes averted. Lee must not see the little triumphant expression on her face. So she had told Mark, and Mark wasn't catching the train to Scotland after all! He had preferred to stay with her. Now everything would be easy.

As soon as Lee had left and Sally, pleading a sudden change of attitude, had said it might be wiser to stay in bed after all, she finished her breakfast and hurried over to her dressing-table. She made up her face with great care, her heart singing happily within her. It had all worked out so much better than she would have believed possible when she had suddenly thought of an illness to get her way with

Mark. Lee was aiding and abetting as if she were party to the plan.

Not really mean in her selfishness, Sally did have a moment's compunction about Clare, but she gave it no more than a thought. Clare would get over it quick enough, she told herself, placing Clare's capacity for loving on a level with her own.

Half an hour later, there was a knock on the door and Mark came in. She smiled at him and told him to sit down on the end of the bed. She was quite confident of the outcome of this little talk and conscious that she was looking more attractive than usual in a fluffy pink bed jacket and her fair hair curling over her forehead.

"I hear you aren't well, Sally," Mark began awkwardly. "I'm – I'm terribly sorry. I mean – Sally, it's no good beating about the bush. Lee told me. You've got to see a doctor."

The smile left Sally's face and her lips were sullen with disappointment and annoyance.

"Lee had no right to tell you, Mark," she said. "I didn't want anyone to know. I don't want you to feel sorry for me. Nor to live the few months of my life I have left with both of you badgering me to see doctors and specialists and people."

Mark got up quickly from the bed and paced up and down the room, feeling that he was incapable of handling this, yet knowing perhaps this girl's life lay within his hands.

"Sally," he said at last, "neither Lee nor I want to keep 'badgering' you, as you put it. Just see one man, one good specialist. Perhaps that doctor in America made a mistake. It could be. If so you're only causing yourself dreadful and unnecessary worry – and all of us, too."

Sally looked straight at him.

"Are *you* worried, Mark?" she asked pointedly.

"But of course, my dear. We all are," Mark said.

"I thought you didn't care any more, Mark – that I didn't mean anything to you?"

Mark turned away and went to the window. He couldn't lie – it was beyond him to lie about his feelings for Clare. Sally would read the truth in his face. And yet if he did not pretend, this might ruin his chances of getting her to see a doctor.

"Sally, you mustn't be so silly," he said as gently as he could. "You know how fond of you I am – I always will be. Shane, Lee, all of us care about you – deeply."

Sally frowned as she stared at Mark's back. So this was not quite so easy after all. Mark could only have meant by that last remark that he cared about her, but only as the others cared; not that he loved her.

"It doesn't really matter very much, I suppose," she said in a tired little voice. "It won't be for long."

Mark turned round and stared at Sally's fair head buried in the pillow. A feeling of perplexity stole over him – and compunction. Sally must be feeling ghastly – alone and needing all the love and sympathy she could get.

"Sally, don't talk like that, please," he begged her. "I can't bear to see you so down. And of course it matters. It matters to us even if it doesn't matter to you. Won't you see this doctor for our sake, if not for your own?"

Sally did not reply and Mark, desperate, went over to the bed and laid a hand gently on her shoulder.

"Sally, please, my dear. Won't you do this much for me?"

She turned round then and almost inaudibly, said, "I'd do anything for you, Mark, if I thought you really cared."

She kept her eyes averted, knowing the struggle that was going on inside him. The very fact that he was in doubt about what he should do and say, only made her the more convinced that she wanted him – whatever the cost. It didn't matter if he married her out of pity now. Once he had done so, he would soon forget Clare and

222

fall in love with her again. Pride didn't matter. Nothing mattered now except getting Mark back.

"Sally, you know I care. But everything's different now. There's Clare—"

She purposefully misunderstood him.

"Oh, Mark, darling, Clare would understand, I'm sure," she said hurriedly. "She knew all along that we loved each other. She must have guessed you just turned to her on the rebound. She'll want to release you. Then we can be together again—"

"But Sally, I didn't—" Mark broke in, but Sally interrupted him.

"Oh, I know you didn't mean to hurt her – or me," she said. "Clare knows that, too. It was all my fault. But I'll make it up to you, Mark – going away with Lyndon like that. I'll be a good wife to you as long as – as I live."

She could not have ended on a better note. Mark's anxiety over her misinterpretation of his words and his desire to put things right, were silenced immediately by Sally's reminder that she hadn't very long to live. Poor little kid. Perhaps Clare would understand and – and wait. And if this way he could persuade Sally to see a doctor, they might even discover she was not so terribly ill – not dying. Then he could tell Sally the truth without any danger to her, and it would be all right.

"Sally, does that mean you will see a doctor?" he asked.

Sally looked at him with shining eyes.

"I'll do anything – anything in the world you want, Mark darling," she cried. "I'll see every doctor there is – anything that will keep me alive. Oh, Mark, I want so much to live now – and last night I wanted to die. I'm so happy."

Mark, in an agony of perplexity, knew that somehow or other he had committed himself. It was too late now to go back on it. He could not be such a beast as to say to Sally now, "But I don't love you. I love Clare. I can never

marry you, Sally, feeling as I do about her." It might kill
her – or cause her to continue refusing to see a doctor.
At least, now, she was willing to do that.

"Mark, when will we be married?" Sally asked
suddenly. "It'll be soon, won't it? You won't ask me
to wait – when we may have so little time together?"

"No, no of course not."

"Then we can be married immediately – by special
licence?"

Mark bit his lip.

"I'll have to see about things, Sally," he said nervously.
"But before anything, we must get you to a doctor. Are
you well enough to come up to town this afternoon?"

It was Sally's turn to be embarrassed. That Mark
would suggest such a thing had never entered her mind.
Whatever happened, they must be married before she saw
a doctor. She could, after all, always put the blame on the
American doctor when it became obvious that she was
perfectly fit. But Mark must not be allowed a loophole.
They must be married first.

"Mark," she said, thinking quickly, "I don't think
I ought to travel again today. I'm still terribly tired
after yesterday. But I might feel better tomorrow, or
Wednesday. Why don't you go up today and see about
the special licence? Then we'll do both things the same
day. Get married and immediately afterwards I can go to
the doctor."

Mark listened aghast. Sally was really rushing things.
It seemed almost as if she had foreseen his last hope – that
she might not be so ill – and had decided to crush it.

Then the nastiness of such thoughts horrified him and
he tried to remember again that this girl's life was in his
hands – that no matter what the cost to himself or Clare,
he must put Sally first.

"Sally, I'll try to get a special licence. It may take a day
or two. I would like you to see that doctor without delay
– before our wedding if necessary. Your health is more

important than anything. You must realise that. Every day may count. Lee says the right treatment might cure you – perhaps a trip to Switzerland or something . . ."

"You mean you want to send me to a sanatorium – send me away from you?" Sally cried. "You don't want to marry me after all, Mark. You want to get rid of me. I can see it all now . . ." her voice rose and Mark watched her anxiously, afraid that she might start a high temperature or something of the sort. He felt hopelessly at a loss to cope with the situation and could not think of anything with any kind of coherence. He must see Lee, talk to her and see what she advised.

"Sally, don't get upset. It may be bad for you. You're not to worry. Please, my dear. I want you to get well – that's all. That's what we all want. Now try and rest. I'll come up and see you again this afternoon."

And with that, Sally had to be content.

Chapter Nineteen

"Lee, I just don't know which way to turn," Mark said hopelessly as he recounted the details of his talk with Sally. "Somehow it just doesn't seem to add up."

"You mean Sally's illness?" Lee asked.

Mark shook his head.

"I didn't mean that, although I have misgivings about that, too. She seems to get so easily upset – excited. I mean, it's not like Sally to be nervy and neurotic, is it?"

Lee shrugged her shoulders in a bewildered gesture.

"I was really referring to her – her emotions," Mark went on. "You see, when one stops to think about it, she left so suddenly with Lyndon and seemed so certain that she had chosen him in preference to me. She barely had time to give it a trial out there before she had left him and was on her way home. Do you suppose he let her down? Or could he really be such a cad as to have found out about her illness and decided he didn't want an ailing wife or fiancée hanging about him? Somehow I can't believe it. I never really disliked the chap and he didn't seem the sort to rat on Sally."

"Perhaps she didn't tell him . . . just left leaving no address or inkling as to her whereabouts."

"Surely he wouldn't leave it at that? Knowing him reasonably well, I should imagine that was just the sort of action to make him raise heaven and hell to find her. He really loved her, I'm sure of that."

"Yes, I think he did," Lee agreed. "Still, this isn't getting us very far. The thing is, Mark, what are we to do? I personally rather dislike the responsibility we've taken on ourselves. I think Sally's parents ought to be told, and Shane. After all, it's ridiculous to keep such a serious and vital matter from them. They have every right to know. Why, what must her parents feel being away at a time like this! They'll want to be with her, advise, comfort, look after her. Sally can't shut herself away at such a time. It's wrong – quite wrong."

"Yet she has bound us to secrecy," Mark said quietly.

"All the same, Mark, I feel we would be justified in speaking out. Her very life may be at stake – is, in fact, as far as we know. That surely is sufficient reason for telling her people."

"I think I agree," Mark said. "Personally I'm afraid I can't see what to do and I want advice – and help. Sally seems to expect me to marry her immediately, by special licence – before she sees a doctor. It's as if she wants proof of my feelings before she's prepared to put up a fight for her life. It places me in the very devil of a position, Lee. I love Clare. I know I can't hide it from Sally indefinitely. If it were to come out after I'd married Sally, immense harm might come of it – more even than if I were honest now. On the other hand, as you said, it seems as if I have influence over her. She has at least agreed to see a doctor – on conditions."

"If one didn't know Sally to be incapable of such an action, one might almost start believing it was blackmail," Lee said thoughtfully. "You know, Mark, that Clare is on her way south?"

Mark's dark face lit up in a smile of surprise and pleasure.

"You spoke to her?"

"Yes, first thing this morning. She says she'll come to my flat right away, and await developments there. She wants to see you as soon as you can get away and told me to tell you that she loves you very much and will understand no matter what happens."

"Oh, Clare!" Mark murmured huskily, his heart filled with a sudden unbelievable longing for her.

Lee watched his expression, feeling a little of his love and pain and longing. So she, too, felt about Shane. Now that he had at last discovered his love for her, it was only with the greatest difficulty that she could conceal her happiness and subdue her longing to become his in marriage and in every way a woman can belong to a man. It seemed so hard that after so long a wait, she must wait yet longer, perhaps a year or more, before they could be married.

Suddenly she decided that Shane must be told the truth. He was, after all, Sally's twin. He could take the responsibility of telling his parents or not as he thought fit. It was not her place nor Mark's, neither of them being members of the family, to keep such a ghastly secret to themselves.

Mark fell in with her suggestion and they went together to Shane's studio and found him busy with a new portrait of Lee he was doing from memory.

He looked up as they came in and his glance went instantly to Lee, a flicker crossing his face as if to say to her, If Mark were not with you, I'd come over and kiss you, my darling.

She smiled back at him and Mark gave him a friendly hello.

"How's Sally this morning?" Shane asked, as he went over to his miniature kitchen to make coffee.

Lee sat down in one of the armchairs and lit a cigarette.

"We've come to talk to you about Sally," she said quietly. "She's not well, Shane."

He came out from behind the screen, kettle in hand, something in Lee's voice striking a note of seriousness.

"You mean she's really ill?"

"Yes!" Lee said. "She told me last night, Shane, and asked me not to tell anyone. I promised I wouldn't, but

I felt I ought to tell Mark because Sally spoke of him in such a way as to show he had some considerable influence over her."

"Look, I don't get this," Shane said. "You mean Sally thinks she's in love with Mark?"

Lee nodded.

"But that's crazy!" Shane said, and with a quick smile at Mark, he added, "I don't mean that personally, Mark, old chap. I meant she'd already thrown you over for Lyndon. Besides, I thought you and Clare—"

"Yes, I'm in love with Clare all right," Mark broke in. "But Sally seems to think she loves me. I know it's crazy, Shane. It just doesn't add up anywhere. But she won't go to a doctor unless we're married first."

"See here, I'm completely in the dark," Shane said. "Start at the beginning. Just what is wrong with Sal?"

"She – she went to a doctor in America," Lee said as gently as she could. "He told her she had TB."

Shane's face whitened and he drew in his breath.

"But that's impossible. She's far too healthy. Why, Sal's never had a day's illness in her life . . ."

"TB can sometimes produce that appearance of good health," Lee explained.

"But she doesn't cough – or anything. Lee, are you certain? Is Sally sure?" Shane asked, his voice hard with anxiety.

Lee nodded.

"But it's curable," Shane said. "Taken in its early stages it's easily curable. I knew a chap who only had to rest up a bit for a few months and he was all right."

Lee wished herself at the bottom of the sea. Shane's affection for his twin was very deep and it was almost beyond her to have to tell him the rest – the worst of the story. But for his own sake – and Sally's, she knew she had to.

"Shane, I wish I hadn't to be the one to tell you," she

229

said quietly. "But Sally told me the doctor said it was too far gone to be curable."

Shane's face whitened and then a flush spread across it.

"That can't be true. Sally must see a specialist right away. Father will get the best opinions in the world. Everything will be done and she'll pull through. Sally can't . . . she can't be as ill as that. She can't. Lee, you're certain that doctor hasn't made a mistake?"

"I'm by no means certain," Lee said, glad to be able to give him this much consolation. "As a matter of fact, I think myself that he *must* have made a mistake. Perhaps she may have it – slightly. But I can't believe any more than you do, that it's so far gone as to be fatal. If only she would see some reputable doctor right away, I am positive this whole thing will show up in a far more hopeful light. She would be a different person if once she knew that there was no danger."

"Then I'll telephone the family doctor right away and ask him who's the best chap to see her. If he's in London, I'll have the car bring him down right away. Otherwise the plane can fetch him. He could see her today – right away." Shane spoke hurriedly.

"The trouble is, Shane, she refuses to see a doctor. She says she doesn't want to spend weeks with specialist after specialist always reminding her that she's ill. She wants to pretend nothing is wrong for as long as she can."

Shane sat down heavily on the stool in front of the fire and his face was thoughtful. At last he said, "I see! You mean you think only Mark can persuade her!"

"Mark has just been speaking to Sally. She says she'll see a doctor as soon as they are married."

"Then she doesn't know about Clare?"

"I think she doesn't quite realise that I'm serious about Clare," Mark said with difficulty. "I tried to tell her when we were coming back in the car from the airport. But since

Lee told me about – about Sally's illness, I haven't liked to be too pointed for fear of losing the chance of being able to make her see a doctor. Lee thought I was the only one who could persuade her."

Shane frowned.

"It's not like Sally to be so stubborn about such things. I don't understand. It's easy enough to make her see reason about little things."

"This is hardly a little thing." Lee pointed out. "It's a matter of life and death, Shane."

Shane stood up.

"I utterly refuse to believe that," he said suddenly. "I'm going to see Sally myself – talk to her. She must see a doctor whether she wants to or not. Her behaviour is childish. There's something behind all this and I'm getting to the bottom of it."

And before either Lee or Mark could recover enough from their surprise at this unexpected action to stop Shane, he had hurried out of the room and was on his way to Sally.

Sally was sitting up in bed reading a book. Shane did not knock at the door but walked straight in so that she was startled and unprepared for his arrival. She saw instantly by his expression that he was upset and wondered if Lee or Mark could have been talking to him. It was not going to be so easy to pull Shane's leg and she resolved to tread warily.

Shane stood by the bed for a minute and then sat down abruptly.

"Sal," he said, "I want the truth . . . about what that American doctor said. You're to tell me everything."

"So Lee broke her promise," Sally said, her voice sharp with annoyance. "I'll never forgive her."

"Don't be childish, Sal," Shane said. "Lee was quite right to tell me, and it was utterly wrong of you to try and keep such a thing to yourself – wrong and selfish. Now out with it, Sal. I want the truth."

Sally felt unnerved by his tone. It was hardly that of a twin brother condoling with his sister over her fatal illness. Could Shane suspect her of lying? She bit her lip nervously. For the first time she began to regret this ruse to get Mark back. One little lie led to so many more and now she was inextricably involved.

"If Lee has told you already, I can't see what more there is to say," she said, and added with a catch in her voice, "I can't see why you all want to keep talking about such an awful thing. I want to forget it."

Tears of self-pity came readily to her eyes. Nothing was working out right. Mark had not, after all, fallen readily into her trap. Lee had broke her promise and told Shane, and now Shane was obviously going to insist on a doctor.

Shane stared at his sister with a little frown of puzzlement. He hated to see her crying. It was unlike Sal, too, and he felt a sudden stab of anxiety in case perhaps this was all true. He had hardly been tactful or sympathetic – and yet he could still not believe it. Sally looked well – rosy cheeked, bright-eyed, and she had not coughed once since she had come home as far as he knew.

"Look here, Sal," he said, his voice more gentle. "I'm quite convinced this American doctor has made a mistake. In fact I'm practically certain. You simply must let me get a good specialist down here right away. It's ridiculous to torment yourself with all this fearful anxiety – and us, too, when it might none of it be true. He might well have made a mistake and the sooner we rectify it, the better."

Sally dashed the tears from her eyes and stared up at Shane, fear written obviously in their depth; fear that Shane believed to be caused by the outcome of the doctor's visit but which was really at the sudden nearness of discovery of her ruse.

"No, no, I won't see anyone," she cried. "Oh, leave me alone, Shane. I don't want to be worried and miserable. I want to be left alone."

Shane put out a hand and touched her arm but she shook him off. He stood up, looking down at his sister's curly head in much the same bewilderment as Mark had stood there an hour earlier.

"Then there's nothing else for me to do but to fetch Father and Mother," he said.

Sally sat up and stared at Shane aghast. That would be the last straw – the end of all her hopes. She knew her parents too well to suppose they would fall in with a death-bed marriage to Mark before seeing a specialist. Whatever happened, they must not be brought into it. Even if she did not get Mark after all, she must at least avoid the disgrace and dishonour of having her lies and ruses discovered by them all. Shane must be handled – anything to put a stop to this before it was completely out of hand.

For the first time, Sally realised how far-reaching were the results of her own selfish desires. She had thought it would be so easy, and it was proving hopelessly difficult.

She burst into tears and Shane paused in the doorway. On a sudden impulse, he came back and sat down on the bed and turned Sally round to face him.

"Look, Sal," he said. "Is there anything you want to tell me? I have a feeling there might be. You know we never used to keep secrets from each other as kids. Must you have any now from me? You can trust me, Sal. You know that. I won't let you down, whatever it is. Why not tell me what's troubling you? Come on, Curly-locks. Have it out."

The unexpected use of his childhood nickname for her and his strange intuitive understanding that there was something more in this than she had told him, decided Sally that her last hope lay in Shane. If he would co-operate with her, she might still get through this whole business and get Mark, too.

She flung her arms round him and sobbed frantically for a few minutes. Then she said between sobs, "Oh,

Shane, I'm so ashamed of myself. You'll never forgive me. But I had to do it. I couldn't lose him. Why should Clare have him when he's really mine? I didn't mean to upset everyone. I thought at first that I'd just have a slight illness – enough to keep Mark from going up to Scotland to Clare. Then somehow it grew and grew and tuberculosis was the only thing I could think of. Then it all seemed to fit in so well and Lee telling Mark and everything. I never meant to worry you all. I just wanted Mark back . . ."

Shane said nothing as he sat there, holding Sally's shaking form in his arms. For a moment, he almost hated her. It would not be difficult to hate someone who could destroy in one minute all that you had believed them to be. He had thought so much of Sal – idolised her, adored her, felt that he would one day want to be married to a girl like Sal – if there were ever anyone as perfect. Now suddenly, he had seen her through her own confession, to be what she really was – selfish, thoughtless, deceitful, scheming, petty and mean. In that minute, Shane struggled with himself, trying not to believe, but knowing he was no longer able to deceive himself; trying not to condemn and yet finding no excuse. Sally wasn't a kid; she was the same age as himself. Or perhaps at heart, she had never grown up.

He jumped at this excuse for her because it helped him to bear his own pain, and enlarged on it quickly. That must be the truth of the matter. It was really his parents' fault – and his. They had all spoilt her. She had always had her own way and this was the first time in her life she had come up against denial of her wants. So she had done what many a child might have done – lied and schemed to get it.

He had to know, though, before he could really excuse her and try to help her out of this mess, if she had any scruples at all. What, for instance, had she thought of Clare? Had she given her any thought at all or had she

234

blatantly decided that if she, Sally, wanted Mark, Clare must go without.

"Sally, tell me truthfully, what about Clare? Don't you see how this might have harmed her?"

"But she'd get over it, Shane," Sally said, her voice now confident and persuasive. "After all, look how easily Mark got over me when I went away with Lyndon. Don't you see? As soon as anyone realises how impossible it is to get the person they think they love, then they just turn round and look for someone else. You got over Clare, too. There's proof of it. Life's like that, Shane. Besides, Clare hasn't known Mark anything like as long as I've known him. She'd get over it much more easily than I would."

So that was it! Sally judged others on her own capacity for loving, on her own rules for life, yet without applying them to herself. If Clare could get over it easily, then so could Sally, and this, he knew now, was what she must do. It would show her once and for all that lies and deceit could not get her the things she did not deserve. And he knew, too, that Sally did not deserve a fellow like Mark. She wasn't good enough for him. Besides, Mark and Clare loved each other.

He released Sally and said sternly, "I said I'd help you out of this mess and I intend to, Sally. But before we decide what's to be done, I want to say one thing – and you're going to listen. Your whole attitude has been disgraceful and dishonourable and wrong – utterly wrong. You're selfish, Sal, and mean and petty. You treated Mark like dirt, flew off to America and then because, no doubt, you weren't getting things all your own way with Lyndon, treated him as badly and came home. It's a pity he didn't stop you. You've very nearly ruined three lives besides your own, but thank goodness you've been stopped in time. You know very well Mark is in love with Clare and Clare with Mark – not just a selfish emotion such as you are only capable of feeling. Well, you're going to find a way of getting out of this so that they can be together again or else I shall tell them what you've just told me. Now, think, Sally, and think hard."

Sally was staring at Shane, her face white, her heart pounding with a mixture of annoyance and unhappiness in which lay, too, the beginnings of shame and self-dislike. It was not easy for Sally to hear Shane talking to her like this – and to know in the depths of her heart that everything he said was true. Nor was it easy to know that now she had really lost her battle and that although Shane would help her, he did not intend to help her get Mark. Life seemed suddenly black and hopeless and beyond bearing. How could she get herself out of this whole business now without Mark and Lee and Clare – indeed everyone knowing she had lied to them? There was no way out and she would never be able to look any of them in the face again. It was awful – awful, and there was no one in the world to help her – except Shane.

In a rush of real feeling for him, she flung herself into his arms, sobbing incoherently.

"Oh, I'm sorry, Shane. I'm sorry and ashamed," she cried. "I didn't mean this to happen. I didn't mean to be so selfish. I'll go away. I'll kill myself – then you can all be happy without me."

A smile flickered across Shane's face, hearing this tearful avowal. Sally was only too apparently still a child. 'You'll be sorry when I'm dead' was always her baby retort to minor punishments. 'I'll kill myself' was only an adult repetition of the same words. Then the smile left his face as he thought again of the mess she had got herself into, and how difficult it was going to be to extricate her without too much loss of face. A pretended trip to the doctor, perhaps, and they could all be told that the American doctor had made a mistake. They must never know the truth.

And afterwards, what then? Mark would marry Clare and he, Shane, would marry Lee. But what would become of Sally? Would she pick up the threads of her old life at home?

"Look, Sal, don't cry any more. We must just try to make the best of it. We'll go up to town and see a doctor tomorrow. That is to say, we'll pretend to go to one, and come back with the news that you're all right. Then we'll have to think of something to do with you. Perhaps you could go away for a holiday somewhere. Although you don't deserve it, you little minx."

Sally stared at him, her eyes filled with tears.

"You're being much too good to me, Shane. I know I'm horrid and beastly. I don't deserve a wonderful brother like you."

And Shane, realising her self-abasement, wondered if after all, this had not all happened for the best. It might result in a more worthwhile Sally, and the anxiety and worry she had caused Mark and Clare and Lee and himself, was, after all, only of a few hours duration. The damage had not been so serious, thanks to his intervention.

"There's the telephone bell. I'll go and answer it," he said, glad of an excuse to be going. The interview had taken more out of him than he realised. He, too, had grown up a little in this past half-hour.

He went downstairs and lifted the receiver. Then his face flushed and his voice when he spoke was ringing with genuine surprise and pleasure.

"Of all the people I least expected it to be you. You've come in the nick of time, old chap. Yes, she's here. And she needs you badly . . .

"No, nothing like that. Look, you come straight here and try not to see anyone before you have a talk to me. Yes, all right. Half an hour!"

He replaced the receiver and stood in the hall, realising that Fate had played into their hands. Lyndon had refused to accept Sally's rebuff. He had come across the Atlantic to knock a bit of sense into her and take her back – as his wife. Judging by the tone of his voice – he meant it, too, and that was just the sort of treatment Sally needed. She had had her day of adoring slaves, of playing off one man against another. Now she would have someone who had learnt his lesson and meant to stand no more nonsense from her. Sally was going to be all right – and the future, which had been bothering him most about this whole affair, had been firmly taken out of his hands.

"Gee!" he said aloud with a smile, repeating Lyndon's words over the phone. "If that isn't just swell!"

And he went in search of Lee.

Chapter Twenty

Lyndon's face was drawn and unhappy as he walked slowly up the stairs to Sally's room. That hour with Shane in the library had been more than a little disturbing. He had surmised on the discovery of Sally's note, left behind for him at their New York hotel, that she had not been finding life quite as exciting or interesting as she had hoped. He knew this was partly due to the fact that he had had a tremendous number of business appointments and Sally had had to be left a great deal alone. In a strange country among strangers, it was only natural she should be homesick and even bored.

He had told her in detail that he hated leaving her, even for an hour or two; that only the great importance of his business could have kept him from her and that as the outcome would be important to both of them for their future, she must just try to make the best of it until they could leave New York for California, get married and start having fun.

Her note had been a big shock, even with his knowledge of her discontent. He had not really believed she would leave him and go back to England, and he was both angry and deeply hurt. After a week's reflection, he had decided that such an impulsive action was typical of Sally. An idea would come into her head and she would act on it without thought. He refused to accept the fact that she had returned to Mark. Everything he knew about her and her former fiancé only served to assure him that they were in no way suited, and that Sally did not really love him. She had been too responsive in his arms; too happy and vivacious in those first days abroad to have been regretting leaving Mark. After that momentary hesitation at the airport, Sally had not seemed to worry about their elopement, and had seemed excited and happy about their forthcoming marriage once the business was dealt with in New York.

Having decided it was not Mark who had been the reason for Sally's return to England, but his own neglect of her at a time when she most needed him, Lyndon lost no further time in finishing off his business and booking himself a plane to England. He did not intend to give Sally up. He loved her far too deeply for that. He knew his Sally well, and did not try to blind himself to the fact that she was spoiled and wilful. In his eyes she was charming and amusing and very, very beautiful and he believed that she would one day grow up a little and achieve more depth of character and with it would come a bigger capacity for loving.

Then he had seen Shane; had heard the truth of Sally's efforts to retrieve Mark, and for the first time in his life, he felt that it was, after all, going to be difficult to achieve what he wanted. From her brother's conversation, he did not doubt that Sally would be glad of this chance to leave the country with him and get herself out of the scrape she had landed herself in. But he wanted more than that from his future wife. He wanted Sally's love, and it seemed to him that he could never really have held it. All the time when he had felt so sure of himself, her heart must have still been with Mark. It made everything so difficult. It made this coming interview with her a painful one for him, too.

He opened the door as she answered his knock and went into the room. Sally was up and dressed and sitting in a chair by the window, staring out across the lawn with red-rimmed eyes. She turned her head to see who it was and the colour flared into her cheeks.

240

"You!" she cried in a muffled voice.

"I've come to fetch you back, Sally," Lyndon said, his voice low with the sudden emotion this fresh sight of her caused him. She turned her head away and he stood there silently, waiting for her to speak. At last she said, "I suppose you know – what I've done?"

"Yes! Shane told me."

"And you still want me to come back with you?"

There was a new note in her voice, a quiet, thoughtful note which he had not heard before.

He moved across the room and stood behind her chair, staring down at her fair curly head.

"I thought you might want to get out of all this," he said at last. "Naturally, I understand you won't want to marry me now. Shane says you're still in love with Mark but that you're leaving him to Clare. Under the circumstances, you must want to get away. I was going to suggest that you come to California and stay with my sister awhile. Then we'll see later how you feel about things."

Sally listened in silence, shame covering her slowly from head to foot. She had treated this man abominably – as badly as she had treated Mark – and Clare. And yet he still wanted to help her. Shane, too, was trying to help her out of the mess she had got into through her own selfishness – selfishness which had no real foundation or cause, as she now knew. She had only wanted Mark once she had known him to be beyond her reach. Had Mark been at the airport waiting for her with open arms, she wouldn't have behaved any better to him than she had before she left the country. It was finding him engaged to Clare that had piqued her pride and caused her to think she wanted him after all.

But she didn't – not deep down inside her. She knew that life with Mark would be routine and quiet and ordinary and that she didn't want any of those things. She wanted the life Lyndon had offered her, and yet she had thrown away her chances because he had had to neglect her. Her

241

own selfishness and pride had been responsible for that, too. She had known very well that Lyn had had a great deal of urgent business – that it was partly her fault as he had stayed in England longer than he intended, in order to win her from Mark.

But she had been annoyed because he wouldn't give in to take her to some party or theatre when it meant cancelling a business date and in a fit of temper, she had left him . . . left the one man who really cared deeply enough about her to come after her; who cared enough even after knowing what sort of a person she was.

She buried her face in her hands and tears of utter wretchedness and self-deprecation stole through her fingers. In a moment, Lyndon was on his knees beside her, his arms gathering her to him and his soft drawl soothing in her ear.

"Honey, don't! It'll be all right. You'll get over the way you feel about Mark. I feel the biggest heel for ever having parted you from him. It's all my fault. But I'll make it up to you, honey. One day I'll give you everything you ever wanted of life."

"Oh, Lyn, don't say any more, please," Sally cried. "You don't understand. I'm not crying for Mark. I'm crying because I'm so terribly ashamed. I've behaved so badly and yet everyone is being wonderful to me – you more than anyone. I don't deserve it. You can't still care about me. I'm not good enough for you."

The light sprang into Lyndon's eyes and his grasp on her tightened.

"You mean – you aren't in love with him?" he asked, hardly daring to believe his ears. "You mean you just decided to make a bid for him because some other girl had snapped him up while you were gone?" And as Sally nodded, he laughed joyously and shook her a little. "You little minx!" he said, half amusedly, half in reproach. "But it's the last time you'll get away with anything like that,

242

Sal. From now on, you're mine and you'll do what I say and like it. No more nonsense. This time we're going to be married before we leave the country. I'm not taking any more chances. Then we'll fly straight to California and start all over again. Now stop crying, honey, and get on your glad rags. We're going to town."

"To London?" Sally choked. "What for?"

"To make believe we're seeing a doc," was Lyndon's reply. "And then to get a special licence."

"But I haven't packed!" Sally gasped. "I'll have to see Shane – and Lee, and tell them. . . ."

"You're not seeing anyone, Sally. We're just going and I'll wire them from London to say the report says everything is OK so you're back to America – as my wife. That's all they need to know."

"You mean I shan't have to face them – with any more lies?" Sally cried. "Oh, Lyn, I don't deserve it – to get out of it all so easily."

"I guess you don't, you little wretch," said Lyndon with a grin. "But there again, I think you might have learnt your lesson. Landsakes, honey, I'm going to have to keep my eye on you!"

Sally stood up and with a sudden sweet smile, she reached up on tip-toe and kissed him gently on the lips.

"Thank you, darling," she whispered. "And I'll try to be a good girl in future."

"You bet you will!" said Lyndon, and gathered her into his arms.

Downstairs in the lounge, Shane and Lee read Lyndon's telegram together. Shane's face was drawn but a faint look of relief crossed over it and he turned to Lee with a smile.

"So that's that!" he said non-committally.

Lee gave a sigh of relief.

"Oh, I'm so glad, Shane – so terribly glad. I felt all along that the American doctor must have made a mistake. The only thing that doesn't make sense is Sally's behaviour over Mark. I suppose thinking she had only a few months to live could have had such an effect on her. It's quite conceivable that one would turn to one's family and to those who had been near and dear at such a time. She must have felt very lost and afraid in New York. Well, it's not much use wondering. Life never seems consistent and the more one thinks about it, the odder it all appears. Let's just be thankful they're both so happy."

Shane listened to Lee's quiet, kindly voice and his heart quickened with tenderness and love. It was not in Lee's nature to look for the worst in people. She had never suspected Sally's deception and he would never tell her. Sally could keep her secret. It didn't matter any more now, anyway. Sally had gone and Mark could go to Clare. And now nothing lay between himself and Lee – nothing in the wide wide world.

"Lee, I asked you two days ago if you would marry me – soon," he said abruptly. "Then you said one year – perhaps less. Could you make it much much less – say a couple of weeks perhaps?"

Lee stared up at him, her eyes starry, her heart singing inside her.

"Oh, Shane, my dearest," she whispered. "We'll be married as soon as we can."

He smiled down at her and reached for her hand and held it tightly in his own.

"I'll write to Father and Mother tonight. Perhaps we could make it a double wedding with Mark and Clare. Let's ring Mark now and tell him the news. The poor chap will be eating his heart out and not knowing which way to turn. It isn't fair to keep him in suspense."

"Nor Clare!" said Lee. "She's sitting alone in the flat in town, waiting for me to ring her and give her the news."

"If Mark hurries, he could catch the four-thirty and be up there by six," Shane said. "Come on, darling. We'll get the car out and run him down to the station. I know what he'll feel like if he misses that train. Every minute counts when one's in love."

Lee linked her arm through his and walked slowly out of the house with him knowing that for her, life had only just begun.

London was in the grip of a heavy fog. Mark swore softly under his breath as he stared out of the window into the inky blackness. The train was crawling along and he felt in his impatience that he might walk the distance quicker.

"Got a connection to catch in town?" asked his travelling companion.

"No, a date!" Mark replied, pulling out his pipe and lighting it with unsteady hands.

The older man smiled.

"Won't she wait?" he asked.

Mark relaxed a little and smiled.

"I've kept her waiting too long as it is," he replied. "That is, if I'd had any sense, I'd have married her months ago. Still, she'll be waiting. That's the kind of girl Clare is."

"Well, best of luck to you both," said his companion. "I've been married twenty years and never regretted it. Wonderful state to be in if you pick the right woman. That's the trouble nowadays. Too many young people rushing into marriage before they know what they really want. Was engaged three times myself before I finally went through with it. Jilted one girl at the church, too."

Mark laughed, glad to have this conversation to take his mind off the absurd speed at which they were travelling; take his mind off Clare who might even be waiting for him on the platform if Lee had managed to reach her on the telephone.

"That took some nerve, didn't it?" he asked the older man.

"Yes! But I'm not sorry. Nor was she. She's been married twenty-two years now and is as happy as I am.

245

We often meet. My wife and she are great buddies. It's strange how much courage it takes to make the right move sometimes. Still, you don't look the sort of fellow to lack courage . . . Were you in the war?"

Reminiscences of the army took up the remainder of the journey to Victoria Station, and then Mark, bidding a hasty good-bye to his travelling companion, jumped out of the carriage and walked hurriedly along the platform, searching amongst the crowds for Clare's tall, slim figure.

The fog hung heavily round the station and the milling crowds took on eerie phantom shapes with white, blotchy faces. Clare was not to be seen at the barrier. He looked for her under the great clock – the traditional meeting place at Victoria Station – and at last, his heart sinking a little in disappointment, joined the queue for taxis.

He stamped his feet a little, half in cold, half in impatience as he moved slowly forward. At last he stood first in the queue; a porter opened the door of the waiting taxi and Mark stepped in, closing the door behind him.

Suddenly it was wrenched open and a figure in a white mackintosh almost fell in on top of him.

"Mark, Mark, I thought I'd missed you!"

"Clare!"

He caught her in his arms and stared down into her upturned face, seeing the light in her large grey eyes, the soft, misty dampness of her dark hair as it framed her pale sweet face.

"Clare, oh Clare!" he said, as if he could only believe in her reality by voicing her name.

"Where to, sir?" asked the grinning taxi driver.

Mark gave the address of Lee's flat, and then the window closed behind the driver's head and they were alone – alone in the darkness and soft enveloping fog, alone together at last.

"Mark, I'm so happy," Clare whispered as she leant her face against his tweed coat, sniffing in the faint odour of country and tobacco and dampness. It reminded her sharply of Scotland and the brief weeks there with Mark, nearly four months ago now. It had seemed so long – so interminably long since she had seen him, sat beside him, heard his voice, been able to reach out and touch his hands.

Instinctively, his hand moved over and clasped hers.

"Clare! Where were you? I must have missed you on the platform. I was so disappointed. Worried, too, until I remembered that Lee might not have been able to contact you on the phone in time to meet the train."

"I was there, but I couldn't see you!" Clare said softly. "I knew I must have missed you when the last people went through the barrier. Then I was afraid you might go to the flat and not find me and think I'd gone back to Scotland or something silly. I was in such a panic."

"I don't think I should have been able to bear it if I'd found the flat empty!" Mark said huskily. "Clare, darling. It's so wonderful to see you; so wonderful to know that it's all going to be all right after all."

"Don't let's talk about that," Clare said vaguely. It was enough for her to know that Sally was well and had left with Lyndon after all. The past no longer mattered – only the present and the future.

"I'll never risk losing you again, Mark," she said urgently. "It was so stupid of me. I should have trusted in you – in your love. I should have known it was something very, very special which nothing – nothing from the past and nothing in the future – has the power to destroy."

"Clare, I'll have to find a hotel room for tonight – but first I want to see you – really to see you; to hold you in my arms and tell you until you're tired of hearing it how much I love you."

"That could never happen," Clare said dreamily. "We'll have supper at the flat, Mark. You must be hungry. I'll rob Lee's larder. How is she? She didn't talk about herself but she sounded very excited. It's unusual in Lee. Has something happened?"

"Didn't she tell you? She and Shane are engaged and are going to be married shortly."

"Oh, Mark how wonderful. I'm so very happy. Lee's been in love with him such a long while. They'll be a wonderfully happy couple. How well everything has turned out after all. I'm glad for Shane, too. He and Lee are two of a kind."

"And so are we, Clare," Mark said, drawing her close against him. "I've realised that more acutely than ever since – since Sally came back. Perhaps it was the best thing that could have happened. It laid the ghost well and truly. I shall always be fond of her. How could one help liking her? But it's you I love, Clare. I love you so much that it hurts. I'm so afraid I can't possibly deserve a wonderful girl like you."

"Mark, you're a dreadful flatterer. But I understand because that's the way I feel about you. Do you suppose we shall always be so much in love?"

"Always!" said Mark with a tender smile.

Clare sighed contentedly.

"You know, darling, I had a good deal of time for thinking while I was alone in Scotland after you came south," Clare said softly. "It frightened me sometimes to imagine how easily we might have missed one another."

"What do you mean?" Mark asked.

"I was thinking about our first meeting – and before that – three children making a childhood tryst to meet again in ten years' time in that funny little tea-shop. We might so easily have broken that tryst, and if any one of us had done so, you and I might never have had another chance to meet."

"We'd have met some time, somewhere," Mark said with conviction. "We were meant for one another, Clare. Fate could not have been so cruel as to keep us apart for long. I should have found you."

"But it might have been too late," Clare said without fear, for it could never happen now. "I might have been married. You might have married Sally."

"Clare, darling, don't talk about such things. We must talk of the present – of our future. When are we to be married, and where? In Scotland? I'd like to be married there. I want to leave Hannington behind me with all its associations. Of course, there's my job but I rather think I can get a transfer up north. You know, darling, I'd love to have our home in Scotland – way up in the Highlands. It's my spiritual home, I think, or perhaps it's just that a Highland nymph I know has bewitched me."

Clare laughed at him, her face radiant.

"I think if we could live in Scotland, I could ask nothing more of life for I should be completely and utterly happy," she said. "Unless it were for a few young Marks around the house to keep me busy while you were at work. Oh, Mark, isn't life truly wonderful!"

For answer, he put his arms round her and heedless of the jolting of the taxi-cab, he bent his head and kissed her passionately. When at last he released her, the taxi had stopped and the driver was smiling at them from his seat.

"Reckon you two've got it bad!" he said with another friendly grin.

"We're going to be married!" Mark said inconsequently.

"We're very much in love," said Clare.

"So nothing else matters – even the clock ticking up to three shillings," remarked the practical Cockney. "Oh, well, we're only young once I says. So you can 'ave this ride on me, and the best of luck to you both. It's a sight for sore eyes to see such happy faces. After all the tears and partings I saw in wartime, it's good to see the brighter side of life. Warms the cockles of me heart, that it does."

"It's very kind of you," Clare said, putting a restraining hand on Mark's arm, for she knew it would hurt the driver's feelings if they were to insist on paying for their fare. "Perhaps you'd like to come to our wedding."

"Yes," said Mark. "Please do. You'll be the first guest we've invited."

So they took his name and address and promised to send him an invitation, and he sat there, beaming and shaking his head as he watched Mark and Clare climbing the stairs to Lee's studio.

"Looked as if they were climbing up to 'eaven," he told his wife later.

And he wasn't so far wrong after all.